RUN, FLINX, RUN!

The Qwarm were out to assassinate a foolish and seemingly harmless alien that went about babbling meaningless phrases. But that made no sense, and Flinx had to know why.

Both Qwarm were standing by a window. While her companion held back the shade, the woman was readying a black pistol. Without doubt, she was going to murder that alien.

Flinx started to retreat, but suddenly a woman in the corner noticed him and drew a startled breath. For the Qwarm, it might just as well have been a scream . . . both whirled from the window.

Instantly, Pip was off Flinx's shoulder. There was a *phut* from the Qwarm's dart pistol and then Flinx threw the knife. The man went down. The female assassin hesitated, and Pip's venom struck her eyes.

Fifteen seconds later she was dead.

Flinx staggered. To anger a Qwarm was certain death. To kill two Qwarm foretold a fate far worse.

And in a galaxy headed for destruction, there were going to be very few places to hide!

THE END
OF THE
MATTER

Alan Dean Foster

A Del Rey Book

BALLANTINE BOOKS • NEW YORK

A Del Rey Book
Published by Ballantine Books

Library of Congress Catalog Card Number: 77-6128

ISBN 0-345-25861-4

Manufactured in the United States of America

First Edition: November 1977

Cover art by Darrell Sweet

For Tim Kirk,
with thranx . . .

Prologue

Take a God-sized bottle of hundred-proof night, spill it across a couple of dozen light-years, and you have the phenomenon humanxkind called the Velvet Dam. A dark nebula so dense that no near star was powerful enough to excite it to glow, the Dam drew an impenetrable curtain across a vast portion of the stage of space. No sun shone through it to the inhabited region known as the Humanx Commonwealth. No broadcasts, transmissions, or birthday greetings could be sent from beyond the vast ebony wall.

It lay far above the burgeoning ellipsoid of the Commonwealth, and ran roughly parallel to the galactic equator. Yet since that which is unseeable is ever the most attractive, humanx exploratory efforts had already begun to probe persistently at its flanks.

One mission was the same as any other to the drone. Whether it sought out new information behind the as-yet-unexplored Dam or above the surface of Earth's own moon made no difference to its tireless mind. Not that the drone was ignorant, however. The enormous distances traveled by such long-range sensor vehicles

rendered constant monitoring impossible. So in addition to the plethora of precision recorders and scientific
instrumentation provided for sampling the far reaches
of space, the independent robotic drones were
equipped with sophisticated electronic brains. Of necessity, they also possessed a certain amount of decision-
making ability.

Its own incredibly complex collage of minute cir-
cuitry was what changed the drone's preprogrammed
course. In its limited mechanical fashion, the drone had
determined that the new subject was of sufficient importance to dictate a shift in plans. So it broke from its
assigned path, fired its tiny KK drive, and relayed its
decision to the drone mother monitor station.

Though small, the tiny drive could push the un-
manned vehicle at a speed no humanx-occupied craft
could attain. As it raced toward the source of the extraordinary disturbance, it continued to relay its readings back to the monitoring station. Before very long
(drone time) it had approached a spot where visual
recording was possible. Without judging, without evalu-
ating, the drone worked hard to send a flood of information back to the station hanging just at the corner
of the Velvet Dam.

What the drone recorded and relayed was consump-
tion on a cosmic scale. It hunted through its memory
for records of similar phenomena, but came up empty.
This was shattering, since in its ultraminiaturized files
the drone retained some mention of every variety of as-
tronomical occurrence ever witnessed and noted by
humanxkind.

The drone-mind worked furiously. Preliminary surveillance was complete—should it depart now and return to its original task or continue to study this momentous event? This was a critical decision. The drone
was aware of its own value, yet it seemed unarguable
that any additional bit of information it could obtain
here would be more valuable to its makers than everything else it might accomplish elsewhere. So the crucial
circuits were engaged, locked with religious fervor. The
drone moved nearer, closer, ever studying and trans-

mitting new knowledge until, without so much as an electronic whimper, it too was devoured.

The drone protested electronically its own destruction, but its message was not heard or seen. That wasn't the drone's fault. There was, at the moment of ingestion, simply nothing to see. But other instruments were better equipped to tell of those last seconds, and they told the drone station all that was necessary.

Several months passed.

In the station's center a circuit closed. Powerful machinery was engaged. All the information gathered by a dozen far-ranging drones was concentrated into a tight beam for deep-space transmission. With a violent belch of energy, the station spat the knowledge to an occasionally manned station on a far-distant humanx colony world. That station shunted the transmission on to another world, and then on to another, and finally on to Earth, one of the Commonwealth's two capitals. Commonwealth Science Headquarters was located there, on the outskirts of a city on a high mountain plain whose inhabitants had once practiced human sacrifice.

Patiently computers decoded, unraveled, and otherwise made the transmission comprehensible. One small portion of that information was marked for special notice. In due course it reached the eyes of a competent but bored human being. As she examined the information, her eyes grew wide and her boredom vanished. Then she alerted others—human and thranx—and initial puzzlement became panic, then metamorphosed into stunned resignation. The information was reprocessed, rechecked, reexamined. The science staff of the station became re-resigned to the situation.

A meeting quickly convened on the other side of the world. The four people present—two human, two thranx—were very important—important enough to have passed beyond arrogance to humility.

One of the thranx was the current President of the Commonwealth, the other head of all Commonwealth-sponsored scientific research. One of the humans was the Last Resort of the United Church. The other would not normally be considered as important as the other three beings assembled in that room, but circumstances had temporarily made him so. He was the technical supervisor in charge of processing drone information at the Mexico City complex.

When the discussion finally had run out of new things that needed saying, the aged President trieint Drusindromid folded truhands over his thorax and sighed through his spicules. His chiton shone violet with many years, and his antennae drooped so low they hung before his glowing compound eyes. He turned multicolored ommatidia on the waiting human technician. "The information is accurate. There are no mistakes. This you are sure of?"

Both the human technician and the thranx science chief nodded, the human adding: "We are running another drone to the area, sir. It will move on a projected intercept path. Since by the time the drone reaches the region the sun which was being absorbed will have been completely destroyed, we will have to depend on nonvisual instrumentation to detect the wanderer. But I don't really think all this is necessary, sir. The first drone's report is unchallengeable."

"I know the speed of which those drones are capable," the President murmured. "Yet this object is so massive that it surely will have sucked an entire star into itself by the time the new drone arrives?"

"Yes, Honored One," the thranx science chief admitted dolefully. "The radiation that first led our drone to it was from the last of the sun's plasma being drawn off from the surface. That portion of space was full of a *ginhought* amount of particulate radiation, especially gamma rays. It—" The science chief respectfully halted, seeing that the President was absorbed with less technical worries.

The old thranx shook his head slowly, a gesture the insectoids had picked up near the beginning of the Amalgamation, the joining of human- and thranxkind several hundred years ago. "This course," he said, gesturing with a foothand toward the three-dimensional star projection floating above the center of the table, "how long?"

Brushing back white-brown hair, the human technician replied mechanically, "Unless for some unimaginable reason it alters its path, sir, the massive collapsar will emerge from the Velvet Dam in seventy-two point one standard Commonwealth years. Fifteen point six years thereafter, it will impact tangent to the projected critical distance from the sun around which the twin Commonwealth worlds of Carmague-Collangatta orbit. We estimate"—he paused to swallow—"that the sun of the twin worlds will have completely vanished down the hole within a week."

"So fast," the President whispered, "so fast."

"Twenty-seven point three years later," the technician continued remorselessly, "the same catastrophe will befall the star around which the world Twosky Bright circles." He paused a moment, then went on. "No other Commonwealth suns or worlds lie within crisis range of the collapsar's projected path through our galaxy. It will continue on through the galactic axis. Several thousand years from now, it will leave the Milky Way, traveling in the general direction of RNGC 185."

"How can the collapsar move so fast?" the President asked.

The technician glanced at his superior; it was the science chief who replied. "We still do not fully understand all the mechanics of collapsars, Honored One. Such radical distortions of the stellar matrix retain many secrets. It is enough to know that it *is* moving at the indicated speed, on the predicted path."

The President nodded and touched a switch, throwing a vast semicircular map onto the ceiling. He studied the map, ignoring the view of sweltering jungle and marshland visible through the window below the ceiling screen. "What of the three worlds, then?"

Rising, the Last Resort moved to stand next to the science counselor. A tall human, he towered over the President—but only physically. One of the three endangered worlds was inhabited almost solely by thranx, yet they were as much a part of his flock, as devout and inspiring, as was his own family. His robes, in the aquamarine of the Church, were simple and comfortable. Only a single gold insignia on sleeve and collar indicated that he was the ranking member of the Commonwealth's major spiritual organization.

"Carmague and Collangatta are the fourth and twelfth most populous worlds in the Commonwealth, sir," he declared. "Twosky Bright is the twenty-third, but ranks fifteenth in real economic production. Together, the three endangered planets have a population of over three and a half billion. From both a humanxistic and an economic standpoint, their destruction would be a stunning blow."

Great compound eyes stared expectantly up at him. The President hoped wisdom was shining from each of them, instead of the anxiety and helplessness he felt. "What can be done for them?"

The supreme spiritual leader of the Commonwealth turned eyes downward but found no inspiration in the tiled floor. "The Church's logisticians tell me . . . very little, sir. Even given the nearly ninety years left to us, actual evacuation is not practical. It would take the resources of the entire navy plus every Church peaceforcer to shift even a fraction of the populations safely and successfully to other worlds. As soon as such a movement was initiated, the reason behind it would be impossible to keep secret. There would be panic of the worst sort. Naturally, we cannot consider such action. And with the Commonwealth so weakened, there are those who would take advantage of our absent defense."

"I know," murmured President Drusindromid. "What is the maximum number that can be saved without weakening our forces to the point of inviting scavengers?"

"The figures are not exact . . ." the Last Resort began apologetically.

Abruptly, the President's voice cut instead of soothed: "I dislike inaccuracy where humanx lives are concerned, Anthony."

"Yes, sir. If we are lucky, I am told, we may hope to rescue as many as five percent."

There was silence in the tower chamber. Then the President mumbled to himself in High Thranx. Aware that no one had heard, he raised his voice. "Set the necessary events in motion. If it were but one percent, I would still consider the effort worthwhile."

"The problem of panic remains, sir," the Last Resort pointed out.

"We will think of a suitable excuse," the President assured him. "But this must be done. Five percent is nearly two hundred million. Saving two hundred million lives is worth the risk of panic. And we may be lucky and save even more."

"Science does not allow much leeway for luck," the Commonwealth science chief muttered, but only to himself. The President was eyeing them each in turn.

"If there is nothing else, gentlesirs?" Silence in the room. "We have much to do, then, and I have another meeting in half an hour. This one is at an end."

At that signal, the Last Resort, the science chief, and the technician started from the chamber. The President saw them out, using foothands in addition to all four trulegs to support himself. As always, everything rested finally on those aged antennae, the technician thought as he was about to bid the President good-bye. But a truhand reached out and stopped him.

"A moment, young man." The technician was nearly seventy. The President was, however, a good deal older. "There is, of course, no way of stopping, turning, or destroying a collapsar?"

Remembering to whom he was talking, the physicist kept any sign of condescension from his voice. "Hardly, sir. Anything we could throw at it, whether a million SCCAM projectiles or another star, would simply be sucked in. The more we tried to destroy it, the larger it would become, though we wouldn't notice its growth, since it would still be only a point in space. Furthermore, we already know from measurements sent back by the first drone that this wanderer consists of much more than a single collapsed star. Much more.

Perhaps several hundred suns." He shrugged. "Some of my colleagues believe that because of the wanderer's speed and theoretical mass, it may be an object only guessed at by recent mathematics: a collaxar. A collapsed galaxy, sir, instead of a single star."

"Oh" was all the President said immediately. Upper mandibles scraped at the lower pair as he considered this information. "There is a political analogy, young man," he finally ventured. "Something like an idea whose time has come. The more insults and arguments you throw at it, the more powerful it becomes, until one is overwhelmed by it."

"Yes, sir," the technician agreed. "I wish all we were dealing with here was an idea, sir."

"Don't underestimate the destructive power of an idea, hatchling," the President admonished him. He glanced at a wrist chronometer banding a truhand. "Twenty-four minutes till my next appointment. Good day, gentlesir."

"Good day, Mr. President," the technician said; then he left the chamber.

Each of the beings who had joined briefly for the momentous meeting returned to his own task. Each had much to do that did not relate to the subject of the meeting, and glad of it. Being busy was a blessing. It was not healthy to dwell on the unavoidable premature death of over three billion of one's fellow creatures.

Chapter One

"Your offer," the withered woman screamed, "is worthy of a kick in the groin!" She lowered her voice only slightly. "However, I am an old, weak woman. You are younger, larger, stronger, healthier, and wealthier." One hand curled defiantly around the hilt of a crooked blade jutting out from a hole in the dirty brown rag of a skirt. Her other hand held the object under discussion. "So what am I to do?" she finished expectantly.

"Please don't get so excited," the young man standing across from her pleaded, making quieting motions at her with his hands as he looked nervously from side to side.

No one in the shifting mob of sidewalk vendors and buyers was paying any attention to the argument. But, being an outworlder, the young man was sensitive to the old lady's accusations. After all, he and his bride were scheduled to be on Moth for only three days before moving on to New Paris with the rest of the tour. The last thing he wanted was to be thrown in jail, on his honeymoon, for fighting with one of the locals.

"Really," he explained desperately to her, adjusting his rain-soaked mustard-and-puce weather slicker, "thirty credits is all I can afford. Have some sympathy for me. My wife is back in our hotel. She's not feeling very well. The daily rain and constant cloud cover is depressing her, I think. I want something to cheer her up. But we have a long way to travel yet. Thirty credits is all I can afford for a trinket."

The old woman proudly drew herself up to her full height. Her eyes were now level with the young man's chest. She held the object of contention firmly in one hand as she shook it accusingly at him. The slim, graceful bracelet of some silvery metal was inlaid with fragments of polished wood and stone.

"This wristlet was worked and set by Cojones Cutler himself, infant! Do you have any idea, *any idea*, what that signifies?"

"I'm sorry," the youth tried to explain, sniffing, "but I've been trying to explain all along that I am only a visitor here."

Clearly the woman restrained herself only by some great inner effort. "Very well," she said tightly, "never mind the honored name of Cojones Cutler." She indicated the oval bulges set in the bracelet. "Look at these whirlwood cabochons—forget the topazes for now." As she turned the bracelet, the naturally hardened, polished sap facing the wood broke the dim daylight into points of azure-and-green fire.

"Hardly a tree in a million has the genetic deficiency necessary to produce such colors, boy. Hardly one in a million, and those grow only in the far north of Moth, where the nomads hunt the Demichin devilope. Why, it takes—"

"Oh, all right." The young man sighed, exasperated. "Anything to get this over with. Thirty-five credits, then." He couldn't have been more than twenty-two or twenty-three. His face was soft and earnest. "We'll just have to stay at a lower-class hotel on New Paris, that's all."

The old woman stared up at him and shook her head in disbelief. "You talk of hotels, and me with three starving children and a husband long dead. You can stand there and talk of hotels, brazen child, while offering me thirty-five credits for the finest bracelet I've been lucky to get on consignment in twenty years. Twenty years!" Her voice rose to a hoarse shout again. "Make me a decent offer or go room with the devil, I say!" she screeched, loudly enough to turn a few heads in the crowd. "But don't stand there innocently and insult a poor old woman!"

"For Church's sake," the youth pleaded, "lower your voice."

Sheltered beneath a rain cape of violet-gray charged slickertic, the young man who had been idly observing the noisy byplay of buyer and seller licked the last sweet traces of thisk-cake honey from his fingers. Then he rose and sauntered toward the quarreling pair.

Slightly under average height, with smoothly arcing cheekbones and deeply tanned skin, he did not present a particularly eye-catching figure. A thatch of curly red hair roofed his skull, hair the color of a field of fireweed on the open tundra. It tumbled over his forehead and ears. Only the odd movement of something under the right side of his rain cape indicated anything out of the ordinary, but the object—whatever it was— was too well concealed to be identified.

". . . and if there's nothing better you can say," the old woman was raving on, "then you'd better—"

"Excuse me," a quiet voice interrupted. "I'd say thirty-five credits for that bracelet is a fair price."

Mouth agape in puzzlement, the young husband stared, uncomprehending, at the slim youth, and wondered why a native should interfere on his behalf. The old vendor turned a furious gaze on the brazen interloper.

"I don't know who you are, sir," she rumbled dangerously, "but if you don't mind your own business I'll—" She stopped in mid-sentence, her mouth frozen in an *O* of shock.

"You'll do what, old woman?" the youngster asked. "Send me to bed without supper?"

Sensing an advantage without knowing its origin, the

dazed bracelet-buyer was quick to act. "Thirty-five credits is really a fair price, as he says."

"Yes ... I ..." The old woman, appearing a little stunned herself, hardly seemed to hear the offer. "Thirty-five, then, and be done with it."

"You're certain?" The outworlder, now sure of his purchase, was anxious to ingratiate himself with the seller. Since he was a good deal bigger than the new arrival, he took a step forward. "If this boy is intimidating you, I'd be glad to ..."

Something moved and partially emerged from cape folds. It was leathery, thin, and brightly colored. Without actually recognizing the object, the outworld tourist nonetheless had an immediate impression of serpentine lethality. His hand proffered his credit slip instead of closing into a fist.

"Here's your money, then."

Mesmerized by the caped figure, the old woman mechanically processed the credit slip through her cardmeter; she handed it back to the buyer without even troubling to check the reference number.

"The bracelet," the young visitor urged impatiently.

"Hmmm? Oh, yes." She handed it over. Flushed with pleasure at his imagined bargain, the tall tourist vanished into the milling crowd of humans and aliens.

Slowly the old woman studied the unimposing figure standing before her. Then she abruptly threw thin but still muscular arms around him and squeezed tightly. "Flinx!" she shouted exuberantly. "Flinx, boy, you've come home!" She shook the lanky youth out of sheer joy, for the familiar feel of him. Jostled, Pip the minidrag shifted uncomfortably on Flinx's shoulder and attempted to tolerate the roughhousing with fine reptilian indifference.

"For a little while, Mother Mastiff," the youth replied quietly. He grinned and nodded in the direction of the departed outworlder. "I see you're having as much fun as ever."

"Fun!" she snorted derisively, making an obscene gesture in the general direction of the marketplace into which her customer had disappeared. "Pathetic, most of them. They suck the enjoyment from trading. Sometimes I wonder how the Commonwealth hangs together, with cement like that." A triangular head flanked by eyes of fire peeked out from beneath the slickertic. The old woman eyed it with evident distaste. "See you're still dragging that creature around with you."

Pip responded with a nasty hiss. There had never been any love lost between Mother Mastiff and the minidrag.

"Many times I think it's Pip who drags me, Mother," the youth argued.

"Well, no matter perversions I can't cure you of, boy. At least you're here." She whacked him on the left shoulder in mock anger. "Here you are ... you good-for-nothing, forgetful, heartless lump of immature meat! Where have you been to? It's been over a year. A year, paragon of ingrates! Not a tridee tape, not a card, nothing!"

"I am sorry, Mother Mastiff," he confessed, putting his arm around her bony shoulders. She shrugged angrily, but not hard enough to dislodge his arm. "It wasn't that I didn't think of you. But I was far from modern communications."

"Ah, in trouble again?" She shook her head. "Is that the way I raised you?" He started to reply, but she cut him off hastily. "Never mind that now. Where were you? Come, tell me back at the shop."

They started down the street. Aromatic scents and the cries of Drallar's inner marketplace filled the air around them. "Come, boy, tell me, where were you, that you couldn't let me know if your worthless carcass was still intact?"

Flinx considered his response carefully. He had good reasons for wanting to keep his whereabouts of the past year secret. What Mother Mastiff didn't know she could never reveal.

"I took a job, sort of," he finally explained.

She gaped at him. "You ... a job?"

"I'm not lying," he argued uncomfortably, unable to

meet those disbelieving eyes. "I set my own hours and work pretty much as I want to."

"Now I just might, just *might* believe you. What kind of job?"

Again he glanced away evasively. "I can't say exactly. I'm sort of a teacher, a private tutor."

"A teacher," she echoed, evidently impressed. "A private tutor, eh?" She let out a snicker. "What is it you teach? Pickpocketing, breaking and entering, or general theft?"

"Now what would I know about such things?" he countered in astonishment. "Is that how you brought me up?" They both chuckled. "No, I'm kind of a general-purpose instructor in basics."

"I see" was all she said this time, so he was spared the difficulty of explaining what kind of basics he taught, and to whom. Especially to whom; it was not time for Mother Mastiff or anyone else to know about the Ulru-Ujurrians, the race he had adopted and which had adopted him. The race that could turn this corner of creation inside out.

"Never mind me," he insisted, staring at her. "Here I take money and set you up in one of the fanciest shop districts of Drallar, with top-flight stock, and how do I find you? Like this!" He indicated her ragged clothes, torn skirt and overblouse, the ugly muffin of a hat perched precariously on long, straggly hair. "Out in the street in the rain and damp, clad in scraps."

Now it was Mother Mastiff's turn to glance away. They turned up a cobblestone street and entered a less frenetic section of the city.

"I got itchy nervous, boy, sitting in that fancy store all day. I missed the streets, the contacts, the noise—"

"The arguments and shouting," Flinx finished for her.

"And the gossip," she went on. "Especially the gossip." She eyed him defiantly. "At my age it's one of the few disreputable delights I haven't grown too old for."

Flinx indicated the street ahead. "So that's why we're not headed for the shop?"

"No, not that stuffy snuffbox, not on a beautiful day

like today." Flinx studied the gray, overcast sky, blinked at the ever-present mist, but said nothing. Actually, it *was* a rather nice day for Drallar. It wasn't raining. He had been home for two weeks and had yet to see the sun.

"Let's go to Dramuse's stall. I'll treat you to lunch."

Flinx expressed surprise. "You buy someone else lunch? Still, after the profit you made on that bracelet . . ."

"*Pfagh!* I could have gotten that callow stripling up to fifty credits easy. Knew it the second he set eyes on that bracelet. Then you had to come along."

"One of these days, Mother, you'll go too far with some knowledgeable offworlder and he'll turn you in to the King's police. I broke in because he seemed like a decent man on his mating flight, and I didn't want to see him cheated too badly."

"Shows what you know," she snapped back. "He wasn't as ignorant as he made *you* think. You weren't there to see his eyes light up when I mentioned the street my shop is on and told him that's where it was stolen from. He knew what he was about, all right. Did you see him shout for the police? No, he was cuddling his hot property like any decent good citizen. Here." She stopped and gestured beyond a gate to tables covered with brightly dyed canopies.

They had entered the last of the concentric rings that formed Drallar's marketplace. This outermost ring consisted entirely of restaurants and food stalls. They ranged from tiny one-being operations with primitive wood-fired stoves to expensive closed-in establishments in which delicacies imported from the farthest corners of the Commonwealth were served on utensils of faceted veridian. Here the air currents stalled, weaving languorous zephyrs of overpowering potency.

They entered a restaurant that used neither wood nor veridian plates and was somewhere between the opulent and the barely digestible in terms of menu. After taking seats, they ordered food from a creature who looked like a griffin with tentacles instead of legs. Then

Mother Mastiff exchanged her gentle accusations for more serious talk.

"Now, boy, I know you went off to look for your natural parents." It was a sign of her strength that she could voice the subject without stumbling. "You've been gone for over a year. You must have learned something."

Flinx leaned back and was silent for a moment. Pip wiggled out from beneath the cape folds, and Flinx scratched the flying snake under its chin. "As far as I know," he finally responded tersely, "they're both long dead." Pip shifted uneasily, suddenly sensitive to his master's somber mood. "My mother ... at least I know who she was. A Lynx, a concubine. I also found a half sister, and when I found her, I ended up having to kill her."

Food arrived, spicy and steaming. They ate quietly for a while. Despite the heavy spices, the food tasted flat to both of them.

"Mother dead, half sister dead," Mother Mastiff grunted. "No other relatives?" Flinx shook his head curtly. "What about your natural father?"

"Couldn't find a thing about him worth following up."

Mother Mastiff wrestled with some private demon, and finally murmured, "You've run far and long, boy. But there's still a possibility."

He glanced sharply at her. "Where?"

"Here. Yes, even here."

"Why," he said quietly, "didn't you ever tell me?"

Mother Mastiff shrugged once. "I saw no reason to mention it. It's an obscure chance, boy, a waste of time, an absurd thought."

"I've spent a year pursuing absurdities," he reminded her. "Give, Mother."

"When I bought you in the market," she began easily, as if discussing any ordinary transaction, "it was a perfectly ordinary sale. Still don't know what possessed me to waste good money."

Flinx stifled a grin. "Neither do I. I don't follow you though."

"Find the dealer who sold you, Flinx. Perhaps he or she is still in business. There's always the chance the firm kept decent records. I wasn't too concerned with your pedigree. Might be there's some additional information in their records that wasn't provided with the bill of sale. Not likely, now. But all I was interested in was whether or not you were diseased. You looked it, but you weren't." She sipped from a mug. "Sometimes those slavers don't give out all the information they get. They've got their reasons."

"But how can I trace the firm that sold me?"

"City records," she snuffled, wiping liquid from her chin. "There would have been a tax on the business. Try the King's tax records for the year I bought you. Waste of time, though."

"I've plenty of time now," he said cryptically. "I'll try it and gladly." He reached out across the table and patted a cheek with the look and feel of tired suede. "But for the rest of the day, let's be mother and son."

She slapped the caressing hand away and fussed at him . . . but softly.

Chapter Two

The following day dawned well. The morning rain was light, and the cloud cover actually showed some signs of clearing. Flinx was spared the shocking sight of sunlight in Drallar when the clouds thickened after he started toward the vast, rambling expanse of official buildings. They clustered like worker ants around the spines of their queen, whose body was the King's palace.

Damp, cool weather invigorated Flinx. Moist air felt familiar in his lungs; it was the air of the only home he had ever known. Or could remember, he corrected himself.

He stopped to chat with two side-street vendors, people he had known since childhood. Yet at first neither of them recognized him. Had he changed so much in one year? Was he so different at seventeen from what he had been at sixteen? True, he had gone through a great deal in that year. But when he looked in the mirror it was no stranger he saw. No fresh lines marred his smooth brown skin, no great tragedy welled out of cocoa eyes. Yet to others he was somehow not the same.

Possibly the crashing kaleidoscope that was Drallar simply made people forget. Resolutely he shut out the shouts and excitement of the city, strode past intriguing stalls and sights while ignoring the implorings of hawkers and merchants. No more time to waste on such childish diversions, he instructed himself. He had responsibilities now. As the leader of an entire race in the Great Game he must put aside infantile interests.

Ah, but the child in him was still strong, and it was a hard thing to do, this growing up . . .

Like a granite ocean the myriad walls of Old Drallar crashed in frozen waves against the sprawling bastion of bureaucracy which was the administrative center of Drallar and of the entire planet Moth. Modern structures piled haphazardly into medieval ones. Beyond towered the King's palace, spires and minarets and domes forming a complex resembling a gigantic diatom. Like much of the city, the building looked as if it had been designed by a computer programmed with the *Arabian Nights* instead of up-to-date technologies.

Flinx was crossing the outermost ring of stalls when two striking figures passed in front of him—a man and woman, both slightly taller than Flinx but otherwise physically unimpressive. What was striking about them was the reaction they provoked in others. People took pains to avoid the couple, even to avoid looking in their direction. But they did so carefully, to be certain of not giving offense.

The couple were Qwarm.

Barely tolerated by the Commonwealth government, the Qwarm were a widely dispersed clan of professional enforcers, whose services ranged from collecting overdue debts to assassination. Despite being shunned socially, the clan had prospered with the growth of the Commonwealth. Since the beginning of time, there had always been a market for the services they chose to provide.

Flinx knew that the two walking past him were

related in some fashion to every other Qwarm in the Commonwealth. Both wore skin-tight jet-black jumpsuits ending in black ankle boots. Those boots, he knew, contained many things besides feet. A decorative cape of black and rust-red streamers fluttered from each collar to the waist, like the tail of an alien bird.

Having heard of the Qwarm but never having had the opportunity to see one, Flinx paused at a small booth. Pretending to inspect a copper-crysacolla pitcher, he surreptitiously eyed the two retreating strangers.

Standing behind them now, he could no longer see their faces, but he knew that the bodies inside the jumpsuits would be as hairless as their heads were beneath the black skullcaps. Red foil designs marked each cap, the only decorative touch aside from the streamers on their clothing. Various pouches and containers hung from each black belt—pouches and containers which held a great many varieties of death, Flinx knew. If he remembered correctly, each belt would be joined in front by a buckle cut from a single orange-red vanadium crystal, which would be inlaid with a gold skull-and-crossbones. Their uniform was sufficient to identify them.

The crowd parted for them without panic. To run might be to give offense. No one desired to give offense to a Qwarm.

Flinx took a step away from the booth—and froze. Unbidden, as it often was, his talent had unexpectedly given him an image. The image was of incipient murder. He hadn't sought the information. The most frustrating feature of his peculiar abilities was that they often functioned most effectively when he had no need of them.

Instantly he knew that the man and woman were a husband-wife team and that their quarry was very near. He tried for a picture of the quarry and, as he half expected, saw nothing.

Even more bewildering were the waves of curiosity and confusion that emanated from the Qwarm couple. Flinx had heard that the Qwarm were never puzzled about anything, least of all anything related to their work. Someone was nearby whom they had to murder, and this puzzled them. Strange. What could so puzzle a pair of professional killers?

Flinx cast about for an explanation and found only a mental blank. He was human and only human once more. So he found himself torn between common sense and his damnably intense curiosity. If only that powerful sensation of uncertainty from the couple hadn't leaped into his mind. Nothing should puzzle a Qwarm so. Nothing! Cause concern, yes, because murder was still illegal and if caught they could be tried and punished by the authorities.

But confusion? Impossible!

Suddenly Flinx found himself walking not toward the receding solidity of the administration center but back into the depths of the sprawling, chaotic marketplace. The black-clad pair were easy to follow. They were utterly devoid of suspicion. Qwarm stalked others; no one followed a Qwarm.

Despite Pip's nervous stirrings on his shoulder, Flinx moved closer. Still the Qwarm gave no indication that they were at all aware of him. At the moment he had nothing in mind beyond following the two killers to the source of their confusion.

A small crowd formed a bottleneck just ahead. The black-clad couple paused and talked together in whispers. Flinx thought he could sense muscles tensing. They ceased conversing and seemed to be straining to see over the heads of the cluster of beings ahead of them.

Moving forward, Flinx encountered a low section of ancient wall off to one side. Part of it was occupied by seated figures staring over the heads of the crowd. No one spared him a glance as he mounted the wall and joined them. Seated securely on the damp, slick stone, he found he could easily see over the heads of even the tall avians in the crowd, which consisted mostly of local humans sprinkled with a few warmly bundled thranx and a smattering of other alien types. His position afforded him a clear view of the center of attraction. He could also keep an eye on the Qwarm, off to his right.

In front of the crescent of laughing, appreciative creatures was a small raised stage. Flinx experienced a jolt of recognition. Jongleurs, magicians, and other entertainers were using the public stage to perform their various specialties for the entertainment of the crowd and the enhancement of their own empty pockets. Not much more than a year and a half ago, he had been one of those hopeful, enthusiastic performers. He and Pip had gone through much since those days. He felt the snake relax, responding to his nostalgic mood.

A juggler currently working the stage finished manipulating four brightly colored spheres. One by one he tossed them into the air, and one by one they vanished, to the apparent mystification of the performer and the appreciative oohs and ahs of the crowd. The watchers applauded; the juggler collected. Life advanced.

Flinx smiled. The material of which the balls were composed remained visible only when heat was steadily applied—such as that generated by the juggler's rapidly moving hands. When that activating body heat was removed, even for a couple of seconds, the spheres became invisible. Behind the stage, Flinx knew, the juggler's assistant waited to catch the carefully thrown invisible objects. Timing was essential to the act, since the assistant had to be in just the right position to catch the spheres.

The juggler departed. As the next act came out on stage, Flinx felt a supple dig at his mind. For a brief instant he was experiencing the same feeling as the Qwarm. Looking over, he felt that they were straining to see a little harder.

He turned his attention to their intended victim.

A tall, robust-looking individual, the figure on stage was not as dark-skinned as Flinx. Black hair fell in greasy strands down his neck. He was dressed simply in sandals, loose slickertic pants, and a shirt opened to show a mat of thick curls on his chest. The shift sleeves were puffed, possibly to hide part of the act.

Try as he would, Flinx could see or detect nothing

remarkable about the man—certainly nothing that might require the attention of two Qwarm instead of one. Yet something here worried someone enough to engage the services of those dread people.

Holding on to a shiny cord, the man was pulling at something still hidden behind the stage backdrop. The jokes and insults he alternately bestowed on whatever was at the other end of the cord were not particularly clever, but the crowd was well baited, anxious to see what could absorb such comments without responding.

It was beginning to drizzle again. The crowd, used to omnipresent precipitation, ignored the rain. The jokes started to wear thin, and the crowd showed signs of restlessness. Having built the suspense, the rope-handler vented a violent curse and gave a hard yank on the cord. Flinx tensed slightly, now really anxious to see what was at the other end of the tether.

When the creature finally wobbled unsteadily around the backdrop, its appearance was so anticlimactic, so utterly ludicrous, that Flinx found himself laughing in mixed relief and disbelief. So did the rest of the crowd.

What emerged from behind the wall was probably the dopiest-looking creature he had ever seen, of a species completely unknown to him. Barely over a meter and a half tall, it was shaped roughly like a pear. The ovoid skull tapered unbroken into a conical neck, which in turn spread out into a wide, bulbous lower torso. It stumbled about on four legs ending in circular feet tipped with toe stubs. Where the neck began to spread into the lumpy body, four arms projected outward, each ending in four well-developed, jointless fingers. The thing gave the impression of being rubbery, boneless.

The creature was dressed in a vest with holes cut at equal intervals for the four arms. Baggy, comical trousers completed the attire. Four large holes were set around the top of the head. Flinx guessed these were hearing organs. Beneath them, four limpid eyes stared stupidly in all directions. Occasionally one or two would blink, revealing double lids which closed like shades over the center of each pupil.

A single organ like an elephant's flexible trunk protruded from the top of the bald skull. It ended in a mouth, which served, Flinx guessed, as both eating and speaking organ ... assuming the thing was capable of making noises.

As if this grotesque farrago of organs, limbs, and costume wasn't hysterical enough, the creature was colored bright sky-blue, with green vertical stripes running from neck to feet. Its owner-manager-trainer gave the cord another sharp yank, and the apparition wobbled forward, letting out a comical honk. Those in the front of the crowd burst into laughter again.

Flinx only winced. Although the tugs on the cord didn't seem to be injuring the creature physically, he didn't like to see anything mistreated. Besides, no matter how hard its owner pulled, Flinx had the feeling that the creature was moving at its own speed, in its own time.

Then, abruptly, Flinx wondered what he was doing there. He ought to be hunting down officials and records, not watching an unremarkable sideshow. The training which had preserved him as a child in Drallar began to reassert itself. It was none of his business if the Qwarm wanted to kill an itinerant animal trainer. He could gain nothing by intruding himself into this affair, Flinx reminded himself coldly. His curiosity had gotten him into trouble often enough before.

He began to slip from his perch as the man in question ran through his routine, prancing about on stage while the crowd laughed at his antics and at those of the poorly trained but funny-looking creature. As the owner attempted to get the creature to execute various movements and the thing clumsily tried to comply, the laughter rose steadily.

Flinx was about to abandon his place when something happened to give him pause—at a command from the owner, the creature spoke.

It had an arresting, well-modulated, and undeniably intelligent voice, and it spoke quite comprehensible Terranglo despite its alien vocal organs. At another command, the creature switched to symbospeech, the commercial and social dialect of the Commonwealth. The alien's voice was a high, mellifluous tenor that bordered on the girlish.

It was reciting gibberish. The words each meant something, but the way the alien was stringing them together made no sense. Over this rambling monologue, the trainer was speaking to the crowd. "Alas," the man was saying, "this strange being, who lives to delight and amuse us all, might possibly be as intelligent as you or I. Yet it cannot learn to speak understandably, for all that it could be our superior."

At this the alien produced—on cue from its trainer, Flinx suspected—another of its hysterical honks. The crowd, momentarily mesmerized by the trainer's spiel, collapsed with laughter again.

"Unfortunately," the trainer went on when the roar had subsided, "poor Ab is quite insane. Isn't that right, Ab?" he asked the alien. It responded with more of its nonstop gibbering, only this time all in rhyme. "Maybe he's glad, maybe he's sad, but as the philosopher once said, he is undoubtedly mad," the trainer observed, and the alien honked again, beaming at the crowd.

Flinx made an attempt to plunge into that alien mind. He achieved just what he expected, which was nothing. If an intelligence capable of something greater than mimicry existed there, it was hidden from him. More likely, there was nothing there to read.

Flinx pitied the creature and idly wondered where it had come from as he jumped down off the wall and brushed at the seat of his clammy pants. No doubt the Qwarm were going to perform their job soon, and he had no morbid desire to stay around to discover what method they were going to employ.

It hit him like a hammer blow when he was halfway up the street. The imagery had come from the Qwarm. Turning and walking quickly back toward the crowd, he had a glimpse of them heading for a nearby building. The image they had unexpectedly projected explained the cause of their confusion: Their intended victim was not the simple animal trainer but rather his subject.

It was reputed that the Qwarm did not hire themselves out for killing cheaply or frivolously. Therefore, one had to assume that in utter seriousness, and at considerable expense to someone—they were about to murder a foolish, seemingly harmless alien.

There was no hint of worry or suspicion in the trainer's mind, and nothing at all in that of his muddled ward. The minds of the Qwarm held only continued confusion and a desire to complete their assigned task. They could not question their task aloud, but they wondered privately.

The stone-and-wood structure they vanished into was slightly over two stories tall, backed up against several other old, solid edifices. As if in a daze, Flinx found himself moving toward the same building. Listening with mind and ears, hunting with eyes, he stopped at the threshold. No one was standing guard inside the doorway. And why should they? Who would trail Qwarm, especially these Qwarm?

He stepped into the building. The old stairway at the far end of the hallway showed one of the Qwarm ascending out of view. It was the woman, and she had been pulling something from a pouch. Flinx thought the object she removed might be a very tiny, expertly machined pistol of black metal.

Cautioning Pip to silence, Flinx approached the railing and started upward, alert for any movement from above. As he mounted the rickety spiral he ran his last image of her over again in his mind. Probably a dart pistol, he mused. He knew of organic darts that would dissolve in a victim's body immediately after insertion. Both the dart and the toxin it carried would become undetectable soon after injection.

The staircase opened onto a second floor. Flinx turned his head slowly. Both Qwarm were standing by a window. One of them pulled the shade aside and peered through cautiously.

A quick glance revealed that this floor was being lived on. It was sparsely but comfortably appointed. In a far, dark corner an attractive but tired-looking young woman was huddling on cushions, cuddling a much younger girl protectively in her arms. She was staring fearfully at the Qwarm.

Flinx returned his attention to the assassins. While her companion held the shade back, the woman was readying the black pistol, her arm resting motionless on the windowsill. Without question, she was about to murder the alien.

He had learned everything he could here; there was no point in staying around. As he started to retreat back down the stairs, the woman in the dark corner saw him and drew in a startled breath. No normal person would have noticed it, but to the Qwarm it might just as well have been a scream. Both whirled from the window, startled. Pip was off Flinx's shoulder before the youth could restrain the minidrag.

Reaching for his boot top, Flinx heard a slight *phut* from the supposed dart pistol. The explosive shell blew apart the section of floor he had just been leaning against. Then he rose and threw the knife in one smooth motion at the other Qwarm, who was fumbling at a belt pouch. It struck the man in the neck. He went down, trying to staunch the flow of blood from his severed artery.

The female hesitated ever so slightly, unable to make up her mind whether to fire at Flinx or at the darting, leathery little nightmare above her. The hesitation was fatal. Pip spat, and the minidrag's venom struck the woman in the eyes. Unbelievably, she didn't scream as she stumbled about the room, clawing frantically at her face. She banged into the wall, fell over the twitching body of the man, and began rolling on the floor.

Fifteen seconds later, she was dead.

The man continued to bleed, though he had stopped moving. Flinx entered the room and rapidly inspected side rooms and closets. He was safe—for the moment. The little girl in the corner was crying softly now, but the woman holding her merely stared wide-eyed at Flinx, still too terrified to scream.

"Don't tell a soul of this," Flinx admonished her as

a nervous Pip coiled once more around his right shoulder.

"We won't ... please, don't kill us," the woman whispered in fear. Flinx gazed into blank, pleading eyes. The little girl stared at the two motionless bodies, trying to understand.

Flinx found himself staggering back toward the stairway. Without even bothering to recover his knife, he plunged down the steps. Somehow he had completely lost control of events and as had happened too often in the past, events had ended up controlling him.

At the bottom of the stairs he paused, regarding the open doorway as an enemy. A glance right and left showed that this floor was still deserted. There had to be a back way out; he went hunting and found a little-used exit opening onto a narrow, smelly alley. The pathway appeared empty. After a careful search, he started down it at a brisk trot. Soon he was back on the streets. The moment he was convinced he wasn't being followed, he turned and angled back toward the stage, approaching it from a new direction.

As for the woman with the child, he suspected she would find new lodgings as quickly and quietly as possible. She might notify the police and she might not.

By the time he reached his destination, the show was concluding. He slipped easily into the protective wall of bodies. Nothing had changed: The trainer was still making jokes at the dopey alien's expense and the alien was bearing it all with the serenity of the softheaded. And that oval head *did* look soft, Flinx reflected. So why had the Qwarm felt it necessary to use such dangerously identifiable explosive projectiles?

A respectable amount of applause and some tossed coins were awarded at the end of the show, as much for uniqueness as for polish, he suspected. The trainer scrambled about after the coins without regard for dignity.

The crowd started to disperse. Apparently the alien act was the last for the afternoon at this location. Flinx sauntered casually backstage, where he found the trainer counting his money and inspecting his few

props. Almost at once, the man grew aware of Flinx's
attention and looked up sharply. On seeing that it was
only a youth, he relaxed.

"What do you want, youngling?" he inquired
brusquely.

"We have something in common, sir."

"I can't imagine what."

"We both train aliens." Pip moved suddenly on
Flinx's shoulder, showing bright colors in the cloud-fil-
tered light. The man frowned, and squinted as he
peered close.

"I don't recognize your pet, boy."

Whoever this fellow was, Flinx thought, he wasn't
well traveled or informed. Minidrags were not common, but their reputation far exceeded their numbers.
Yet this man obviously didn't know one when he saw
one.

Flinx found his attention shifting to the alien, which
stood patiently to one side, muttering rhythmically to
itself in some unknown language. "In any case," he explained, "I'm curious about *your* pet. I've never seen
anything like him." To make conversation, he went on,
"Where did you get its name from?"

Flinx's politeness disarmed the man a little. "It came
with the poor dumb monster," he explained, exhibiting
more sympathy than Flinx would have suspected of
him. "I bought it from an animal dealer who thought it
no more than that. But the creature has some kind of
intelligence. It can speak as well as you or I, and in
many languages. But in none of 'em does it make
sense. Oh, Ab's quite mad, it is, but he can learn.
Slowly, but enough to serve in the act." He smiled,
now filled with pride. "I was smart enough to recognize
his uniqueness. No one else has ever been able to identify Ab's species either, boy. I hope it's a long-lived
one, though, since this one's irreplaceable.

"Far as the name goes, that's kind of a funny tale.
Only time he's ever made sense." He frowned. "I was
trying to decide what to call 'im when he gave out with
one of his crazy ramblings." He turned and eyed the
alien. One egg-yolk eye watched him while the other

three operated independently. Flinx considered that a creature capable of looking in four directions at once must have a mind of considerable complexity, simply to monitor such a flood of neural responses.

"What's your name, idiot," the trainer asked, pronouncing the words slow and careful. "Name!"

"Mana, Orix, Gelmp nor Panda," the liquid tones ventured promptly, "my name is Abalamahalamatandra."

While the creature continued to mumble on in verse, the man looked back at Flinx. "Easy to see why I call 'im Ab, hey?" he bent over and wiped at his muddy boots. "Dealer I bought him from had no clue to his species. Just assured me he was docile and friendly, which he is."

"It's remarkable," Flinx observed, flattering the man as he studied the blue-and-green lump, "that as mad as Ab is, you've managed to teach him so much."

"Told you, boy, all I've taught Ab are the rules of the act. He's a mind of his own, of sorts. I said he can talk in many tongues, didn't I?" Flinx nodded. "Terranglo and symbospeech are just two of 'em. Every once in a while Ab gives me a start when I think he's said something almost sensible." He shrugged. "Then when I try to follow it up he goes on blabbin' about the taste of the sky or the color of air or stuff I can't make any sense of whatsoever. You're curious about 'im, are you? Go over and say hello, then."

"You're sure it's all right?"

"I said he was friendly, boy. In any case, he's got no teeth."

Flinx approached the alien tentatively. The creature observed his approach with two eyes, which crossed as he neared. Flinx smiled in spite of himself. Experimentally, he extended a hand as if to shake the alien's.

Two eyes dipped downward. One smooth hand came up and slapped Flinx's palm. Flinx drew his hand back sharply, more surprised than hurt. As if in admonition, another hand came around and slapped at the one which had struck Flinx. Apparently enchanted, the alien commenced slapping its four palms together, entirely ignoring Flinx.

The alien palm had been hard, flat, and cool to the touch.

The owner was speaking again. "Ab will eat just about anything except," he finished with a smile, "me and thee." Rising, he walked up to Ab and booted the creature hard. It ceased slapping itself and resumed mumbling steadily, like an idling engine. "C'mon, sit down for a while, you stupid monstrosity."

Showing no sign of pain, Ab sat down on the ground and began cleaning its feet with all four hands. In that position it looked like a demented triclops trying to pull its toes off. Again Flinx found himself grinning unintentionally.

"Have to do that when I'm not watchin' 'im," the man explained, "or he'll wander off."

"I can see why you use Ab in a comedy act," Flinx observed readily. "What I can't understand is why anyone, least of all a Qwarm, would want to kill it."

At the mention of the assassin clan the trainer lost his composure, his emerging friendliness, and most of the color in his face.

"Qwarm?" he stammered.

"Two of them," Flinx elaborated. He nearly turned and indicated the building with its window facing on the stage. Then he thought better of it. "I don't know why they changed their minds," he lied, "but I know for a fact that they want your pet dead."

"Qwarm?" the man repeated. At that moment, Ab appeared to be the more balanced of the two. Looking around frantically, the man grabbed a small black satchel. A couple of coins fell from a half-open pocket. He ignored them.

"You train aliens too?" he bleated hurriedly. "Good. He's all yours now, boy."

"Wait a minute!" Flinx protested. Things were happening too quickly again. "I don't want to—"

" 'Bye and luck to you, boy!" the man shouted back to him. He put out a hand, vaulted a nearby railing, and vanished on the run into the milling crowd nearby.

"Hey, hold on!" Flinx shouted, rushing to the railing. "Come back, I can't take care of—"

There was a tentative honk from behind. Flinx turned and saw Ab staring blankly at him while mumbling steadily. When he turned back to the crowd, the trainer was out of sight, though his terror still lingered like the scent of cloves.

Flinx stared over and down at the striped blue alien. "Now what am I going to do with you?" The fix he now found himself in was his own fault, of course. If he had taken care not to mention the Qwarm by name . . . Well, no matter now. He started to walk away. A fresh, louder honk stopped him.

Ab had stood up and was following Flinx. At the sight of that utterly open, helpless face, Flinx's coldness shattered. Whatever else he did he couldn't leave the poor thing alone. It would probably remain where it was, cleaning itself, until someone took charge of it or it starved to death.

Served him right. He had started the day in an attempt to find out something about himself. Instead, he'd killed two Qwarm and acquired an alien simpleton by default.

"I can't keep you," he told the bubbling creature, "but we'll find a place for you as quickly as possible." One big eye blinked disarmingly at him.

"Mur'til hurtill?" he sang.

"Yeah, come on," Flinx instructed. "I'm going to finish the day the way I should have started it." He started off; a glance behind showed the creature following dutifully, weaving on its four legs. Spouting sing-song nonsense, it trailed Flinx through the crowd, apparently as happy with its present master as it had been with the former one.

Flinx was not happy with the stares his strange companion drew, but there was nothing that could be done about it. As soon as he finished with the records department, he would get rid of the creature.

There was a knock at the door.

The woman sent her silent little girl into the bathroom. Then she walked over to lean against the door and listened with one hand on the bolt. "Yes?" she finally asked quietly.

"You have a delivery," a soft voice replied.

That was the code sentence. She glanced at the covered bodies of the black-clad man and woman lying beneath the window and threw the bolt sharply.

"Thank you for coming so quick," she said gratefully. "I don't care how you dispose of them, just—" She choked on the rest of the words.

The man on the other side of the doorway was not from the discreet service she had contacted. Dressed entirely in black, devoid of hair even to the shaved eyebrows, he was clearly a mate to the corpses in her chamber.

His gaze indicated that he bore her no animosity, but that he would as soon kill her as talk with her. Her hand went to her lips, and she slowly backed away from the door as the man entered. He was tall—very tall. He had to bend to fit beneath the portal.

His stare traveled across the room, lingering momentarily on the two shapes beneath the blankets. Embroidered red whirls on his skullcap caught the afternoon light, as did the skull engraved into his belt buckle. It gleamed like alien blood in the room.

"I didn't," the woman started to say, then she slumped inwardly, her hands falling limply to her side. "What does it matter now," she muttered, with the resignation of those who have no hope. She sank down on the pillows in the far corner, where she entertained business far too frequently. "It's a rotten life, probably hopeless for the poor child, too. Kill me if you want. This is all too far above me. I can't fight any more."

Ignoring her, the man strode past her to kneel above the two bodies. He did not seem to believe these two could be dead. When he finished, he rose and turned to her. The fury in his eyes was so bright that in spite of her declaration she shrank back a little deeper into the cushions.

"I have no quarrel with you or your child," he explained, with a curt nod in the direction of the bathroom. "Why, though, did you not notify us instead of calling for others to take away the dead?"

The woman laughed hollowly. "Nobody contacts the Qwarm if it can be avoided, no matter what their situation."

"True. I note your point," the tall specter acknowledged without humor. "I suppose it would have been too much to expect." Moving to the window, he leaned out and made a beckoning motion.

Shortly, four men entered the room. They were not Qwarm. Carefully they loaded the bodies into two long cylinders. When they departed, the tall hunter turned his attention back to the silent woman in the corner. There was a soft murmur from the region of the bathroom.

"Mommy . . . can I come out now?"

Suddenly the woman looked frightened again. Her gaze shifted rapidly from the tall figure to the bathroom door and back again.

"I said I have no quarrel with you, woman." He leaned close over her, ice-eyed, hollow-cheeked. "Our quarrel is with whoever was foolish enough to have done this thing." Reaching into a pocket at his belt, he brought out a fistful of metal bars.

In spite of her fear, the woman's eyes glowed. Here was more money than she had ever seen at one time in her life. It represented many, many weeks during which she would not have to entertain visitors in the room.

"Describe them," the Qwarm said tightly, extending the metal.

The woman licked her lips as she considered. She did not have to consider long. "Not them," she corrected. "Him."

For the first time since entering the apartment, the specter showed some emotion: surprise. "Only one?"

he inquired in a disbelieving, warning tone. "You are certain? Might he have had friends, accomplices?"

"I don't know," she insisted. "I saw only one man. Boy, maybe. He was young, less than twenty for certain." She grimaced. "I'm good at estimating such things. No taller than myself, dark skin, red hair ..." She went on describing Flinx as best she could, from clothing to demeanor.

When she had finished, the man handed her the metal bars, not throwing them at her feet, as her visitors did. Exhibiting an unnerving politeness, he murmured a startlingly gentle "Thank you" and turned to leave.

"You're not ... going to kill us?" the woman wondered, still unable to comprehend her good fortune.

For the second time the tall figure showed surprise. "You have been only a witness to unfortunate events you could not affect. You have done nothing detrimental to me or mine, and you have been helpful. We will not see you again, and this business will be concluded satisfactorily very soon now." He closed the door behind him quietly.

Stunned, the woman sat on the pillows and stared at the gleaming metal in her hands. She tried not to think about the promise of silence she had made to the youth as he fled from her rooms. But what could she have done? Money or not, she eventually would have told the Qwarm anything he wanted to know, voluntarily or—she shuddered—otherwise. And she had the child to think of.

She managed a slight smile. At least she might have given the boy a chance, through one slight oversight on her part. She had told the Qwarm the truth when she said she had seen only one man. But she had failed to mention the small flying dragon that had slain one of the two dead ones. Let the Qwarm form their own conclusions from the state of the two corpses.

The tall man had carried through on his other promises, so she assumed he had told the truth when he said he would never see her again. Nevertheless, after letting her frightened daughter out of the bathroom, she set about making preparations to find new lodgings. The money represented by the metal bars would permit them to leave Moth, and she was in a rush to do so.

Chapter Three

Administrative offices wove in and about one another like copulating squid. Though raised on Drallar, Flinx still had a terrible time trying to locate the offices he wanted.

At first sight, minor bureaucrats were inclined to regard the persistent youth with contempt. Such bellicose thoughts, however, always brought a quivering, questioning little head out from beneath the folds of Flinx's clothing. It was amazing how rapidly once-indifferent civil servants took an interest in Flinx's problem. Helpful as they tried to be, he still found himself shunted from one department to the next. Planetary Resources bounced him down to Taxation, which kicked him up to Resources again.

Finally he found himself in a small, dingy compartment occupied by a sixth-level bureaucrat in the King's government. This lowly tape-twister was a tired, withered old man who had started life with great expectations, only to turn around one day and discover that he had become old. He sighed unencouragingly when Flinx once again explained his request.

"We don't have slave records here, boy."

"I know that, sir," Flinx acknowledged, settling himself into a chair so ancient it was actually made of real wood instead of plastic. "But money changed hands not just between seller and buyer, but between seller and the government in the form of taxes. Slave sales still require more documentation than most today. I'm assuming that hasn't changed in the past, oh, dozen years."

"Not that I know of, boy, not that I know of. Okay, we'll give it a try. What do they call you, and what is the name of the one whose sale you wish to trace?"

"I'm called Flinx. The name I wish to trace is Philip Lynx, and I have the exact date of the transaction." The man noded when Flinx gave him the date.

"Couldn't do much without that," he admitted. He rose and tottered to the wall behind him. It was lined from wall to wall, floor to ceiling, with tiny squares. Examining the wall, he finally touched several minute buttons. One of the squares clicked and extended itself into a meter-long tray. A single thin piece of dark plastic popped out of the tray.

Removing the thin square, the old man inserted it into a boxy machine on the left side of his desk. Then he turned it to face the left-hand wall, which was coated with a silvery-white substance.

At that point he paused, one wrinkled hand hovering over the controls of the machine. "I need to know the reason and justification for showing this, boy," he announced pleasantly. Flinx laid a discreet but ample bribe in the hovering palm. After transferring the money to a pocket, the hand activated the controls on the device.

"You don't have to tell me," the old man went on, "and it's none of my business, but why this transaction, exactly?"

"You're correct, it's none of your businsss." The old man looked resigned and, disappointed, turned away from Flinx. Motivated by some perverse impulse, Flinx blurted it out: "It's myself that was sold. I'm that same Philip Lynx."

Rheumy eyes squinted at him, but the man said nothing, merely nodded slowly. Aware that he had learned more than he was entitled to, he activated the projector. A series of seemingly endless tiny figures appeared on the wall. The oldster was experienced at his task. He scanned the figures and words as they flashed past on the wall faster than Flinx could follow. Abruptly, the flash flood of figures slowed, then began to back up, and finally it stopped.

"Here we are," the clerk declared with satisfaction, using a built-in arrow to indicate one thin line. "A tax of twenty-two credits paid to the municipal fund on the sale in the city of one boy Lynx, Philip. Selling price was . . ." and he ran off figures and facts Flinx already knew. Date of transaction, time . . . Flinx grinned when the name of the purchaser was read. So, Mother Mastiff had paid the tax under a false name.

"That's all?" he inquired when the wall unexpectedly went dark. "Nothing on the origin of the shipment, where it arrived from?"

"I'm truly sorry, boy," the old man confessed, sounding as if he meant it. He turned and folded his hands on the desk. "What did you expect? This department holds only financial records. But . . ." He hesitated, then went on. "If you want more information, if I were you I'd look up Arcadia Organics in the slave traders' offices. That's the firm that sold you. They might still retain some records themselves. They're not the largest concern of that type on Moth, but they're not the smallest, either. That's what I'd do if I were you, boy."

"I'd rather not," Flinx admitted. Returning to the slave market under any circumstances was a disquieting prospect. "But since that's where my only remaining hope leads, I suppose I must." Rising, he nodded thankfully to the old man. "You've been very kind, old sir." He turned to go.

"Just a minute, boy." Flinx turned, and winced reflexively as he caught something thrown at him. It was a small but still substantial credit chip—the same one he had given the oldster moments ago. His gaze went to the aged clerk, who could expect little more in the way of promotion or money in his lifetime. His eyes framed an unvoiced question.

"I don't have much drive, never did, and I'm a stranger to greed, I'm afraid," he explained slowly. "Also, compassion—that's out of keeping with being a successful bureaucrat."

"I can see that, old sir," Flinx acknowledged, respectfully tossing the chip back. It clattered faintly on the table top. "That's why you're going to keep this."

"I don't take bribes," the old clerk said firmly, ignoring the chip, "from those more unfortunate than myself."

"Appearances can be deceiving, old man," Flinx insisted, giving the impression that he wasn't boasting. "Keep it." He turned and left the room, left an uncertain yet gratified human being staring after him.

Flinx spent the night with Mother Mastiff, regaling her with tales of his trip to Earth. He detailed his visit to United Church headquarters on the island of Bali, told of his eventual discovery of who his natural mother was, and something of her death.

He told a carefully edited story, for he left out his encounter with the daughter of Rashalleila Nuaman, who had turned out to be his half sister. Nor did he mention the Baron of the AAnn, Riidi WW, or Conda Challis, or that unfortunate merchant's mysterious offspring, Mahnahmi—the girl with the angelic visage and wild talents. Most important, he left out any mention of his journey to Ulru-Ujurr and his commitment to educate the innocent geniuses who were the Ulru-Ujurrians themselves.

Whether she could figure out that there was more to his tale, Flinx could not tell. With Mother Mastiff, one was never certain whether a lie had been believed or tolerated. In any case, she did not comment until he mentioned his intention of looking up the slave firm which had originally sold him.

"I don't know, boy," she muttered. "Do you think it wise?"

"Why not? All they can do is refuse to talk to me."

"It's your state of mind that concerns me, Flinx. You've been throwing yourself into this search for a long while. I worry what you'll do if this last trail dead-ends on you."

He did not look at her. "Let's see what Arcadia Organics tells me, first."

She tapped the arm of the plush chair she sat in. "Better to leave yourself some hope. You'll drain it too quickly."

Now he stared at her in surprise. "Mother Mastiff, what are you afraid of? Of what I might find?"

"I haven't stood in your way during this mad chase of yours, boy. You know that. Though I'd rather you spent your time looking for a fine young lady of wealth and form to settle down with." She leaned forward out of the chair. "It's only that I don't like to see so much of you put into a wild-drizer chase. By your own admission, it has left you almost dead several times now." Flinx wondered what she would say if he told her about the encounter with the two Qwarm he—and Pip—had killed this morning.

"I'm sorry, Mother Mastiff. It seems this search is controlling me, not the other way around. I've *got* to know. My mother I found out about. Suppose . . . suppose my father is still alive?"

"Oh, what of that!" she shouted angrily. "What would that mean? Would it change you any, boy? Would it affect your life?"

Flinx started one reply, settled himself down, and switched to another. "I tell you what, Mother. If he's a fine man of wealth and form, I'll bring him back here, and maybe then I can finally get you to settle down."

She gaped at him momentarily, then broke into a robust cackling laugh which did not seem to die down until the last vestiges of daylight did. "All right, boy, you go," she finally agreed, sniffing and blowing her nose. "But be certain you take that gargoyle with you." She pointed to a far corner of the room, where Abala-mahalamatandra was honking and rhyming steadily to himself. "I will not have that monster living in my house, and I certainly can't keep him downstairs in the store. He'll scare away customers."

"Who, Ab?" argued Flinx desperately. He had hoped to unload the helpless tag-along on Mother Mastiff. "What else can I do with him? I can't let him follow me around."

"Why not?" she countered. "He seems happy enough doing so."

"I was thinking maybe you could take care of him for a while," he pleaded. "Besides, Ab doesn't frighten people; he makes them laugh."

"Maybe he makes you laugh," she snorted, "maybe he makes others laugh." She jabbed a leathery thumb at her bony sternum. "But he doesn't make me laugh. I want him out of my house and out of my shop, boy." She thought a moment, then ventured brightly, "As to what you can do with him, well, you're going to the slave market tomorrow. Sell him. Yes," she finished, well pleased with herself, "maybe you can make a profit on your inconvenience."

"I can't," he whispered.

"Why not?"

He thought rapidly. "Having once been sold myself, Mother, I can't see myself selling another creature. I'll let him follow me, I guess, until I can find him a kind home."

Flinx turned to eye his new ward while Mother Mastiff grunted in disgust. There was no way he could tell her that he was keeping Ab around because he was still curious as to why the Qwarm wanted him dead.

Ab honked and gazed cryptically back at him with two vacant blue eyes.

The following day dawned damp and drizzly. That was not the reason behind Flinx's shivers, however. A modest walk had brought him to the outskirts of the slave market, and he was discovering that, despite his determination, the atmosphere was having a chilling effect on him. Pip squirmed anxiously on his shoulder, uncomfortable at his master's state of mind. The only member of the little group who remained unaffected was Ab, singsonging irrepressibly behind Flinx: "Neutron, neutron, who you are, why is an organ camelbar?"

"Oh, shut up," Flinx muttered, aware that his admonition would have no effect.

He made his way, frozen-eyed, through the stalls. The beautiful maidens and dancing girls were present, just as in the old spacers' tales and marketeers' stories, but they danced much more reluctantly and unenthusiastically than those stories would lead one to believe. Nor were they as sensuous and appealing as in those tales, neither the men nor the women.

They were here, though. That Flinx knew. Drallar was a prime market world, a crossroads of the Commonwealth. Whether male, female, androgynous, or alien, the prime product was not put out on the avenue for the common herd to gawk at. In the streets around him, such dealings were consummated quietly, in secret. It was better that way, for it was rumored that sometimes there were souls who were not sold freely or honestly.

There were various beings for sale, as the Commonwealth boasted a glut of organic power. A few thranx were present, though not many. The clannish insects who had amalgamated with mankind tended to care better for their own. He saw a thorps and some seal creatures from Largess, the latter looking more comfortable in the dampness of Moth than they would have on most Commonwealth worlds.

One covered balcony provided seats for a handful of well-dressed prospective buyers. Few if any of them would be the ultimate owners, he knew. Most were merely intermediaries for respectable employers who wished not to be seen in such a place.

Presently he noticed spirited bidding on a bewildered, narcotized boy of six. For all his blondness and differing features, the lad reminded Flinx of a similarly lonely child of many years ago. Himself.

For a crazy instant he thought of buying the child and setting it free. Free on whom, though? Mother Mastiff would certainly never take in another foundling; he'd never understood what had possessed her to buy him.

Ab knocked Flinx back to reality, bumping clumsily into him from behind.

"Watch where you're going, you opinionated piece of elastic insulation!"

A bulging blue orb winked at him, lids fluttering uncertainly. "To give offense in any sense," he began sensibly, only to finish with "lox are a very metaphysical bird, it's heard."

"No doubt about it," Flinx shot back distastefully. He forced himself to a faster walk. He was anxious to leave this place.

The sign over the office door in the street behind the stalls was tastefully lettered—not flashy, but eye-catching. It bespoke a firm of moderate status, one which took a certain amount of pride in itself. The door was clean, polished, and made of intricately carved wood brought down from Moth's snow-clad northern continents. It read: ARCADIA ORGANICS.

Home to the helpless and homeless, Flinx thought. The name sounded much better than Slave Dealer.

He reached out and touched the silent buzzer. After a brief wait, the door slid aside silently. It turned out to be much thicker than it looked from outside. The delicate woodwork was a thin veneer laid over metal.

Completely filling the portal was a massive humanoid of solemn demeanor. He glanced down at Flinx and addressed him in a deep, throaty voice: "Your business here, man."

"I've come to see the owner, about an earlier sale of his."

The giant paused, appearing to listen. Flinx noticed a small glint of metal, some sort of transmitter, built into the left side of the humanoid's skull. The installation looked permanent.

"The nature of the complaint?" the giant inquired, flexing muscles like pale duraplast.

"I didn't say it was a complaint," Flinx corrected cheerfully. "It's just something I'd like cleared up." With Pip's aid, he knew, he could force his way past even this brute, but doing so would not help him gain the information he sought. "It's a question of pedigree."

Once more the man-mountain relayed the information to parts unseen. His response this time was to move aside with the same mechanical precision as the door. "You will be attended to," Flinx was assured. He would have preferred the invitation to have been phrased otherwise.

Nevertheless, he stepped into the small chamber. Ab followed, his rhyming loud in the confined space. The room was empty of furniture.

A hand the size of a dinner plate gently touched Flinx's shoulder—not the one Pip rested on, fortunately, or circumstances might have become awkward. "Stand, please." Seeing no place to go, Flinx readily complied.

A polelike finger touched a switch. There was a hum, and Flinx felt himself dropping. Forcing himself to be calm, he affected an attitude of pleasant indifference as the floor and room sank into the ground. Before very long he found himself in a much larger room. It was spacious and neatly decorated, and it fit the man who moved around the table at its far end to greet Flinx as he stepped out of the elevator.

Twisted and braided dark ringlets cascaded over forehead and neck. The man was a little taller than Flinx and roughly three times his age, though he looked younger. A pointed vandyke and curled-up mustache gave the slaver the appearance of a foppish raven with clipped wings. A very large star-ruby ring on the man's pinky was the only meretricious detail in the office.

After greeting Flinx politely, the man escorted him to a lavishly brocaded chair. A proffered drink was declined. Flinx thought the fellow looked disappointed at the youth of his visitor, but he tried hard not to show it. After all, Drallar was home to spoiled children as well as spoiled adults.

"Now, what can I do for you, young master? My name is Char Mormis, owner and third generation in

Arcadia Organics. Don't tell me—it's a young lady you're looking for. I knew it! I can always tell." While Char Mormis spoke his hands charted each sentence like a seismograph measuring tremors. "I can always tell when they're hunting for comforting." He winked lewdly across the desk. "Name your tastes, young master. Arcadia can supply you."

"Sorry, Mr. Mormis," Flinx said, "but I'm not here to buy."

"Oh." The slaver looked crestfallen. He leaned back in his chair and tugged at the point of his beard. "You're here to sell?" he asked uncertainly, eyeing the rhyming Ab, who stood by the elevator entrance.

"Neither," Flinx informed him firmly.

Mormis let out a reluctant sigh. "Then you really are here over a question of pedigree. Oh well. How may I help you, young master? Is there some question of inaccuracy?" He appeared genuinely distressed at the prospect. "It pains me to think we might be responsible for such an error. We are not dealers in the highest-priced merchandise, but," he added conspiratorially, "we have the advantage of being honest."

"Relax," Flinx advised the slaver. "I'm not accusing you of anything. I just need some information. It concerns a boy named Philip Lynx you sold to a woman named"—he grinned—"it wasn't her real name, but that doesn't matter. The boy's name is correct. He was four, five years old at the time of sale."

Mormis spread his hands. "I'll tell you what I know, of course. We retain permanent records of every one of our transactions." Faith, but he was so smooth, so polite, Flinx mused. "But first, young master, you must satisfy me that you have a right to such information. Slaves have a right to their privacy too, you know. We respect the rights of our purchased as well as those of our purchasers."

"Glad to hear it," admitted Flinx.

Mormis studied the confident youth seated across from him. "Let me guess. The boy was bought to be a companion for you. You've grown up with him. Now you've become curious about his original background.

Or maybe he's asked you to inquire about it to satisfy his own curiosity. You look to be about his age."

"I am," agreed Flinx. "I'm him."

Mormis did not appear as surprised as the elderly clerk had been at this information. He simply slumped into his chair and looked weary.

"I was afraid it might be something like that. You must realize, Mr. Lynx—"

"Just Flinx."

"Very well. You must see, Flinx, that we have clients to protect in such cases. If it is revenge you seek, if you are on some kind of personal vendetta . . ."

Flinx shook his head impatiently. "Nothing of the sort. I give you my word, I'm only trying to find out what happened to my natural parents."

Now Mormis looked sad. "Such cases are known. Very persistent people who gain their freedom often seek such information. All such searches I know of come to naught. If the sale of the child was voluntary, the parents go to great pains, usually successful, to conceal their identities forever. If the sale was involuntary, then the seller goes to the same lengths to disguise *his* identity. Even if you were to get into the archives on Terra itself—"

"I've already done that," Flinx informed him.

Mormis's eyes widened slightly. "You've been to Earth?"

"I've been in the Church archives on Bali itself. Eventually I managed to find out who my mother was. She'd already been dead many years." Surprisingly, he found he could relate the information without pain. It was as if he were talking about someone else, not himself. There was only a cold emptiness in him.

Mormis looked at him with fresh respect. It was evident in his tone as well. "You are an unusual young man."

"So I've been told," Flinx commented drily. "Now, about my request?"

"Yes, certainly." Mormis activated an electronic filing system rather more modern than the one Flinx had visited yesterday. It coughed up a tiny rectangle, which the slaver inserted in a projector.

"Here is the original record of sale," Mormis told him, pointing to the wall screen. "Look for yourself."

Flinx was already doing so, raptly. His early self was spelled out on the wall, a human being metamorphosed into figures. Height, weight, hair and eye color, and every other vital statistic imaginable was shining brightly on the wall. He had to smile again when he saw the name of his buyer: the Grand Ladyess Fiona Florafin. Mother Mastiff was right—slavers were concerned only about the legitimacy of a purchaser's credit.

Once again, that which he most hoped to find was absent. Remuneration was recorded as having gone to the House of Nuaman, presumably to enrich the coffers of his now-deceased aunt, the murderous Rashalleila. That fitted with what he already knew.

Of his natural parents he found less here than he already knew; there was nothing about his mother to match what he had spent a year learning, nothing at all about his still-mysterious father.

"Thank you, Char Mormis," he forced himself to say tightly, struggling to hide his disappointment. Finally, he had reached the dead end he'd feared. There was no place else to go, nowhere more to search.

The matter was finished.

"I appreciate your kindness." Flinx's hand moved in the direction of his credit cardmeter.

Mormis waved the gesture off. "No, thank *you*, Flinx. The pleasure was mine. It's always heartening to see merchandise that has done well for itself. You are an independent citizen?"

"Have been since the day I was bought, thanks to my buyer."

"You know, it's odd ... Can't I persuade you to have a brandy?"

Flinx shook his head. Despite Mormis's courtesy, the man was still of a breed for whom human lives were chips on a gaming table. He wanted out.

But there was something prodding at Mormis. "It's strange ... I have an excellent memory for people—

nature of the business, you understand." Flinx nodded without speaking. "But ... I think I remember your sale."

Flinx sat down abruptly.

"Yes, I'm sure of it. At that time it was my father, Shan Mormis, who was running Arcadia. I was still learning. But your sale, your sale ... it sticks in my mind for some reason. You've brought the memory back to me, for two reasons. The first concerned your buyer. An old woman?"

Flinx nodded vigorously.

"That grandiose name on the manifest"—the man gestured toward the wall—"didn't match her appearance. Does that make sense to you?"

"A squat, heavy woman dressed in neat rags, with a vocabulary like a spacer?"

"That description seems to fit," Mormis confessed, caught up in Flinx's excitement. "You keep in touch with your former owner?"

"She was never really an owner in the usual sense," Flinx explained, a pugnacious yet affectionate picture of Mother Mastiff forming in his mind.

"I suspected as much, considering your present status. Such a contrast between appearance and given name—how could one forget? The other memory concerns the one other person who was bidding for you." Mormis looked embarrassed. "You were not a quality item."

"My value on the scale of such things doesn't depress me," Flinx assured him.

"Self-deprecation ... a good trait in mer—in a citizen," the slaver corrected himself hastily. "It was the spirited bidding for your unremarkable self between two extraordinary persons which remains in my memory."

"What of the other bidder?" insisted Flinx eagerly.

"Well, he was human, quite human. Huge he was, built like a city wall. Would have fetched a pretty price on the stage. Sadly, he was on the wrong end of the business. He must have weighed as much as two good-sized men. Heavy-planet upbringing, no doubt. All white-haired he was, though I think it was premature. Two meters tall, easily." Mormis paused, and Flinx had to urge him to continue.

"There *must* be more."

Mormis strained at his memory. "So many over the years ... that face, though. A cross between a libertine's and a prophet's. And I think he wore a gold ring in one ear. Yes, I'm sure of it. A gold ring, or at least one of golden hue."

"A name, Char Mormis, a name!"

The slaver rambled on. "You weren't sold very high, Flinx. I think the fellow had reason to leave the bidding when he did. He left in a rush, and as I recall there were an inordinate number of soldiers milling about. But I shadow-play a scenario. I never heard him mention a name."

"Anything else?" Flinx pressed him, refusing to be discouraged. "Why did he want to buy me?"

Mormis looked away, as if Flinx had touched on something the slaver would have preferred not to discuss. "We do not inquire into the motives of our customers. Once the transaction is completed, subsequent events pass into the jurisdiction of the authorities. Our business is to sell, not to judge."

"But he left before the bidding closed," Flinx mused. "Then it's conceivable he could have outbid the woman who bought me?"

"Naturally, that's possible."

"You can't remember anything else about him?"

Mormis pursed his lips in disapproval. "After twelve years? I think it's remarkable I've remembered what I have. If you will entertain a hypothesis, I would say that, considering the limited bidding for you, the fellow looked on you as an investment."

Flinx didn't reply. He was thinking. A very large human, prematurely white-maned, gold ring in one ear ... He grimaced. It wasn't much to go on.

"I need more information." Pip, aroused from his nap, poked his head out.

Mormis started. "By the chains of the sky, there it is!"

"There what is?" a puzzled Flinx wondered.

"Your quest is impossible, young master, but I will not dissuade you. That—that is the other thing." He was pointing at Pip. Intrigued, the minidrag stuck a questioning tongue out at the slaver. Ab sang on in the background.

"It is the second one I have seen. The other . . . the other rode on the shoulder of the bidder who ran. I swear it would be the same creature, save that I think his was smaller!"

Flinx's neatly organized thoughts collapsed like a bridge whose foundation had failed. In their place turmoil reigned.

So far as he knew, Pip was the only Alaspinian minidrag on Moth. If another lived on the winged world, he was sure he would have learned of it by now. Suppose Pip was the same minidrag which Mormis insisted had ridden his would-be buyer's shoulder? That implied that for Flinx to have ended up with the flying snake was a coincidence too extreme to be believed. Could his unsuccessful purchaser have planted Pip in the alley where Flinx eventually discovered him, for Flinx to find?

If that was what had actually happened, it indicated much more than a casual interest in Flinx, from a person not connected with Nuaman Enterprises. An employee of his aunt's? But to what end, what purpose?

I will go mad, he silently screamed.

"A name," he demanded, "give me a name, Char Mormis!"

The slaver recoiled at the youth's violence. "I told you, he never voiced one. Nor could I tell where he was from. I recall no distinctive accent. Beyond his size and the earring, I can tell you nothing."

"I understand, I understand," Flinx said carefully, trying to control himself. Words stormed through his brain.

Alaspin, Alaspin, old friends a-claspin.

"Recipe for salad dressing . . . two SCCAM bars without messing." Ab rambled nonsensically. "Shirted on conclusion of the composition, wise not to bear a

cockatrice," the alien finished. He continued in an unknown language.

When Flinx finally got his raging thoughts under
control, he forced himself to speak slowly. "What
would you do if you were in my place?" he asked the
slaver. "I value your advice."

"Were I in your position," Mormis instructed him
through thoughtfully steepled fingers, "I would go to
wherever home is, return to your work, and save your
money and possibly your sanity."

"Next suggestion."

"Assuming you have unlimited time and funds,
young master, I would go to Alaspin. That's where
your little beast comes from, is it not?" Mormis extended a paternal hand in Pip's direction, but drew it
back hastily when Pip hissed sharply at him. "If the
creature is as rare as it is reputed to be, and as dangerous . . ."

"It is," Flinx assured him.

". . . then you might have a chance of locating one
other who once also kept one."

So, Flinx thought, it had come to this: a search for a
man who twelve or so years ago had appeared on
Moth with a minidrag on his shoulder. A man who
might never have been to Alaspin but who might have
acquired his lethal pet elsewhere. But a destination was
better than nothing.

"Thank you again, Char Mormis." Flinx rose to
leave, and saw that the elevator had returned, along
with its hulking operator. "I just wish," he offered in
parting, "that one as nice as you were engaged in some
other business."

"The morality of it can weigh heavily at times," the
slaver confessed as the lift door closed on Flinx and Ab.
"But not," he concluded softly after the elevator was
on its way surfaceward, "enough to make this one want
to quit."

Chapter Four

It was a busy, fruitful day, and Mormis thought no more of his interesting visitor. By the time darkness had come and he locked up for the night, he had forgotten the incident completely.

The modest Mormis tower home lay in a nearby inurb, one of many such restricted enclaves in Drallar. It was a pleasant evening, and Mormis decided to walk. His monolithic manservant strode comfortingly alongside.

Out of necessity, the streets were relatively well lit. Perpetual cloud cover hid any light the planet's bright moon, Flame, might have thrown on the pavement.

Mormis tugged his thick cloak closer about him. He was afflicted with bursitis, an ancient disease. Mournfully he mused that the only part of his life which was not well lubricated involved his aching joints. Physicians and wishans, none could help.

When he was halfway home, a strong yet gentle voice called out of shadows to him: "We would request of you a few minutes of your time, Char Mormis of

53

Arcadia. We wish minimum delay in your homeward journey."

Despite the assurances in that voice, Mormis reacted as any man in his profession might. Voices in the night usually meant only one thing on Moth, where darkness was the shield of beings with less-than-civil intentions.

Throwing aside his cloak to give himself maximum mobility, he turned, hunting for the source of the request. As if in response, a figure emerged from the fog around him. It approached on four legs, foothands and truhands all extended in a pose of insectoid placation. Vast compound eyes shone bright with reflected light from the street illuminators.

Mormis took in the shiny, exfoliating chiton, the deep purple coloring. But neither the thranx's obvious age nor his conciliatory manner served to relax him. He hadn't had any dealings with a thranx in some time. Not that they didn't own slaves. For all their vaunted logic, the thranx were still a race of individuals, some of whom were as subject to vice as their human counterparts were.

So he retreated from the advancing figure and ordered his manservant to take defensive action. When the insect was pinioned, then, perhaps, he would talk.

The massive, blue-cloaked golemite lumbered forward. The slaver was not eased in mind when the fragile-looking insect stood his ground. "Really, Char Mormis," he observed in the delightfully musical voice of the thranx, "inhospitality is hardly the mark of a successful businessman. I am disappointed. And this looking for a hidden weapon on my person . . ."

Mormis was about to interrupt to say that it was the thranx who was about to be disappointed when his fears were partially confirmed. A second figure emerged from the fog to intercept his servant.

The new figure was human, somewhat taller than average but slim and unimpressive. His advanced age was belied by the suppleness of his movements. He looked like an ambulatory birch tree. Gray hair, cavernous wrinkles, and other age signs were held at bay by eyes that were coal-black shards.

This steely-looking scarecrow blocked the advance of the servant, who reacted rapidly and directly. A short but furious scuffle followed in the middle of the street. The great mass of Mormis's servant seemed to obliterate his opponent, but when movement ceased, it was to reveal the tall, lanky stranger standing over the motionless bulk of the golemite.

The tall man, part Oriental, shook his left arm. There was an audible popping sound as joints rearranged themselves. When he spoke it was without panting, and in the same reassuring tone as that used by the watching thranx: "I have not injured him. He will wake soon, after we have finished."

Mormis's left eyelid twitched uncontrollably. His fingers quivered.

"You would not reach the beamer," the thranx told him, in a voice so confident that Mormis lost all hope. "Please be so kind as to refrain from such irrational hostilities and listen to what we have to ask."

The slaver considered. Then he slowly slid his hand away from the concealed weapon within his shirt. He consoled himself with the fact that this odd pair, whatever their intentions, looked neither brutal nor immune to some common-sense reasoning. So he tried to calm himself as the elderly thranx moved toward him. The slim human, he noted with relief, remained next to the motionless body of his servant.

The thranx was tall for one of his kind, Mormis observed, tall enough so that the rainbow-hued compound eyes were nearly level with the slaver's own. The thranx was bundled tightly against the chill, though Mormis knew the dampness was to the insect's liking. They were hothouse-world creatures. He could hear the soft puffing as air moved through the insect's spicules.

"You have me at a disadvantage," he declared, dropping his hands to his sides. "I can do nothing but what you wish." Meanwhile he searched for identifying signs. Both sets of vestigial wings were present, protruding from shiny wing cases on the thranx's back. A never-mated bachelor, then.

The insect noted the slaver's gaze, "No, you do not know me. We have never met before, Char Mormis." An impressed Mormis realized that his questioner was speaking perfect Terranglo instead of the galactic lingua franca, symbospeech. Few thranx could master the smooth vowels of mankind's principal language. For the first time a little of the tenseness left him. Violent beings were usually not this well educated.

"You have the advantage of me, sir."

"We require some information," the insect responded, showing no inclination to reveal either his name or that of his human associate. Mormis masked his disappointment. "We have learned that earlier today you had a visitor."

"I've had many visitors," Mormis countered, stalling.

"This one was a young man. Or an old boy, depending on your perceptiveness. The boy had as companion a small, dangerous flying reptile and an alien of peculiar type."

Since the thranx already knew this, Mormis saw no sense in denying it. "I admit to receiving the person you describe."

In an oddly human gesture, the thranx cocked its valentine-shaped head to one side. "What did the boy want of you?"

Natural caution took over for Mormis, and he replied without hesitation. "I said I remembered the boy," he declared slowly, finding apparent fascination in the patterns water made on the street. "But I also had many other visitors. It's impossible to remember the details of every conversation. My days are hectic, and talk tends to run together."

The tall human took several steps forward. "We are wasting time with this one." He extended a hand and flexed long, skilled fingers in a way Mormis didn't like. "I could always—"

"No, no complications," the thranx interrupted, much to the slaver's relief. "But, as you say, we waste time. Rather than debate morality . . ." He reached into his thorax vest and brought forth a credit cube of fair size. A glance assured Mormis it was genuine.

"Still," Mormis said smoothly, "in my business it is necessary from time to time to reconstruct certain conversations. Odd, but suddenly I find the one you mention coming back to me."

"A remarkable surprise," the tall man commented sardonically.

Anxious now that he had managed to turn a dangerous situation into an opportunity for profit, Mormis spoke freely. "It was a trivial matter, interesting for one reason. The boy was originally sold by Arcadia."

"What did I say?" the tall human told his companion.

"It seems the lad has done well since then," Mormis went on.

"Well enough," the thranx commented enigmatically.

"Now the orphan is hunting diligently and foolishly for his natural sire and dame. A harmless but expensive obsession. He searches now for his father."

"And you were able to give him information?" the man asked.

"No, I had no such details. However, I did relate to him an intriguing anecdote involving the circumstances of his sale. If you wish it, I can—"

The thranx cut him off impatiently, checking a wrist chronometer as he spoke. "That is not necessary. We need to know only what he intends to do now, where he is going."

Mormis backed off. "Revealing that information would be unethical, sir." He glanced significantly in the direction from which credit cubes of impressive size came. "To reveal such would be a violation of confidence."

"You are neither physician nor padre," the tall man rumbled, "so don't prattle to us of confidentialities and revelations."

"You have been paid enough," the thranx declared quietly, adding in a politely blood-curdling way, "we are through wasting time."

"The boy might," the slaver ventured as quickly as he could, "be traveling to Alaspin. He seemed anxious enough to go there. Driven, one could almost say. I would guess that at this very minute he is on his way to Drallarport."

"Your civility and common sense are respected," the thranx told him, finishing a touch sarcastically, "along with your wonderfully responsive memory. We will bother you no longer. Go home, Char Mormis."

Turning in the way of the thranx, the insect started off into the fog at a fast jog. The tall human followed him easily, stepping over the body of Mormis's manservant.

The slaver watched as the odd twosome was absorbed by the mist. "It's sure I won't bother either of you," he muttered to himself, slipping the credit cube into his shirt. His slave was breathing noisily now. Mormis walked over and kicked the recumbent bulk hard in the ribs. A second kick produced a weak groan.

Then the massive humanoid sat up. He blinked and looked up at Mormis. "I request abjuration, master," he muttered dully. "I no excuse, but opponent was much more than—"

Mormis kicked him again. "I know that, idiot. Get up." He found he was shivering, though not from the dampness. "I'm in a hurry to get home . . ."

"Exalla Cadella morphine centalla, espoused lost in the woods. A time to conjure redonjure skull face from under the hoods," Ab hummed softly.

Flinx turned and called back to his dutifully trailing acquisition, disgust plain in his voice, "If you have to ramble, can't you at least say something sensible once in a while?"

Four arms made incomprehensible, meaningless gestures. The upper half of the blue torso leaned slightly forward. One bright-blue eye winked blankly at him, and the trunk atop the smooth skull weaved in time to some unspoken alien rhythm.

Flinx sighed and continued trudging up the road. Carts were scarce this late at night—early in the morning, rather. Since taking leave of Mormis's place he had seen none plying the streets.

Supper still sat warm and heavy in his belly. He had eaten in a small comestabulary partway out of the city proper. *Quda* chips had come with his stew, and he had amused himself for a while by throwing the circular chips into the air, whereupon Pip would launch himself, lightninglike, from his shoulder to snatch them before they could hit the floor. The minidrag was extremely fond of anything heavily laced with salt. Flinx had halted the game only after the owner approached him to plead desperately for an end to it. It seemed that the venomous flying snake's dives and swoops were unnerving the rest of his customers.

It should be light soon, Flinx mused as he neared the major route leading from Drallar to the city's shuttleport. There landing craft transferred local goods to great KK-drive starships waiting in orbit and brought outworld goods into the city. Along this broad avenue he was sure to encounter either a jinx driver looking for a first-morn fare or one of many huge powered cargo transports. The latter he could always obtain a ride on, sometimes with the knowledge and consent of the operator, often without. In spite of his present relative affluence, he knew, old talents often came in handy.

As morning neared, the mist-fog thickened. To an outworlder it presented an imposing obstacle to travel. To a native of Moth, it was as natural and expected as a sunrise. Drizzle ran steadily off Flinx's slickertic cape. At least, that was the way it appeared to an onlooker. Actually, the drops never touched the material itself. A steady static charge kept the rain from ever making contact with the always-dry cape.

Flinx noticed a huge skimmer parked close by the last warehouse bordering the busy right-of-way. It was stacked with many tons of cargo.

A bipedal figure suddenly appeared out of the fog, stumbling toward him. Pip was off his shoulder in an instant. Flinx started to reach for the fresh blade in his boot, then hesitated. He sensed no aura of danger about the figure. A shouted command brought Pip back; the anxious minidrag hovered in a tight spiral over Flinx's head. Pip's response assured Flinx that the weaving form ahead wasn't dangerous; if it had been, Pip would have ignored the command.

The figure stumbled onward, something gripped tightly in one hand. As the man neared, he seemed for the first time to take notice of Flinx. His glazed eyes appeared to clear slightly. Summoning fresh strength, the man increased his pace and steadied himself somewhat. For a minute Flinx thought he might have to free Pip after all. Then the man's pupils filmed over again. He tripped on nothingness and fell sideways into the drainage ditch lining the right-hand side of the access road Flinx was walking on.

His body formed a dam for the running water. The runoff rose and began to flow around the man's arm and shoulder, the limp limb a long, slowly bleeding dike. Nor was the shoulder wound the only one visible on the man. He had been badly hurt in an efficient, professional manner.

Sidling cautiously up to the corpse, Flinx found he was trying to watch every direction at once. His erratic talent, naturally, revealed nothing at the moment. Yet no one, injured or healthy, charged from the darkness at him. He returned his attention to the body.

The black skullcap with its embroidered crimson insignia had fallen from the hairless pate when the man fell. Several portions of the tight black suit were soaked with blood. The fringed cloak was torn. It hung loosely from a single neck clasp.

Further examination was unnecessary. The Qwarm was dead. Yet Flinx persisted, disbelieving. It was known that the Qwarm were masters of many bodily functions. Imitating death was a useful way to lull the suspicions of an intended victim. But Flinx was positive this one was not faking, nor would he ever fake anything again.

Curious, he kneeled to examine the object clutched convulsively in the assassin's right hand: a short, grayish metal cylinder that looked much like pewter. A tiny red light was still gleaming near the cylinder's middle.

Flinx found a loose scrap of pavement and passed it carefully between the out-pointing end of the cylinder and the air. There was a tiny *ping*, and a millimeter-wide hole appeared in the thick section of stone.

To protect the many inquisitive children prowling the night streets of Drallar, Flinx touched a stud at the haft of the weapon. The red light went out. A repeat pass with the stone did not produce a puncture. Flinx pulled the tiny device free of its former owner's death grip.

This Qwarm toy was a phonic stiletto. It generated a thin beam of sculpted sound that would put a hole through just about anything. It fit neatly in a man's palm, generator and all, was easily concealed, and was almost impossible to detect or defend against.

Flinx rose and looked around worriedly. Having killed two Qwarm recently, he could understand another one with an activated weapon coming toward him. But this Qwarm had run into something else before he had had a chance to ambush Flinx. Or had he really been after Flinx?

Moving on four stumpy legs, a mumbling Ab walked over and bent to pick, cretinlike, at the clothing of the dead man. Hands and eyes moved, apparently enraptured by the commingling of blood and water in the ditch.

Had the killer been after Flinx, or were they still pursuing the moronic alien in his charge? He didn't like to consider the first possibility, because that would mean they now knew he was responsible for the death of two clan members back in the old house fronting the stage. In that case he had to move faster than he had intended. Once an enemy was known to them, the Qwarm clan would never rest until that enemy or every member of the clan was dead. It would help him to know whether they knew.

Falling mist was rapidly obliterating any hint of a trail, but drops of dissolving blood still showed against the pavement clearly enough for him to trace them around the prow of the huge cargo carrier. They led to the entrance of the warehouse. Careful examination of the personnel door showed that it had been keyed open, and Flinx did not think it had been done by the building's owner.

Every instinct, everything in him, warned against entering the blackness inside. That was countered, as usual, by his relentless curiosity. He slipped through the slight opening. A dim light shone in a near corner, near mountainous heaps of extruded plastic casings. Treading softly, with a dim shape fluttering nervously overhead, he moved toward the light.

Suddenly he could sense unease, even fear. Marshaled against it was a frightening coolness. Both were far from here and moving rapidly away from him. From the lighted region he was approaching he detected nothing. Very slowly, he peered around a last, four-meter-high yellow case.

Six bodies filled the space his astonished gaze encountered. Six! They lay draped over crates, contorted on the metal floor, and bunched beneath overturned casings. Four were women, two men. All were clad in the by now too-familiar black. Several showed naked skulls, their caps missing. Copious amounts of blood lent murderous highlights to the devastated scene. Several of the smaller crates were shattered. It must have taken sòme unknown, awesome force to crack those seamless containers.

In a few hours, Flinx knew, some warehouse supervisor would arrive to open up, and get the shock of his or her life.

There were only dead Qwarm here, no sign of any other intruders. Flinx couldn't conceive of anyone or anything that would attack, let alone destroy, such a large number of professional assassins. He stiffened. A hint of a far-off mental scream had touched him, alerted him once more to something that continued to move away from this place. Whatever it was, he considered, it might not continue to move *away*.

Once again Flinx looked back at the crumpled, silent bodies, some of which were partially dismembered.

Again he noted the cracked plastic casings strewn casually about. Some great force had been at work here, for reasons Flinx could not imagine. That distant mental shriek continued to echo in his mind as he found himself backing away slowly from the nightmarish scene. Darkness closed tight around him once more.

Something touched his shoulder.

His sigh of relief when he found it was only Pip, returning to his perch on his shoulder, was enormous. Then he was out of the structure, running steadily toward the main roadway ahead. The mist was no longer a friend but a deceiver, hiding something terrifying and mysterious from sight.

Moments later he reached the road. From below he heard the bellow of *kinkeez* and other animal-powered conveyances, mixed with the roar and hum of machines. A short climb, a downward slide and scramble, and Flinx was over the embankment and on the roadway itself. Somehow Ab managed to keep all four of his feet under him as he stumbled on without complaint after his new master.

The owner of the *meepah*-rickshaw balked at the sight of Flinx's quadrupedal companion. Credits overcame his uncertainty, however. Soon the two-legged *meepah* was racing toward the shuttleport at its maximum stride, Flinx getting the speed he was paying for. Happily, nothing flew out of the rising mist-fog from behind to strike at either owner or rider.

At the port, Flinx had the misfortune to encounter one of those many bureaucrats whose sole purpose in life seemed to be complicating that of others, from which they obviously derived a false and pitiful feeling of superiority. "Let me see your tunnel pass, boy," the man demanded condescendingly.

Flinx turned and glanced anxiously back the way he had come. The moving walkway leading back into the central terminal building was almost empty. Despite the early hour and the absence of any pursuit, he was expecting one or more black-clad specters to appear among the tired businessfolk and travelers. Drallarport operated round the clock, twenty-eight hours a day.

"I don't have a tunnel pass, sir," he responded, forcing himself to modify the sharpness he heard in his voice. "I . . ."

That was enough to engender a wide leer of satisfaction on the other's fat face. No, he was not stupid, this one. His mental malady ran deeper than simple ignorance. Malice requires a certain amount of intelligence before its wielder qualifies as truly irritating.

"No pass, and attempting to enter a private access tunnel," he snorted through pursed lips. Ostentatiously, he jabbed a button on the callbox at his waist. Two large, no-nonsense humans appeared and glowered threateningly at Flinx. They were soon joined by an out-of-breath, elderly little man. In appearance, he was sufficiently ordinary to make Flinx's plump tormentor look unique.

"What is it, Belcom?" he asked the fat one curiously while eyeing Flinx.

"This child," Belcom declared, as if he had just learned the identity of a multiple-murderer, "is trying to sneak into this restricted area without a pass."

"I wasn't trying to snea—" Flinx began in exasperation, before the newcomer cut him off.

"This is a guarded section, boy. No visitors allowed." While tired, probably from finishing up a night shift, the man was at least polite. "If you want to watch the ships lift, try the cargo landing."

"I don't have a tunnel pass," Flinx finally succeeded in explaining as he fumbled at a belt pouch beneath his slickertic, "because I'm not boarding as a passenger." From the pouch he extracted a small, virtually unbreakable slip of polyplexalloy. The information implanted in it was unforgeable.

Blinking back fatigue, the new arrival studied the card. When he looked up at Flinx it was without lethargy. He turned a vicious gaze on the smug subordinate next to him. That worthy took in his superior's glare and reacted with the attitude of someone who has just discovered a poisonous insect crawling up his leg yet is afraid to swat at it for fear of being stung.

"Of course this *gentleman* doesn't have a pass, Belcom. Don't you ever inquire before you make an idiot of yourself?"

Aware that he couldn't respond without demeaning himself further, an uncomprehending Belcom simply gaped blankly at the little man. After allowing Belcom's embarrassment to last to the point of eyestrain, his superior finally continued: "He has no pass, you damn fool, because he's not a passenger. He's an owner. Private registry vessel."

"I—" Belcom stammered, glancing worriedly at Flinx. "He was so young—I didn't consider, didn't think—"

"Two reasons for not promoting you, and excellent ones at that," his supervisor snapped venomously. Turning to Flinx, he framed sincere apologies with an officious smile. "Terribly sorry for the inconvenience, sir. If there is anything I can do to redress the insult suffered, anything at all . . ."

Flinx thought he saw a commotion at the far end of the moving walkway behind him. "Just let me through," he said crisply. Both guards moved solemnly aside; they watched as Flinx and his odd charge loped up the corridor. Neither turned to watch or listen as additional execration continued to fall on the unfortunate Belcom.

Though he had studied hard the past year and a half, Flinx was still no pilot. But most craft were so complex that manual operation was out of the question for all but the most skilled individuals, and the shuttlecraft he settled into was no exception. So it was fully fitted out with automatic controls. Anyone capable of delivering coherent instructions to the ship's computer could pilot it.

Firm pressure forced him back into the acceleration couch as the little vessel boomed skyward, lifting cleanly out of the reaction pit. Shortly thereafter he was curving out into free space.

Nograv relaxed him physically; the fact that now no Qwarm could slip up behind and stick a sonic stiletto or something equally exotic into his neck relaxed him mentally. Behind, Ab whistled and rhymed cheerfully.

The alien accepted nograv as readily and good-naturedly as it had the damp atmosphere of Moth.

Approaching tangency with a particular orbit, Flinx took a moment to belch once while admiring a great swath of glowing gold splashed across the sky. It was one of the two remarkable "wings" that had given Moth its name. Whichever god had designed Flinx's home world had finished with a flourish of finger-painting. Each fan-shaped wing was composed of highly reflective particulate and gaseous matter, narrow near the surface, fanning out and diffusing as gravity weakened away from it.

Like a dauber wasp, the shuttlecraft nestled itself snugly into the ellipsoidal fuselage of Flinx's ship. From that structure projected a long tube which ended in a fan-shape, something like a wineglass: the KK-drive posigravity-field projector.

Flinx's ship was a gift from his extraordinarily gifted pupils, the race of ursinoids who inhabited the pro-scribed world of Ulru-Ujurr. They had used blueprints and scavenged material to construct it. In shape and capabilities it was much like the racing yacht of Flinx's sometime benefactor, Maxim Malaika. Only the much-less-sybaritic furnishings were significantly different.

The Ulru-Ujurrians had christened it *Teacher*.

Flinx punched in the coordinates of Alaspin, added a maximum cruising speed, and then permitted himself to lie down. With only the most general description to go on, he had to try to find a man who might not ever have been to Alaspin. Added to that was the possibility that the slaver's memory was open to question—not to mention the fact that the Qwarm were intent on preventing him from locating anything ever again.

Some comfort came from Ab's antics. The alien was fascinated by the ship's workings. Certainly Ab had been on at least one other craft before, but slave quarters left little chance for study. Flinx had to be careful. Automatic and foolproof as interstellar navigation had become, the accidental manipulations of an idiot like Ab could delay his trip seriously.

As to what he would do if he reached Alaspin and learned nothing, Flinx had no idea. At such moments Flinx wondered why he bothered so much. What, after all, were a mother and father but an accidental combination of humanity, a chance commingling of chromosomes and such which had produced . . . himself.

Of all the myriad things he was ignorant of, one of the greatest was his own motivations. Beside them, stellar physics was simple child-gaming. Why try to assuage his loneliness? Knowledge of his origin couldn't do that. But maybe, he mused, when he finally knew, it might keep him from crying quietly so often.

Traveling almost as fast as a Commonwealth peaceforcer, the *Teacher* sped through the void, carrying its small cargo of one melancholy human youth, one indifferent flying reptile, and a spritely alien mad poet wrapped in an enigma.

In his long and busy life, the lanky old man had undergone many security screenings. The one he was forced to endure today had proved as thorough as the most extensive he could recall.

Once cleared, he was finally admitted to a very dark office. What furniture lay within appeared placed haphazardly, without regard to esthetics or function. Nothing in the way of decoration showed anywhere.

That extended to the single figure waiting to greet him. Like the room, the thickly hooded shape conveyed a feeling of somber staleness. It stood, rather than sat, behind the single heavy desk. Where a face would have been, darkness and many folds of cloth served instead. They disguised even their wearer's size and form. There was nothing deceptive about the soft voice that issued from beneath the heavy shrouds, though. It was sibilant in a way the taller man could almost place.

"Business has been finished?" the shrouded one asked. No casual greeting, no hopeful hello to waste time. No exchange of names.

From beneath his embroidered skullcap the elder Qwarm responded, "There has been interference." A finger rubbed at an upper lip and obliterated an itch. Hairless lids blinked once.

Beneath its many folds the other speaker appeared to twitch violently, though control of its voice remained unbroken. "It cannot be. Neither the Church nor the Commonwealth government realizes . . . !"

Shaking his head briskly, once, the tall Qwarm leader explained, "There has been no evidence of official interference, or even of interest, insofar as we can discover. Both members of the clan who had been assigned the task were apparently in position and preparing to carry out their work when they were interrupted. Whether they were interrupted on purpose or by accident we have been unable to discover. It does not matter now. Both of the clan are dead."

"It matters very much to *me*," rumbled the hooded shape.

"You will be notified as to the identity of the fool who interfered when we gather in his body," the Qwarm declared coldly. "At present we know no more than you. We thought such knowledge, together with the postponed completion of your assignment to us, was within our grasp. Something . . . happened." Vast unpleasantness burned back of wise old eyes. "Much outrage was felt within the clan at the death of our brother and sister. Such a thing has not happened in a long time. Punishment was decreed. A large group of clan members, the largest gathered together in one place in some time, was assembled to exact proper revenge." Now the Qwarm's anger gave way to confusion.

"It was believed at first that he who interfered acted alone. Such was apparently not the case. He has powerful and as-yet-unidentified associates or allies. All we know is that none of them appear to be associated with the government. All of the assembled were murdered mysteriously." Long, deceptively thin fingers opened and closed slowly.

The hooded figure eyed the movements cautiously. This old man was dangerous, like a well-used weapon—worn and dulled on the outside, but still an efficient killer. It would not do to push him, especially in his present mood.

"If no official agency of Church or Commonwealth is involved," the soft voice ventured, "then there is still time for this business to reach a satisfactory conclusion." Then it added, as an afterthought: "There will be no additional money for the additional time involved, you realize."

"That is of no import."

"Really?" Now a hint of disdain crept into the whisperer's voice. "I thought that money was paramount among your kind, businessfolk that you are."

"We are a clan, an extended family first," the Qwarm corrected him, "businessfolk second. Our reputation protects us more than our abilities. That is why anyone who kills a single Qwarm cannot be permitted to live to tell of it. Such a tale would impair our efficiency and place isolated members in danger."

"This business of killing is still a business," the figure rasped from beneath its shrouds.

"Rest assured," the Qwarm leader replied. "Whether we regard it as a matter of business or clan morality should not matter to you. You have hired us. We will carry out the terms of our contract satisfactorily for you—even if it carries us to the ends of the galaxy."

"I wish not to see you again until you can bring me word of that," the figure intoned forcefully, evidently unimpressed by the Qwarm's speech. "Whether you kill this interferer or his friends is your business. Kill however many you must, but kill foremost the creature called Abalamahalamatandra."

"As I have declared, it will be done." That seemed to end the meeting, except that a touch of human curiosity overcame the Qwarm. His professional poise lapsed briefly to reveal an emotional creature beneath.

"I would still like to know why you or anyone else is willing—nay, eager—to pay the absurd sum of one million credits for the killing of a single alien being."

"I am sure you would," replied the hooded shape, a hint of amusement in its voice. When nothing more was forthcoming, it was clear that the discussion was over.

As he turned to leave the room, the Qwarm saw the hooded figure move. Light poured through the open doorway from the hall beyond. Despite the figure's rapid movement, the shaft of fresh light in the dark chamber seemed to sparkle off a cornea that was not human beneath those enfolding shrouds.

Then again, the Qwarm elder reflected as he strolled down the hallway of the eighty-second floor, in the brief instant he could have misinterpreted the effect of the light.

Not that it mattered anyway. The Qwarm clan had often accepted assignments from nonhumans and non-thranx. This present employer's desire for anonymity was hardly remarkable.

Rage boiled within him, though he didn't show it as he left the office tower. So many of the clan dead! People saw his set face and parted to let him pass. This had become much more than a simple job for the clan. It did not matter that no one save a single woman and child—now painlessly if somewhat belatedly—eliminated, had learned of the Qwarm's failure on the commercial world of Moth. It was enough that the Qwarm themselves knew. It was enough that they had been outraged.

So it was that law-enforcement officials throughout the Commonwealth noted the unusual activity among black-clad, skullcapped men and women on various worlds and wondered at it. They would have wondered much more if they had known that all the frenzied activity was caused by the actions of a single innocuous-looking young man . . .

Chapter Five

The *Teacher* slipped into a stabilized parking orbit above Alaspin. A few preparations and then Flinx and Ab were dropping planetward.

Pip hissed softly as Flinx considered what he had learned during their journey to the frontier world they were approaching. The planet was warm, though not especially humid, consisting mostly of patches of jungle spotted about vast, sweeping savannas and reedy river plains. Alaspinport was a small city by Commonwealth standards. In fact, this little-explored globe boasted a very modest humanx population.

Considering that, Flinx had been surprised at the number of ships hovering above Alaspin's surface. There was evidently interstellar traffic disproportionate to the populace. In a way, that should not have surprised him. Alaspin was rich in two things: gemstones and history. The prospectors, mining companies, and many universities and research institutions with interests on the planet could account for the kind of heavy traffic to and from the surface that he encountered.

Despite overcrowding, it was no problem to secure

his shuttle at the port. Lodgings were plentiful, and he got a room in a modest hotel in town.

Walking through the hot streets, he saw that the population was divided almost equally between humans and thranx. If anything, there were more of the busy, active insects than humans. They tolerated the dryness and thrived in the heat of midday.

The mixture of scientists and fortune hunters was a peculiar one. Flinx passed studious individuals arguing alien sociology, then overheard a conversation dealing with the smuggling rates on Catchalot. Alaspin was filled with two institutions: libraries and brothels.

One of the greatest multiple-culture populations in this part of the galaxy had risen and passed on here before the Commonwealth was more than a dream in a few visionaries' eyes. "It's true, Flinx," the Junoesque, henna-haired concierge was telling him upon his return to the hotel. "They say that the Alaspinians explored all through the region of the Commonwealth and beyond."

"Then why aren't there any left?" he asked reasonably.

She shrugged. "According to the research folks I've chatted with, the locals liked long-range exploring, but never gave a thought to colonizin' anyplace else." She made a show of adjusting the complex of straps beneath her yellow-and-silver dress as she explained the function and operation of the water-retrieve and other devices in his room.

"Xenohistorians I've had stay here told me the Alaspinians died out less than eighty thousand Terran standard years ago. They think it was a gradual thing, not sudden like. Almost as if the Alaspinians had lived a full racial life, got tired, and decided to diffuse out." She manipulated the air purifier and tempioner. There was a soft hum, and cool air filled the room.

The hennaed coiffure, the garish make-up were a disguise, he suspected. There was a vulnerability beneath the paint that appealed to him.

"You're a damn sight younger than most of the solitaires I get in here, Flinx. You said you're not a miner?"

"No," he confessed, beginning to wonder if she was as vulnerable as he imagined. He smiled in what he hoped was a pleasant yet neutral manner. "I tend more toward research—you might even say sociology."

"That's okay," the landlady declared amiably, "I like intellectuals too. If they aren't snobbish about it. You're not snobbish, I think."

Ab saved Flinx the necessity of commenting by chiming in with a particularly loud rhyme. Distracted, the hotel owner gazed at the alien with distaste. Mild distaste, because no one could look at Ab and not be amused.

"You going to keep that thing with you?"

"If it's permissible. Ab doesn't get in the way. He won't trouble anyone."

"Doesn't matter to me," the woman responded evenly. "Is it clean?"

"As far as I know."

She frowned. "What's that supposed to mean?"

"Ab performs objectionable bodily functions, if he has any, out of my sight."

"That's okay then. Only thing is, I don't know whether to charge you double room rate for two, or single with a pet. Which is it?"

"Whatever you think appropriate," Flinx advised her.

That was the wrong thing to say. She smiled broadly at him. "Whatever I think's appropriate? I'll remember that." Her gaze traveled over him. Somehow he got the impression she wasn't admiring his attire. "Yes, you're a damn sight younger than most. If you need anything . . . later . . . if the air controls don't work right, you let me know." Her voice dropped an octave. "It's hot during the day, but it can get chilly here at night."

Flinx swallowed. "I'll be sure and let you know, ma'am."

"Mirable," she corrected him. "Mirable Dictu." She sidled toward the door. "It's nice to find someone who's not a fanatic about what they're here for. Scientists get too wrapped up with thinkin', and the prospectors never do. Good to have a guest who embodies a bit o' both."

His last view was of her perambulating form drifting suggestively toward the stairway. He almost called out to her. However ... He sighed. With serious business unfinished, he had no time for such foolery. But if Alaspin proved to be the final dead end, as he half suspected it would, then he might have time and need of some sympathetic company. In that event, he might strike up a more serious friendship with the voluptuous Mirable.

She was the first one he asked about the enormous man with the white hair and gold earring. As expected, Mirable had no knowledge of anyone fitting that description.

Several days of questioning around the town produced memories of numerous men with rings in their ears, some of the ornaments gold or gold-colored. But if the men were the right size they didn't wear the earring, and if they wore one they were never big enough. Or they were large enough and beringed, but their hair was brown or red or black or blond.

A cargo loader finally told Flinx of a friend who almost fit the description. The only thing he was unsure of was the earring's color. In a burst of excitement, Flinx tracked the man down and found that he still worked in Alaspinport.

Unfortunately, he was only twenty-two years old and had never been to Moth in his life. Nor did he know offhand of anyone resembling himself who was older.

That disappointment had nearly caused Flinx to give up.

"Eh, my handsome young guest," Mirable had chided him, "so many years you think on this, and then a couple of days and you're ready to forget it?"

He stayed on Alaspin and kept asking questions.

Various inquiries around the town the next day elicited no leads, but did bring Flinx to the office of a garrulous, enthusiastic clerk. He was in charge of Temporary Residences, and Flinx had to see him to get his permit stamped so he could legally remain on Alaspin.

"Entry to Alaspin is strictly limited and watched," the clerk rambled on. "You already had a taste of our security procedures when you set down at the port." Flinx nodded. They had seemed unusually thorough for a frontier world. "That's because of the gems." The clerk winked. "Local police have to keep tabs on everyone. Claim stealing, robbery—we have our share. Adds to the spice of life here."

Sure, Flinx thought, when you can sit in a nice, cool office and watch the arrests and shootings on the tridee.

"And it's not only the gemstones," he went on. "Oh no. Constant fighting between the research people and the prospectors. Constant. It's not easy keeping peace between them. Each group has little sympathy for the other. The scientists think the miners are destructive Neanderthals, and the miners consider the scientists cloud-walkers each with a fat credit pipeline to some research group."

"I don't understand," Flinx admitted openly. "A little conflict I can see, but persistent battling—what for? Isn't each group after different things?"

The clerk shook his head at the newcomer's ignorance. "Let me give you an example. Have you ever heard of the Idonian Mask?"

Flinx shook his head.

"It cost the lives of sixteen people, on Alaspin and off, before the Commonwealth finally stepped in. Declared it a treasure of the people and appropriated it for the Pre-Commonwealth Societies Museum on Hivehom." He eyed Flinx. "The mask was about your height and twice your width, Flinx, and decorated with sixty thousand carats of flawless blue diamonds set to form the face and history of some long-gone local god or politician or chief thug—they don't know which yet. All done on worked, poured crysorillium."

"Now *that* I've heard of," Flinx interrupted.

The clerk nodded, smiling sagely. "Uh-huh . . . rare heavy metal that looks a little like iridescent azurite, only greener and much tougher. Thranx call it *fonheese*, or Devoriar metal. They prize the stuff, but it's even more valuable to men, because there's none of it on Earth, and little on the other explored worlds. Here they call it blue gold.

"Itinerant old dirt-grubber found the mask first, nearly forty years ago," the clerk went on. "I still remember the first faxes of it. Beautiful thing. The local scientists went crazy on seeing it. They said it held clues to a hundred missing years of Alaspinian history. Of course, the miner and his buddies were only interested in how many diamonds and how many kilos of crysorillium they could get out of it.

"The mask went back and forth, changing hands between miners and scientists and back again, losing a certain amount of metal and diamonds with each transfer and replacing them with blood. Nor were all the deaths between contesting miners and researchers, no. I remember the story of two thranx scientists who published simultaneous identical interpretations of the mask's upper writing. They ended up in a duel and killed each other. That's why the Commonwealth government had to step in and take the thing over, to prevent any more deaths. Even so, the last two people the mask 'killed' were murdered over a plot to break into the museum and steal it."

He waved a hand at the bustling street outside the office window. "From what's been learned, they say Alaspin once boasted several hundred different societies, united by a worldwide system of engineering and weights and measures, that sort of thing. But each society different. There are tens of thousands of mapped ruined structures out there, Flinx, and that's estimated to be only a small portion of the total. Each culture worshipped its own gods. So, you see, it became kind of a sporting competition to see whose temples could be the most lavishly decorated. Jungle and swamp have taken many of them over, but it's still a treasure hunter's paradise out there, for anyone who wants to risk the weather, the hostile flora and fauna, and the aborigines."

"Aborigines?" Flinx exclaimed. That was enough to set the clerk to gabbing again.

"The sociologists working here aren't sure about the abos. They don't seem to bear much resemblance to reconstructions of what the original Alaspinians were like. No one can decide for sure if they're in fact degenerate remnants of the original dominants, or simply another semisentient group that's evolved to take the place left by the vanished major culture." He fumbled with some tapes. "I've got to get back to my own work, young man. Sorry if I bored you."

"No, you've been very informative," Flinx told him honestly.

"That's Alaspin then, son. A place where fortunes and reputations can be made, sometimes together. And I am sorry," he added, remembering his visitor's original reason for coming, "that I don't know of your oversized quarry with the gold ring."

Flinx left the office, and found himself wandering in no particular direction through the town. Casual conversation and random questioning had gained him nothing. His best chance for finding out anything lay with the local arm of the Commonwealth peaceforcers. They should have records of just about everyone who ever set foot on this world and passed through the screenings at the port. But a direct inquiry would likely be met with questions. The police did not supply faxes and biographs to anyone who walked in off the street and asked for them. He didn't think they would cooperate without a few answers—answers Flinx would rather not give.

Passing a street vendor, he palmed a food stick and replaced it without being detected. Old habits were hard to break. But stealing the right fax tape would be hard to do, perhaps even impossible. The local peaceforcers would not be city-soft.

That left him with only the prospect of endless questioning ahead. Angrily he mused that coming here had probably been a mistake. Mother Mastiff was right—he was going to find nothing. In his anger he didn't notice that he was now walking through a section of town he had not been to before.

Besides, there were his responsibilities to the Ulru-Ujurrians. Without his supervision their innocent experiment could prove dangerous, to themselves and to others. They needed him to explain the rules of civilization as they constructed their own.

What was he wasting his time for, then? Probably the man he sought had never set foot on the soil of Alaspin, had acquired his minidrag elsewhere, just as Flinx had. Time was passing. Why, in a little while he'd be twenty. Twenty! An old man.

A tightening on his shoulder caused him to look that way and speak comfortingly. "I know, Pip ... don't worry." The minidrag stared back up at him with slitted, anxious eyes. "I'm just nervous, that's all." But it wasn't Flinx's state of mind which had caused his pet to tense. The source lay ahead.

A group of locals—prospectors, by the look of their clothes—were chatting in front of a business which managed to flourish a garish front even in the still-bright light of late afternoon. Concluding their conversation, one man and the two women miners left and walked on up the street. They turned to wave a good-bye, which the two men who stayed behind returned before entering the building.

Flinx had a good look at one, less so at his companion. The man nearest him was short, his skin darker than Flinx's but not black. That color was reserved for his hair, which fell straight and slick to just above his shoulders. Cheekbones bulged in his face like apples in a child's pocket, and his nose was as sharp and curved as the fins of an atmosphere flier. The other man was not nearly so swarthy, and was of a different ethnic background.

These details were interesting, but they were only incidental to what had caused both man and minidrag to tense. Each man had displayed a curled form on a shoulder, one on the left, the other on the right. Even from a distance there was no mistaking that blue-and-pinkish-red pattern of interlocking diamond shapes.

Minidrags!

Tame ones, probably as domesticated as Pip. His pet was the only miniature dragon Flinx had ever seen. While he had known that Pip came from here, he had had no idea that the practice of domesticating the venomous creatures was popular. Certainly it wasn't widespread, because he had wandered through much of the town without seeing any tame flying snakes. Until now.

He increased his speed and found himself facing the entrance. If nothing else, he would learn something of his pet on this trip. The two men inside, living as they did on the snakes' native planet, likely knew more about minidrags than Flinx had been able to learn on his own. Seeing the two men together, he suspected that the bond achieved between man and reptile led to one between men capable of taming such a dangerous animal. It was a suspicion compounded of equal parts naiveté and reason. If he was right, they would greet him as a friend.

Despite his anxiety, the entrance to the structure still gave him pause—the two men had entered a simiespin. Flinx was familiar with the notorious, barely tolerated simie booths. Places of unrefined amusement often advertised such booths for use.

In a simie booth, an individual's thoughts were read, amplified, and displayed three-dimensionally in the booth user's mind. The dreamlike simulacrum was complete with all relevant sensory accompaniment: sight, smell, touch, everything. All it took was the modest fee.

Naturally, a simie booth was private. Intrusion into a private booth, during which the intruder could also partake of some private dream, was one of the most universally decried offenses in the Commonwealth. This because the most unassuming individual could rid him or herself of the most depraved, obnoxious fantasies no matter how hellish they might be, without harming anyone.

Since booth owners didn't care what fantasies their patrons conjured up, simies were once considered obscene and had been banned. The resultant great legal battle had finally been decided in favor of the simie manufacturers. Freedom of thought, one of the pillar principles of the Commonwealth, was brought to bear on the argument, and it was that which had finally defeated the censors. That, and the solemn testimony of a Church medical team. The team had deplored the uses to which the booths were sometimes put while simultaneously ruling that the booths had therapeutic value.

What Flinx was confronting was something at once less disreputable and more unsettling. In effect, a simiespin was a greatly enlarged simie booth which surrounded an entire establishment—a restaurant, a bar, sometimes even a travel agency. Preprogrammed, the simiespin machinery projected mass three-dimensional illusion. It provided an always-changing environment, keyed by the random thoughts of its patrons but preprogrammed with nondestructive simulacra. The thrill was in never knowing where a visitor might find himself next.

Simiespins vied with one another in the detail of their programming and the intensity of their simulations. Unwary visitors had been known to suffer from spells of madness, unable to cope with the rapid-fire change of environments, but these cases were insufficiently common to close the simiespins down. Ample warnings were posted outside to keep the unwary and uncertain from entering.

There was additional protection, as Flinx discovered after paying the fee and entering. He found himself in a long hallway, dark and lined with fluorescent murals depicting scenes from different worlds. It was more than a mere entranceway. He could feel a tickling at his mind.

Behind those decorative murals lay expensive, sensitive equipment, which the law had determined necessary. If any of them felt that Flinx's mind or that of any other prospective patron was ill equipped to handle the fluctuating environment of the spin, alarms would sound and human or mechanical attendants would appear. They would announce with regret that those so analyzed would have to search elsewhere for amusement.

It was interesting that although a simiespin could serve food and drink that by themselves produced mental effects, there was no age restriction. What was required was a firm grasp on reality. Children were notoriously weak in that area, and so in general were barred from entering. But those children whom the machines passed were welcome within, whereas certain adults were rejected. It could and did lead to occasional embarrassment for overconfident parents, when they were denied entrance and their offspring were passed on.

Flinx found himself wondering how many politicians would be refused admittance to a simiespin. He was not surprised when the machinery also passed Ab. His alien tag-along had *no* grip on reality, and so was freely granted admittance to the lesser madness ahead.

Before him the door pulsed with an internal ruby glow, a promise of pleasure beyond. A sensuous mechanical voice murmured softly, "You have paid for and have been granted permission to sample our palette of a thousand worlds. Your pet"—an apparent reference to Ab—"may enter with you but must be kept under control at all times. You will be charged . . ." and the voice quoted various figures; the rate went down as the length of time increased. "On your way out or in, partake of the invigorating refreshments we offer," the voice concluded. Flinx nodded. It was a bar, as he had suspected.

Smoothly the pulsing red door slid into the floor. Flinx braced himself mentally and walked forward. His initial reaction was one of letdown. The simiespin chamber was huge, a good three stories high inside. Though it didn't look like an ordinary gathering chamber at present. Instead of benches and booths and a bar, he found himself looking at a sloping beach studded with boulders. It was evening. A sun much pinker and hotter than either Moth's or Alaspin's was turning the drifting stratus clouds above the color of wine. The sky matched the ocean, whose purple-lavender waves lapped sonorously at the yellow sands. A few strange plants swung lazily in the hot breeze off the water, almost in time to the humming sound of un-known source.

Nearby a man and a woman lay entwined in each other's arms. Their filthy prospectors' clothing was gro-tesquely out of place in the idyllic scene, but neither appeared to mind. They were elsewhere anyway, no doubt partly as a result of whatever they were sucking from a nearby boulder through a pair of long, sturdy plastic siphons.

"Where are we?" Flinx asked, his curiosity at the vision around him overcoming his unease at invading the couple's privacy.

The man didn't object. Pulling the tip of the siphon from his lips, he eyed Flinx and muttered dreamily, "Quofum, I think. Quofum."

That was a world Flinx had heard of once. It sup-posedly lay far from the Commonwealth's boundaries, somewhere along the inner edge of the Arm. Only a few humans and thranx had ever succeeded in visiting it. Something was wrong with space in that region, something which caused Quofum to appear only occa-sionally at the coordinates recorded.

Fabled Quofum, where the sky was as clear as a vir-gin's conscience and the wine-colored seas tasted of ev-erything from ouzo to Liebfraumilch. For the oceans of Quofum were varied, though the sea-stuff normally ran about nine percent alcohol. In the endless oceans of Quofum, so the tale ran, swam fish who were never un-happy.

Stepping off the wooden landing, he found his feet sinking slightly into warm sand. Then he was by the edge of the sea, which stretched endlessly to the hori-zon. Sunset outdid itself as he kneeled at the edge of the water. Purple comfort ran over his knees and ex-tended hands. Pip stirred uneasily on Flinx's shoulder, shook him with a start back to reality. It was the most perfect illusion Flinx had ever experienced.

Cupping his hands, Flinx dipped them into the sea, brought them up, and sipped a double palmful of ocean. The flavor of the seawater was rich, fruity, and strong, with a powerful bouquet and a gentle perfume caused by the warming effect of his hands.

Rising, he noticed the stains on his jumpsuit and frowned.

Someone chuckled.

Looking behind, he saw the two minidrag tamers he had followed in, leaning up against a wave-worn rock. The one with the aquiline nose called to him. His accent was unplaceable.

"Join us, young dragon lord, and sit with your fellow reptiles."

Flinx started up the beach, brushing fitfully at his pants.

"Don't worry," the swarthy man assured him, "the stains will disappear the moment you leave. They're as unreal as the sand and the drunken oceans."

Even so, Flinx could still taste the smooth wine in his mouth, feel the wetness where it had swirled around his wrists and knees. The sand remained hot underfoot. Yet despite the heat, he realized, he was comfortable. No wonder only those of stable mind were permitted entry into such places! One with a less solid grasp of reality could go quite mad here.

As if to test his thoughts, the sky above suddenly blurred, as did the landscape around him. When the brief moment of disorientation had passed, he saw storm clouds overhead. Rain was falling steadily, and lightning crashed around him as electrons warred in the heavens.

Flinx blinked away drops that he *knew* weren't real, that were only the products of machinery so sophisticated and sensitive that few humanx really understood how they operated. But he had to blink, the water dimmed his vision.

Jungle and high ferns closed tightly around him, the startling climax vegetation of a cold-weather rain forest. He felt stifled, and looked around frantically for the simiespin entrance. Naturally, he could see nothing so out of keeping with the forest simulacrum. Rain continued to pelt his head and shoulders, sending Pip deep into the folds of Flinx's jumpsuit material. Ab singsonged behind them, oblivious to the cold downpour.

Except . . . Flinx wasn't cold.

"We're over here," a laughing voice called to him.

He hunted but saw nothing. "Where?"

"Behind the big tree, straight ahead. We haven't moved."

Flinx walked around a meter-thick bole which looked like a cross between a Terran redwood and a bundle of black lizards tied together. As he walked past, he tapped the trunk. It responded with a stentorian bark that made him jump.

His response prompted another laugh, nearer now. Behind the tree, the two minidrag tamers stood as before, only now they were leaning up against a rotting stump. Rainbow-hued fungi formed a riot of color on the dead wood.

"First time in a simiespin, compadre?" the small man asked with a grin.

"Yes. I had some idea of what to expect but"—he took in a deep breath—"it's still awfully disconcerting. Especially the suddenness of the changes."

"That's one of the attractions," the other man countered. "As it is with everything in life."

"Don't pay any attention to Habib," the short one advised. "One drink and he turns morbidly philosophical." He extended an open hand. "My name's Pocomchi." A nod toward Pip, peeking out from beneath Flinx's shirt top. "You're the youngest I've ever seen with a tame drag."

They were already on a first-name basis—good. As Flinx shook the proffered palm, Pocomchi extended the other. It held a large, fat mushroom. At least, that's what it looked like. Flinx reached for it. As he did so, the large triangular head cradled next to the short man's neck lifted. A slight sneeze from that head and Flinx would be dead. But at a word from its master, it relaxed.

The mushroom turned out to be full of a brown liquid. It looked like gravy, but it held the kick of the whole bull. After a stunned taste, Flinx handed it back.

Meanwhile, Pip's head was weaving back and forth, up and down in jerky, dancing motions. His excitement was understandable. Since Flinx had found him, this was the first time he'd ever set slitted eyes on another of his own kind. The two minidrags opposite were apparently more used to others like themselves. They regarded Pip with only mild interest.

"I'm Flinx," he replied when he had his breath back. As they sat down across from him, Flinx made a seat on the stump of another dead bush; the spongy mold crushed to cushion his backside against the hard wood.

"Tell me, is this a chair I'm sitting on, or . . . ?"

"You guess as well as we," the one called Habib told him languidly. "All life's an illusion."

"There he goes again," grumbled Pocomchi good-naturedly. He pointed behind Flinx. "Since that's remained constant, I assume it's not an illusion." Flinx saw that the man was gesturing at Ab.

"He's a ward of mine. Crazy as a drive lubricator from too many fumes, but completely harmless."

"Funny-looking creature," Pocomchi decided. He swigged his mushroom.

Flinx studied his seat. It looked exactly like a dead stump. As he regarded it, it turned into an eight-legged, blue-furred spider-shape which rolled bug-eyes and hearing organs at him. It didn't move, however, and seemed content to support him. Somehow Flinx managed not to jump.

But his new friends noticed the irrepressible twitch. "First time in a simiespin for sure," Pocomchi chuckled, as the sky turned pale puce above them. Then his expression turned curious, although the friendliness remained in his voice. "And maybe the first time on Alaspin as well? But that makes no sense. Dragon lords are few, Flinx. I don't recall seeing you before."

"I'm from offworld, all right," he admitted. For some reason, he didn't hesitate to reveal information to these men. Anyone who could tame one of the em-pathic telepaths called minidrags could employ them only for defense, never to attack or bully or cajole others. The snakes wouldn't do it. They would never associate with such a being in the first place.

If these men were not informative, they might at least be potential allies.

"Not only is it my first time here," he continued, "but it's Pip's as well. He was abandoned on my home planet when we were both much younger. In a way, I suppose," he concluded, fondly rubbing the minidrag under one pleated wing, "it's more of a homecoming for him than it is anything for me."

"Your dragon is as welcome as you," Pocomchi assured him. He leaned back into the supportive limbs of a multitentacled creature. As Flinx watched, the alien octopus-shape became a small tornado. Wind whistled and howled all around them. The jungle was gone.

"Isn't that right, Balthazaar, old fellow?" Pocomchi had reached up to rub the neck muscles back of his snake's skull. The big minidrag was obviously as much older as it was larger than Pip.

"How does one get a drink in here?" Flinx asked.

"If you don't want to try the mushrooms, or other decor," Habib told him, "you can always tuck-a-tube." He extended a hand downward to pull a red siphon out of the ground. "If this doesn't appeal to you, there's a fairly standard mechbar back there." He pointed at a giant bird, which abruptly turned into an emerald cactus. "I much prefer the tube, because it matches the simie."

"I don't understand," Flinx confessed, taking the tube with one hand and eyeing it uncertainly.

Habib smiled. "The liquid changes to match the new environment. You never know what you're going to be sipping next." Flinx made a face, and Habib hastened to reassure him. "You can't get sick. This is a legiti-mate place. Plenty of modifiers included in the drinks to make sure no one gets ill. The owner's proud of his reputation. Wouldn't do to have customers puking all over his simulacra."

Habib retrieved the tube, stuck it in the corner of his mouth, and leaned back. "How do I get one?" Flinx asked, studying the ground unsuccessfully.

"There's one by your right hip," Pocomchi informed him. "It was sticking out of the left leg of that spider thing you were sitting on a few minutes ago."

Looking down, Flinx saw the whirlwind he was sitting on change into a blue stalagmite. Now they were in a cave filled with chromatically colored formations: stalagtites, helicites, flowstone, and much more. Cool cave air hung motionless around him.

One of the helicites sticking to his seat was longer and straighter than its neighbors. It was also flexible, Flinx discovered when he pulled on it. Sticking it into his mouth, he sucked experimentally. A thin syrup flowed through the tube, with a taste redolent of over-ripe pomegranate. It coated his throat. The sweetness did not make him sick.

There was, he decided, plenty of time to ask the important questions. For now, he would enjoy the simiespin's delights and the company of these two companionable men.

Chapter Six

At least an hour passed, although within the simiespin there was no way of knowing the exact time, before Flinx spoke again.

"What do you two do?" Curious, he examined them,
the quick-moving, enthusiastic Pocomchi and his lanky,
mournful companion. "Surely you're not attached to
one of the scientific teams working on Alaspin?"

"Who, us—archeologists?" gasped Pocomchi, eyes
flashing in the dim light. The cave simulacrum, apparently proving popular, had been returned. "Fine
chance you'd have, Flinx, of finding one of those
brain-cases in a simiespin. No, they get their kicks
down in the town library that the Commonwealth
maintains for them."

"You go to extremes, Poco," Habib insisted. He ran
a hand through thick, curly black hair. "Even the
thranx among them aren't strictly mental machines.
You see thranx in here too, don't you?" With an arm
he gestured toward a cluster of sparkling aragonite
crystals, delicate as flowers. A male and female thranx
were sprawled on their stomachs, immersed in illusion

and each other. The male was caressing his companion's ovipositors suggestively.

The cave vanished as snow started to sift down over them. Now Flinx's seat was a rough block of solid ice. Yet he remained comfortable, even as the breath congealed in front of his mouth.

"We wander around a lot," explained Pocomchi.

Habib leaned back into a snowbank and sucked silver from the siphon. "What we actually do, Flinx, is ... not much." He noticed the youth staring at his associate. "Tell the boy where you're from, Poco. He's shared with us."

"I was born and raised in ..." Pocomchi hesitated. "Just say it was on Earth, near the middle of what teachers call the Hourglass. Near a place called Taxem." Flinx admitted ignorance of the name, though he knew of the Hourglass, where the two smaller continents met.

"It's an old archeological site," Pocomchi went on. "I grew up surrounded by ancient temples. When I was seven I was running the tiller in my family's quarto-maize field when something went clunk and the machine stopped. I sat there and cried for hours, afraid I'd busted the damn expensive thing." He grinned at the memory as he watched Ab's antics.

"My mother finally heard me crying over the locater I always wore ... there were creatures called jaguars living in our neighborhood. When she and my uncle came out and moved the tiller, they found I'd hit a buried stone head about twenty-six hundred years old. It was on our land. The local museum paid one-hundred fifty credits for it. I got ten whole credits of my own to spend. I bought out part of the local sweetshop and for a week I was sicker than a boa trying to swallow a maiden aunt." He took a swig from his tube, which now projected from the head of a glowing fish. They were underwater, Flinx noted with interest. Bubbles rose from his nose and mouth, yet it felt as if he were breathing clean air.

His sensory apparatus was beginning to handle the

extreme shifts in environment. Ab seemed to float in
the water behind him.

"I've been trying to stumble over credit-producing
heads and related stuff ever since," finished Pocomchi.

"In short, he's as money-hungry as I am," Habib put
in with a supple smile. "We're as bad as a Moth merchant."

Flinx bridled slightly at the deprecatory comment directed at his home world, then relaxed. Why should he
take umbrage at the reference? He was no merchant.
And if he had one friend in that trade, it was off-bal-
anced by a dozen enemies.

"So now you know what we're hunting for," muttered Habib, after explaining that he came from a part
of Earth called Lebanon. "What are you hunting
here?"

"A man."

From nearby, Ab let out a startlingly clear bit of
nonsense rhyme. Habib sat forward; he seemed to notice the alien for the first time.

"Why's that with you?"

"*His* associate," quipped Pocomchi. "Both Flinx and
I share the same fate."

"I acquired Ab by default," Flinx explained yet
again, as Habib threw his grinning partner a sour look.
"I haven't the heart to abandon him, and I'm not sure
I could sell him. Besides, Ab's not good for anything
except singing madness and serving as the butt of bad
jokes."

"Never seen anything like it before," Habib admitted.

"Neither have I," added Pocomchi. "The simie admitted him?"

"I don't think environment affects Ab," Flinx theorized, as the subject of the discussion drew lines in the
snow. "Once in a while he almost makes sense. I'm
afraid Ab exists in a universe of his own."

Ab bent over to stare with a single eye at something
on the ground. Apparently the thing was moving, since
Ab's head inclined to follow it between his legs. Slowly
he tucked head and then neck beneath him, until he

fell over on his back—if it was his back and not his front—into the snow. Flinx smiled sympathetically, while both men laughed.

"See?" Flinx said. "He's too pitiful a creature to just leave some place."

"You sure you're not a slaver?" Pocomchi inquired with sudden sharpness. "You don't look the—"

"No, no," Flinx corrected, shaking his head rapidly. "I'm just here looking for a man."

"For what?" Habib asked with unexpected directness.

Flinx hesitated, and finally said, "Personal reasons."

"You want to kiss him or kill him?" Habib pressed disarmingly, not put off by Flinx's disclaimer. But then, Flinx knew, this was a frontier world, where such civilized subtleties as obfuscation were unknown.

"Honestly, I'm not sure, Habib," he admitted, considering for the first time what he *would* do if he actually found the person he sought. "It depends on whether he's the end of a trail or simply another signpost on it." Sighing, he repeated his description of the man in question, for the hundredth-odd time on Alaspin:

"A very big man, age uncertain but not young. Over two meters up, two hundred kilos in between, maybe less. Wears a gold ring in his right ear, or used to. He may or may not have a minidrag with him. Don't tell me about the cargo handler at the port. I've already met him, and he's not the one I'm seeking."

"Sounds like it could be . . ." Habib was murmuring thoughtfully, but his companion was already waving his hands with excitement.

"Sure, we know him."

Flinx started, and slid off his ice block to land in a shallow pool of thick petroleum. They were in a swamp again, a dark morass dominated by carboniferous plants from which swung chittering oil-black creatures with flaming red eyes. A red sun blasted the noon sky overhead, stabbing through black-white clouds.

Flinx saw only Pocomchi.

"Don't look so startled, lad," the Indian urged. "It's

not a common man you've described. The one we're both thinking of fits, even to the gold earring." He shook his head, smiling at some secret thought. "A character, even for Alaspin, he is."

"Could you—where is he?" Flinx finally managed to stutter as he fought to untangle himself from his siphon tube.

Habib made an expansive gesture eastward. "Out there, doing the same things we do. Got a claim of sorts that he works with a partner." He leaned forward slightly. "Personally, the grubbers I've talked with say he's working an empty slot."

"When was the last time you saw him there, or knew for sure that he was at this place?"

"Three, maybe four months ago," Pocomchi considered, scratching the bridge of his impressive nose.

Flinx sagged inwardly. By now the man could be anywhere, even offplanet. But it was something! A reason to remain.

Habib rose and sauntered toward Flinx, waving his tube. "If I were to tell you some of the stories about your man, dragon lord, you wouldn't . . ." His mouth opened wide, and he gaped querulously at Flinx. Then his hands went out in front of him reflexively as he fell forward, metacarpal bones buckling as they hit the now-firm gravel floor of the desert under them. Three suns burned hellishly above; a fourth was sinking over the distant horizon.

Flinx had a glimpse of a hair-thin wire attached to a needle the size of a nail paring protruding from Habib's back, near the spine. A slight *phut*, and the needle and wire were withdrawn. The faint smell of ozone lingered in the air as he threw himself flat.

While Flinx crawled over the sand and gravel toward Ab, Pocomchi was moving toward his friend, calling to him wildly.

The instant Habib hit the ground, a tawny leathery shape had left his shoulder. Now it was joined by Balthazaar, and then Flinx felt a familiar weight leave his own arm. Like leaves in a dustdevil, the three winged demons circled one another in the air. Then they were streaking as one toward a gleaming boulder of solid citrine off to Flinx's right. Several violent hisses sounded behind them, a reptilian equivalent of a sonic boom.

Flinx continued toward Ab, shouting for the alien to lie down. Two blue orbs moved, eyeing him quizzically. The slight puff of displaced air sounded above Flinx. Artificial desert sunlight reflected from a long, silvery thread. The thread ended in a sharp, tiny shape which struck the quadrupedal alien just under one of its four arms. A faint crackling sounded, as if a hand had been dragged across a coarse wool blanket.

Ab stopped in mid-verse and appeared to quiver slightly. Then he resumed rhyming as if nothing had happened. Flinx reached him, got his arms around three legs, and yanked. Ab tumbled to the sand. He stared at his master with a blank but almost hurt expression.

Glancing behind them and to the right, Flinx saw that Pocomchi was kneeling next to the motionless form of Habib. Slowly, as if fearing what he would learn, he extended a palm. It touched his companion's back, rested there a moment, then was brought away.

"Get down, Pocomchi!" Flinx yelled frantically. The Indian didn't look over at him, and made no move to comply. He appeared dazed. Maybe it was unconcern, Flinx thought, when muffled curses and screams began to reach him from behind the tall spire of yellow quartz.

As he waited and watched, the boulder changed into a giant diamond-bark tree, whose brown exterior flashed with blue sparks. Three shapes fluttered out from behind the tree.

Pleated wings braked as Pip came in for a landing, tail extended like a hand. It curled around Flinx's shoulder, the body then folding itself around the youth's extended arm, pleated wings collapsing flat against the cylindrical body. Flinx could feel the tenseness in the minidrag; he noted that his pet was panting nervously. Slitted eyes continued to dart watchfully from side to side.

A second minidrag, the constrictor-sized Balthazaar, draped itself around the back and arms of the grieving Pocomchi. The long, pointed tongue darted in and out worriedly, touching cheek, touching eyes, touching.

Flinx watched Habib's minidrag settle to a curled landing on its master's back. It lay there briefly, then slid forward to examine the head. After several minutes, great pleated wings unfurled. The flying snake fluttered forward until it was hovering in front of Habib's face. Leathery wings beat at the air violently, sending wind into the motionless man's mouth and nostrils.

More minutes, until the minidrag finally settled to earth by the still head of Habib. It coiled itself, and they remained like that, face to face, unmoving.

Flinx finally realized he was still holding on to Ab's legs. As soon as he released him, the alien righted himself. Indifferent to all that had taken place, Ab proceeded to inspect a tree root.

Keeping his eyes on the citrine boulder, Flinx crawled over to sit next to Pocomchi. He was still cautious, but felt less and less that any danger still hid behind the massive yellow rock.

There was no need to state the obvious. He had seen death in Habib's eyes before the man hit the sand.

"Look, I'm sorry," he whispered tensely. "We'd better try to get out of here."

"Why?" Pocomchi turned anguished eyes on Flinx. When he spoke again, Flinx realized his question had nothing to do with a reason for leaving the simiespin.

"We never stole a claim, we made no serious enemies," the little man went on. His eyes returned to the slim prone form below them. The sand and gravel beneath it abruptly, uncaringly, changed and became blue grass.

"Three years. Three years we've been grubbing and carving and stinking on this end-of-civilization world. Three years! Other people hit it big all around us. But not us, never us." His voice rose. "Why not us? *Why not us?*"

Flinx made calming motions. Other patrons were beginning to look in their direction. The one thing he didn't want now was to be asked unanswerable questions. Reaching out, he tried to grab Pocomchi by the shoulders, to turn him toward him.

The moment he was touched, Pocomchi shook the hands violently from him. "Don't touch me!" He trembled; his voice was full of homicidal fury.

After a moment's hesitation, Flinx sat back on his haunches. While waiting, he occasionally eyed the yellow massif, which had now become a cluster of *sutro* branchings. Pocomchi seemed to calm himself a little. Flinx decided to wait, despite possible danger to himself, until the tormented Indian regained a measure of self-control.

So he turned his attention to the corpse at his feet. There was no blood, no visible wound. Leaning close, he saw where the needle-tipped wire had touched. A small hole had been made in the back of Habib's shirt. It was blackened around the edges. The peculiar smell still hung above the spot: ozone.

At least, he reflected gratefully, the philosophical miner had not suffered. Death had been instantaneous, brought on at the moment of contact with the needle.

A hand touched his shoulder. He glanced up anxiously, then relaxed. Pocomchi was standing above him, looking down at the body of his friend. His firm, assured grip was comfort enough for Flinx.

"I'm okay now, Flinx. It's just that—that—" He fought for the words. He wanted them to be right. "Habib was about the only man on this world that could stand me, and he was one of the few that I could stomach. Three years." Abruptly, he rose and turned to face what was now a clump of trees long extinct on Earth but still flourishing in mind tapes.

"Come on," he instructed Flinx as he started toward the small cluster of elms, "I want to see the dirt."

After a last backward glance at the body, Flinx hurried to catch up with the Indian. "What about your friend?"

Pocomchi didn't look back at him. "He'll lie there until the place closes. First the management will run their drunk crew through to help out those able to walk. Then they'll come through again and sweep up the incapacitated.

"Habib would like that, when they find out he's more than drunk. First they'll panic—probably think it's something toxic that's snuck into their siphon mixture. Then they'll locate the real source of death, electrocution, and go crazy trying to find the malfunction in their simie machinery.

"When that doesn't turn up anything," he concluded bitterly, "a few credits will change hands and they'll give him a proper, if circumspect, burial. The Church will make sure of that."

They were almost around the grove of elms when the trees became a pair of enormous mushrooms. Flinx found himself slowing, putting out a restraining hand. "Don't you think maybe . . . ?"

Pocomchi shook his head curtly. "Balthazaar would never have come back if any kind of threat remained. Nor would your drag, I suspect."

Flinx murmured agreement. It was not the time to argue—and he settled for letting the Indian round the corner first. When nothing sent him reeling back in his death throes, Flinx moved to join him.

There were two bodies on the ground. One was clad in a yellow-green dress suit, the other in a casual coolall. Flinx had a bad moment, but it gave way to what he expected to feel when Pocomchi put a foot under one corpse and flipped it over. The dress suit fell aside, revealing a familiar skin-tight blackness beneath.

Barely restrained anger gave way to puzzlement as Pocomchi checked the heads. A floppy green hat fell aside to show a black-and-crimson skullcap beneath. "Qwarm," he muttered with a frown. "We've had no dealing with them. Habib and I hadn't discovered anything worth killing over, nor have we offended anyone that badly. Qwarm are expensive. Why would anyone want to have us killed?"

Something clicked, and he jerked his head up to see Flinx staring patiently back at him. "You. Why do the Qwarm want you dead?"

"Not me," the youth explained, pointing behind him. "It's Ab they want. Though they want me too because I got too curious about why they wanted Ab."

"I'm not sure I'm following you, Flinx."

By way of an answer, Flinx pointed at the two awkwardly sprawled, venom-scarred bodies. "If two of their members," he explained, "hadn't reacted without thinking, I might not be involved with them at all. Habib might still be alive." He gestured loosely at the corpses. "So might they."

Pocomchi's reply was laced with contempt. "What do you care about a pair of soulless murderers like these?"

"They're humanx," Flinx responded quietly.

Pocomchi grunted eloquently. Then he raised one foot over the body he had overturned and brought it down with a hard, twisting motion. There was a cracking sound, as of shattering plastic. Kneeling, the Indian tore open the back of the black shirt. Several square plastic cases were linked together around the assassin's waist. A thin but heavily insulated cord ran from one case to a tiny, childish-looking plastic gun lying on the floor.

"Supercooled dense battery pack," Pocomchi explained, examining the arrangement. He touched a small switch on the cord before picking up the toy gun by its insulated handgrip. "Delivery terminal," he declared. "Fires a small needle attached to a wire."

Flinx had heard of this weapon but had never seen one before. But then, there were many ways of killing, and the Qwarm undoubtedly knew most of them.

"The wire rolls onto a spool inside the handgrip," Pocomchi was telling him evenly. "It serves two functions: to deliver the lethal charge and to guide the needle to its target. A good man with one of these"— he hefted the little weapon easily—"isn't stopped by any kind of shielding. If you're good with the guide system, I understand, you can shoot around several corners. An opponent wouldn't get a shot at you, or even a clear look. Or a chance . . . to fight back."

Flinx knew Habib had been electrocuted instantly. Then why . . . ?

He found himself walking out from behind the mushrooms, to look across a newly born brook. On the far side, Ab had an artificial yellow-and-pink flower in one hand. A big blue eye was bent close, studying the petals.

"I don't understand," Flinx muttered, half to himself.

"I don't understand either," snapped Pocomchi. Then he became aware that Flinx was staring, and not referring to the killing that had just taken place.

"It's Ab . . . my alien," Flinx told him eventually. "That needle hit him. I *saw* it hit him. I heard it. The charge went into him, and he doesn't show any sign of it. I've heard of natural organic grounders before, nervous systems which can shuttle enormous voltages harmlessly through their own bodies—but never in an animal, always in plants."

Pocomchi shrugged. "Maybe your Ab is a plant imitating an animal. Who knows? All that should matter to you is that he was immune to this particular kind of murder."

Flinx was looking around nervously now. "This means they know I'm on Alaspin. I've got to move." He started off to his right. "Are you coming, Pocomchi? I could use your help."

The Indian laughed sardonically. "You're a fine one to be asking for my help, young dragon lord. You're marked for dying. Why should I go anywhere with you? I can think of a dozen simpler ways to commit suicide."

Flinx stopped. He stared hard but unthreateningly back at Pocomchi. "I need to find the man you told me of, even though he's probably just another false lead. You're the only one on Alaspin I know who could find him for me. I don't expect you to come with me out of friendship. I'll settle for hiring you. Why should you go anywhere with me? Why not?" he finished, rather heartlessly. "You have other immediate prospects?"

"No," Pocomchi whispered blankly, "no other immediate prospects."

"But money isn't sufficient reason for you to come with me," Flinx went on relentlessly. "So I'll give you a better reason. I'd be very surprised if they don't try to kill Ab and me again."

Pocomchi rose and brushed at his pants to wipe off imaginary sand. "That's no reason."

"Think, Pocomchi," Flinx urged him. "It means that you and Balthazaar will have a chance to meet some more Qwarm."

The Indian glanced up at him, uncomprehending for a moment. Then his expression tensed with the realization of what Flinx was telling him. "Yes. Yes, maybe we will have a chance to meet some of that kind again. I'd like that." He nodded slowly, forcefully. "I'll go with you and guide you, Flinx." Turning, he spat on the two limp bodies and started to murmur in a guttural, alien tongue.

Flinx reached out, took Pocomchi's unresisting arm, and tugged him toward the exit. The man allowed himself to be led, but never ceased his muttering, which was directed at the two corpses they were leaving behind.

They crossed the small brook. In midstream it turned into a river of molten lava. Flinx felt gentle heat swirling around his legs, when they should have been burned to cinders. But he took only the barest notice of the effect. His mind was full of thoughts unconnected with the sensory gluttony provided by the simiespin machinery.

"Come on, Ab!" he shouted behind him. Blue eyes focused on him. With a good-natured singsong having something to do with vultures and fudge, the alien followed the two men across the glowing pahoehoe. By the time they reached the simiespin exit, Pocomchi had recovered enough to pay for his stay with his own credcard, though from time to time he would resume his muttering.

Finally they were on the street outside. Flinx started back toward his hotel, Pocomchi walking alongside.

The last remaining light of the Alaspinian evening was fading to an amber luminescence. Expecting a new kind of destruction to stab at them from behind every crate and barrel, from every rooftop and floater, Flinx found his gaze shifting constantly at imagined as well as real movements.

A hissing cry sounded suddenly—a reptilian wail. Both men paused. Behind them, a leathery winged shape rose into the sky. It passed over their heads, soaring on brilliantly hued wings as it lifted into the sunset. For a minute it paused there, above and slightly ahead of them, circling as it climbed. A dream-dragon out of a childhood fairy tale, its colorful diamond pattern caught the fading sun.

Abruptly it gave another short cry; it had reached a decision. Wings pushing air, it shot off in the direction of the setting sun. Light and distance combined to obscure Flinx's view of it in a very short while.

Both men resumed walking. "I wondered what Habib's minidrag would do," Flinx murmured thoughtfully. "I always wondered what a tame minidrag would do if its master died."

"Now you know—they turn wild again," Pocomchi elaborated. "Hazarez was a good snake." He eyed the sun, which had swallowed the last sight of the shrinking dark dot. "Balthazaar will miss Hazarez, too."

"We're liable to miss a lot more," Flinx assured his companion, "if we don't get off these streets before dark. The Qwarm prefer two sets of clothing: black cloth and night. I've got a few little things in my room I want to collect. Then we can rent a floater and get out of the city." He increased his pace, calling back over his shoulder, "Get a move on, Ab—I'm in a hurry!"

Four legs working effortlessly, the blue-green alien complied without any indication of strain.

Darkness owned that corner of Alaspin by the time they reached the modest hotel Flinx was staying in. His room pass keyed the transparent doorway. Panels slid aside, admitting both men and Ab to the unpretentious lobby.

Flinx headed straight for the lift; his rooms were on the third floor. Pocomchi and Ab trailed close behind, so close that when Flinx halted as if shot, the Indian nearly ran into him.

"Flinx?" Pocomchi inquired softly, alert now himself.

An amorphous, oppressive something had fallen like a thick curse over Flinx's thoughts. For a moment he had difficulty classifying the source. Then he knew. The mental stench of recent death permeated the entire building.

He told himself it might merely be a lingering aftereffect of the simiespin experience, a sort of mental hangover. It could also be the result of his often-morbid imagination. But he did not think so. He was trying to rationalize away his fear of what must have taken place here.

Instead of taking the lift, he tried to lean in the direction where the brain-smell was strongest. It led him toward the opposite side of the lobby. Mirable's quarters and office were here.

When he placed his palm over the call contact, he heard a reassuring buzz within. But no one came to open the door or check on the caller. He repeated the action, with the same result.

He tried to tell himself she could be out of the building. That must be it. His bill was paid for two more days in advance, but it would only be polite to leave a message explaining his sudden departure.

Picking the light stylus from its holder in the wall, he inscribed his good-bye on the electronic message screen. Then he pushed the transcribe button. When she returned, her presence would activate the screen machinery. His light images would be turned into voice and played aloud for her.

Replacing the stylus, he turned to leave. Pocomchi caught him and nodded at the doorway: "Listen."

Flinx obeyed. He heard something, then realized it was the message he had just left. That meant Mirable had to be in her apartment.

Why didn't she respond?

Experimentally, he placed a hand on the door and pushed. It slid back a few centimeters into the wall. That didn't make sense either. If she was within, surely she would have set the lock. Even on a relatively crime-free world—let alone a boisterous planet like Alaspin—such a device was standard equipment, built into the doorway of every commercial establishment.

The door continued to slide back under his pressure. He peered inward.

A voice called from behind him, "What's going on, Flinx?"

"Shut up."

Pocomchi was the sort of man who had broken limbs for less than that, but something in Flinx's manner induced him to comply without protest. He contented himself with watching the hotel entrance and the lift doors, while keeping an eye on Ab.

Shoving the door all the way into the wall, Flinx noticed a dark spot near its base. A thin stain indicated that a fluid-state switch had been shattered. That tied in with the broken lock mechanism.

Slowly he walked into the room. Internal machinery detected his body heat and brightened the chamber in greeting. It was decorated with the sort of items one might expect to be chosen by a woman whose dreams were rapidly leaving her behind. The flowers, the little-girl paraphernalia, a few stuffed animals on a couch, all were nails desperately hammered into a door against which time pressed relentlessly.

Then he saw the leg sticking out from behind the couch. The trussed body of Mirable lay naked beyond. Most of the blood had already dried.

A vast coldness sucked at him as he knelt over the rag-doll shape. One eye stared blankly up past him. He put a hand up and closed it gently. The other eye was missing. A look of uncomprehending, innocent horror was frozen on her face. About that he could do nothing.

Why she had shielded him, as she apparently had, he could not imagine. Whether out of some strange loyalty or the like, or out of pure stubbornness, she had not talked immediately. That would please ordinary criminal types, but not the Qwarm. True sadism was not a luxury professionals could afford, and they had done a professional job on her. But he did not understand why they had killed her. It was almost as if her obstinacy had irritated them.

Quickly he left the room and the body, surrounded by now-dead dreams. He almost expected to see Pocomchi and Ab lying dead across each other. But both were standing there, Ab mumbling amiably to himself and Pocomchi waiting silently. The Indian said nothing.

Flinx's gaze went immediately to the lift. He did not think anyone had seen them enter the building; if they had, he would not be standing here now.

"They're upstairs, I think," he told the expectant miner.

"I know where we can rent a skimmer now, if you've got the money," Pocomchi told him.

"I've got the money." Flinx took a step toward the lift. Pocomchi caught his arm, hard. Both minidrags stirred.

"You did me a right turn, back in the spin," the Indian said tightly. "Now it's my turn." He jerked his head toward the lift and the floors above. "This isn't the place or time. *They've* chosen both. When the time comes, we'll be the ones who've done the planning."

Flinx stared at him for a long moment. Pocomchi stared back.

"It was the woman who owned this hotel," Flinx finally explained flatly. Pocomchi let go of his arm, and they started slowly for the door. "She should have told them about me immediately."

Both men checked the door and the street beyond. It was empty.

"Then she did tell them," Pocomchi said.

Flinx nodded. "Not right away."

"Why not?" the Indian wanted to know as they exited and turned right down the street. Nothing fell from above to explode between them; no one challenged them from behind a corner.

"I don't know," he admitted, unable to blot the pitiful image of her twisted form from his mind. "It was a stupid, foolish thing to do."

"She must have had some reason," pointed out Pocomchi.

"I think ..." Flinx's tongue hesitated over the words. "I think she liked me, a little. I didn't think she liked me ... that much."

"One other thing." Dark eyes turned to Flinx in the dimness. "As soon as we started for the elevator, you knew something was wrong. How?"

If nothing else, Flinx owed this little man some truth. "I can sense strong feelings sometimes. That's what hit me when we went in. An overwhelming sensation of recent death."

"Good," Pocomchi commented curtly. "Then you know how I feel." He increased his speed, and although Flinx was a fair runner and in good condition, he had trouble staying alongside him. "Let's travel," Pocomchi urged him, seemingly not straining at the wicked pace. "Let's get that skimmer."

As they ran they passed several late-evening strollers. Some examined the racing triumvirate curiously. A few stopped to gawk at the four-footed apparition loping along behind the two men.

But as he panted and fought to keep up with Pocomchi, Flinx knew that no death lay behind any of those staring eyes. That threat was behind, receded with every additional stride they took into the night. As the warm air enfolded him, he wondered how much longer it would stay behind him.

Chapter Seven

In comparative silence, the skimmer drifted across the waving grassland of Alaspin.

Flinx had the feeling he was riding a bug over an unmade green bed. Neither the topography nor the vegetation was uniform in height or color. Here and there the familiar green gave way to a startlingly blue sward, and in other places to a bright yellow. Heavier growth, sections of bush, forest, and jungle, protruded like woody tentacles into the sea of reeds and grass.

He studied the individual seated next to him, in the pilot's chair. Pocomchi seemed to be perfectly normal, very much in control of himself. Still, Flinx could sense the tension in the man, along with the anguish at his partner's death. Both had been pushed aside. To any other onlooker, the Indian's attention would have seemed to be wholly on the rippling savanna beneath them. Flinx knew otherwise.

From their position, roughly a meter above the waving stalks, he inclined his head to squint up at the warm buttery beacon of Alaspin's star. It was a cloudless day, too hot for human comfort, too cool for a thranx to really enjoy.

"I still don't know where we're going, Pocomchi."

"The last I know of your man," the Indian replied conversationally, "he was working his claim near a city reputed to be of Revarn Dynasty. Place called Mimmisompo. We're three days out of Alaspinport—I'm hoping we'll reach the city some time this afternoon." Unexpectedly, he smiled at his companion. His voice changed from the uncaring monotone Flinx had gotten accustomed to over the past several days.

"Sorry if I've been less than good company, Flinx." His gaze turned back to the terrain ahead. "Habib was the type to mourn, not me. I'm kind of surprised at myself, and I certainly didn't mean to shunt my misery off on you."

"You haven't shunted a thing off on me," Flinx assured him firmly. "Intimate deaths have a way of shaking one's ideas about oneself." He wanted to say more, but something ahead caught his attention. Pip squirmed at the abrupt movement, while behind Ab rambled on, oblivious.

Just in front of the leisurely cruising skimmer the sea of high grass had abruptly given way to a winding, curved path roughly a hundred and fifty meters wide. Where the path wound, the tall growth had been smoothly sliced off a couple of centimeters above the ground. Some torn and ragged clumps of uncut reeds pimpled the avenue, which looked to have been created by the antics of a berserk mowing machine.

While Flinx tried to imagine what kind of instrument had sliced away the grasses, which grew to an average height of several meters, Pocomchi was pointing to some gliding, bat-winged avians armed with formidable beaks and claws. "Vanisoars," he was saying, "scavengers prowling the open place for exposed grass dwellers." Even as he spoke, one of the creatures dove. It came up with an unlucky furry ball in its talons.

"But the path, what made it?"

"Toppers. Hexapodal ungulates," he explained, examining the path ahead. He touched a contol, and the skimmer rose to a height of six meters above the topmost stalks. "This grass looks fresh-cut. I think we'll see them soon."

The nearly noiseless engine of the skimmer permitted them to slow to a hover above the herd of huge grazing animals. The largest member of the herd stood a good three meters at the fore shoulder. Each of the six legs was thick, pillarlike, to support the massive armored bodies. Hexagonal plates covered sides and back.

Massive neck muscles supported the lowered, elongated skulls. Most remarkable of all was the design of the snout. What appeared originally to have been armored, the nostril cover had lengthened and broadened to form a horn in the shape of a double-bladed ax.

Flinx watched in fascination as the creatures methodically cut their way through the green ocean. Lowered, ax-bladed heads swung in timed 180-degree arcs parallel to the earth, scything the grass, reeds, and small trees almost level with the ground. Then the lead creatures would pause briefly, using flexible lips to gather in the chopped vegetable matter immediately around them.

Behind the leaders, immature males and females followed in the path of the adults. They consumed the cut-down fodder prepared for them by the leaders. A few small females guarded the end of the procession, shielding the infants from a rear assault. The younger toppers had no difficulty downing their share of food, which had been pounded to soft pulp by the massive footpads of the larger herd members in front of them.

It seemed an ideal system, though Flinx wondered at the need for a few adults to shield the calves. The smallest, he estimated, weighed several tons. He questioned Pocomchi about it.

"Even a topper can be brought down, Flinx," he was told. "You don't know much of Alaspin." He nudged a switch, and the skimmer moved forward slightly. "See?"

Flinx looked down and saw that one of the lead bulls was standing on its rear four legs, sniffing the air in a northerly direction. The enormous nose horns looked quite capable of slicing through the metal body of the skimmer.

"Let's see what he's got," Pocomchi suggested. He headed the little craft sharply north. Flinx had to scramble to keep his seat.

In a few minutes they were above something winding its patient way through the reeds. Flinx had a brief sight of a long mouth lined with curved teeth, and glowing red eyes. It snapped at the skimmer and Flinx jerked reflexively.

Pocomchi grinned at his companion. "That's a lance'el." He swung the skimmer around for another look. They passed over a seemingly endless form laid out like a plated path in the grass. Row upon row of short legs, like those of a monstrous millipede, supported scaly segments. Flinx couldn't make an accurate estimate of its size.

"I knew it'd be well hidden," Pocomchi said easily. "That's why I kept our altitude. We'd have made that fellow a nice snack." A hiss-growl came from below; angry eyes stared up at them.

Pocomchi chuckled. "We've interrupted his stalk, and he's not happy about it. It's unusual for a lance'el to strike at a skimmer, but it's happened." Another growl from below. "They can jump surprisingly well. I think we'd better leave this big one alone."

Flinx readily agreed.

Pocomchi had turned the skimmer and increased their speed. They were back on their southwesterly course once more. As the sun reached its zenith they were racing over bush and tree-lined streams as much as grassland.

"I think we're all right," Pocomchi murmured, checking a chart. "Yes." He shut off the screen and returned his attention forward. "Another ten minutes, I think."

The time passed. Sure enough, Flinx discovered the first reflections from stone and metal shining at them from between tall trees. "Mimmisompo," his companion assured him, with a nod forward. He slowed the skimmer, and in a minute they were winding carefully through soaring trees hung heavy with vines and creepers.

"We're on the edge of the Ingre," Pocomchi informed him, "one of the largest jungle-forests in this part of Alaspin. Mimmisompo is one of many temple cities the archeologists don't consider too important."

They were among buildings now, lengthy multistory structures flanking broad paved avenues. Brush and creepers grew everywhere. The fact that the city wasn't entirely overgrown was a tribute to the skill and precision of its engineers. An abandoned city in a similar section of Earth would have been all but eradicated by now.

It was a city of sparkling silence, an iridescent monument to extinction. Everywhere the sun struck, it was reflected by a million tiny mirrors. Mimmisompo had been constructed primarily from the dense gold-tinged granites Flinx had seen employed in Alaspinport. The local stone contained a much higher proportion of mica than the average granite. Walls built of such material gave the impression of having been sprinkled with broken glass.

The architecture was massive and blocky, with flying arches of metal bracing the carefully raised stonework. Copper, brass, and more sophisticated metalwork were employed for decorative purposes. It seemed as if every other wall was fronted with some intricate scrollwork or bas-relief. Adamantine yellow-green tiles roofed many smaller structures.

As they traveled farther into the city, Flinx began to get some idea of its size. Even that, he knew, was an inaccurate estimate, considering how many buildings were probably hidden by the jungle.

"Maybe it's not an important city," he mused, "but it seems big enough to attract at least a few curious diggers."

"Mimmisompo's been grubbed, Flinx," his companion told him. "No one ever found a thing. At least, nothing I ever heard of."

"What about all those fancy engravings and decorations on the buildings?"

"Simple relics and artifacts are throwaway items on Alaspin," Pocomchi informed him. "This is a relic-rich world. Now if some of those worked plates"—he gestured out the transparent skimmer dome at the walls sliding past them—"were done in iridium, or even good old-fashioned industrial gold, you wouldn't be looking at them now."

"But surely," Flinx persisted, "a metropolis of this size and state of preservation ought to be worthy of *someone's* interest. I'd expect to see at least one small survey party."

Pocomchi adjusted their course to avoid a towering golden obelisk. A broad grin split his dark-brown face. "I've told you, you don't know Alaspin. There're much more important diggings to the north, along the coast. Compared to some of the major temple-capitals, like Kommonsha and Danville, Mimmisompo's a hick town."

"Stomped flat, sit on that, push it down and make it fat."

"What's he drooling about now?" Pocomchi asked, with a nod back to where Ab squatted on all four legs.

Flinx looked back over the seat idly. Ab had been so quiet for the majority of the journey that he had almost forgotten the alien's presence. But instead of playing dumbly with all sixteen fingers, Ab appeared to be staring out the dome at something receding behind the skimmer.

"What is it, Ab?" he asked gently. "Did you see something?"

As always, the alien's mind told him nothing. It was as empty as a dozen-diameter orbit. Two blue eyes swiveled round to stare questioningly at him. Two hands gestured animatedly, while the other two executed incomprehensible idiot patterns in the air.

"Behind the mine the ground has stomped subutaneate residue lingers in the reschedule. Found itself often comatose. If you would achieve anesthesia, take two fresh eggs, beat well, and by and by up in the sky leptones like lemon cream will . . ."

"Well?" Pocomchi asked.

Flinx thought, scratching the scaly snake head, which was curled now in the hollow of his neck. "It's hard to tell with Ab, but I think he did see something back there. There's nothing wrong with his sensory *input*."

Even as he slowed the skimmer and brought it to a hover, Pocomchi considered. He cocked a querulous eye at Flinx. "You willing to waste some time to check out an idiot's information?"

"Why not," the youth responded, "since we're probably on an idiot's errand?"

"You're paying," Pocomchi replied noncommittally. The skimmer whined slightly as its driver turned it around. Slowly they retraced their path.

"Whatever it is has to be on the starboard side now," Flinx declared, carefully studying the landscape "That's the side Ab was looking out."

Pocomchi turned his attention to the ground on his right. In order to see clearly past him, Flinx had to stand. His head almost bumped the top of the transparent canopy. Jungle-encrusted ruins passed by on monolithic parade.

Several meters on, both men saw it simultaneously.

"Over there," Flinx said, "under the blue overhang."

Pocomchi angled closer to the walls, then cut the power. With the soft sigh of circuits going to sleep, the little vessel settled birdlike to the ground. A few shards of rock and shattered masonry crunched beneath the skimmer's weight.

A touch on another control caused the canopy to fold itself up and slide neatly into the skimmer's roof behind them. In place of the steady hum of the engine, Flinx now heard jungle and forest voices emerging into the silence. They were cautious at first, uncertain. But soon various unseen creatures were whistling, howling, cooing, bellowing, hissing, and snuffling with increasing confidence beneath the blue sky.

The noises fascinated Ab (didn't everything?).

"There is a large depression in the sermoid," he began. Both men tuned out the alien versifying.

Their attention instead was focused on the massive azure overhang to their left. It resembled blue ferro-crete, although that was impossible—ferrocrete was a modern building material. It stuck outward, a thrusting blue blade shading a space fifteen meters square. In the sheltered region beneath the overhang was a familiar, self-explanatory outline.

Pocomchi turned his gaze to the depression in the earth. Flinx, his own thoughts still on the blue mono-lith, followed the Indian out of the skimmer.

"I haven't seen that color before," he told Pocomchi.

"Hmmm?" murmured the Indian, intent on the out-line pressed into the ground. "Oh, that. The ancient Alaspinians colored a lot of their formed stone. That overhang isn't granite, it's a cementlike material they also used. Probably a lot of copper sulfate in this one, to turn it that dark a hue." He traced the outline in the ground with his feet, walking around it.

"A pretty good-sized skimmer made this mark," he announced. "Light cargo on board." Turning, he strug-gled to see through stone and jungle, walls and trees. "Somebody's been here recently, all right." Eyes in-tently focused on the ground, he walked away from the outline until he was standing beneath the blue over-hang.

"A good place for a first camp. Here's where they unloaded their supplies," he noted, examining the dirt. He walked out from under the sheltering stone and looked up across dense brush which formed a green wave against the side of the structure. It sounded like corduroy against his jumpsuit.

"They've gone off through here, Flinx." Turning, he eyed his anxious young companion. "Yes, it might be your massive mystery man with the gold earring. Whoever it was, they've spent some money." He pointed to where the brush had been smashed down re-peatedly to form a fair pathway that was only now be-ginning to recover from the tread of many feet. "They made a lot of trips to transfer their stuff deeper into the city. I thought everyone had given up on this location years ago."

He started back toward the skimmer. Flinx was gazing with interest at the azure overhang, wondering at its original purpose. A temple at least a hundred meters high towered behind it. The massive blue form had fallen outward, leaving a gaping hole in the temple wall. Beyond he could barely make out a darkened interior lined with shattered masonry, dangling strips of punched metal, shade-loving plants, and the emptiness of abandonment.

"What do we do now?"

Pocomchi grinned at him and shook his head. "You've hardly heard a word I've said, have you? There's the remnants of a service trail back here, clear enough for us to follow. Since they felt the need to walk it from this point, I think it's safe to assume we can't get the skimmer through. Hopefully your quarry will be at the other end of the trail. Anyway, I'd like to meet anyone foolish enough to think there's anything worth taking out of Mimmisompo. I hope they've got easy trigger fingers and an inviting nature."

"Let's get going, then," ventured Flinx.

"Easy, dragon lord." He indicated the sun. "Why not wait till we've a full day to hike with? No one's running anyplace, least of all the people we're hunting. I think they're pretty deep into the brush." A hand waved in the direction of jumbled stone and bushes where the trail lay. "There are creatures crawling around in there that I'd rather meet in daytime, if I have to meet them at all. I'll set up a perimeter, and we'll sleep by the skimmer tonight."

A radiant fence was quickly erected in a half circle, with the skimmer inside. Another compartment of the compact craft produced inflatable mattresses and sleeping material. It would have been safer to sleep in the skimmer, but the small cockpit was cramped enough with two men. Two men trying to sleep inside, together with Ab and a pair of minidrags, would have been impossible.

Their temporary habitat was topped by an inflatable

dome, which would serve as weather shield in the event of wind or storm. The semipermeable membrane of the dome would permit fresh air to enter and allow waste gases to pass out, but would shunt aside anything as thick as a raindrop.

Outside, the radiant fence would keep curious night-stalkers at bay, while Balthazaar and Pip could be counted on to serve as backup alarms in the event that anything really dangerous showed up. As for arboreal predators, the great majority of them were daylight hunters, according to Pocomchi.

Flinx leaned back on the soft mattress and stared out the dome toward the trail site. He was anxious to be after whoever had made it, impatient to have this search resolved once and for all. But this was Pocomchi's planet. It would be wise to take his advice.

Besides, he thought with an expansive yawn, he was tired. His head went back. Through the warm tropical night and the thin material of the dome he could count the stars in strange constellations. Off to the east hung a pair of round, gibbous moons, so unlike the craggy outline of Moth's own rarely glimpsed satellite, Flame.

The single moon of distant Ulru-Ujurr was larger than these two combined, he thought. Memories of his pupils, the innocent ursinoid race which lived on that world, pulled strongly at him. He felt guilty. His place was back there, advising them, instead of gallivanting around the Commonwealth in search of impossible-to-learn origins.

A fetid breeze drifted through the single window, set above and to the side of his bed. Soft crackling noises, like foil crumpling, drifted in to him. In a little while, the alien lullaby had helped him fall sound asleep.

First sunlight woke Flinx. Rolling over, he stretched once and was instantly awake. Pocomchi lay on the mattress next to him, snoring stentoriously for so small a man. He stretched out a hand to wake the Indian, and frowned as he did so. Something was missing, something so familiar that for a long moment he couldn't figure out what was gone.

He woke Pocomchi, sat up, and thought. The motion of rising brought the absence home to him. All at once, Flinx was moving rapidly, searching behind the mattress, by the skimmer body, on the opposite side of Pocomchi's bed. Nothing.

Zipping open the doorway, he plunged frantically outside, and almost ran toward the jungle before remembering the radiant fence. Standing by the inside edge of the softly glowing barrier, he put cupped hands to his lips and shouted, "Pip! Where are you, Pip!"

His eyes swept the trees and temple tops, but the searching revealed only silent stone and mocking greenery. Though both must have seen what had become of his pet, all remained frozen with the silence of the inanimate.

Turning, he ran back into the dome and climbed into the skimmer. Rubbing the sleep from his eyes as he deflated the mattresses, Pocomchi eyed him but said nothing. Better to let the lad find out these things for himself.

Flinx crawled behind the two seats, back into the storage area where Ab had ridden. "Come on out, Pip. The game's not funny any more. Come out, Pip!"

When he finally gave up and rose, vacant-eyed, from the cockpit, he saw Pocomchi packing away the inflatable dome and taking down the fence. The Indian said nothing, but watched as Flinx moved to the edge of the brush and resumed calling. By the time the youth had shouted himself hoarse, Pocomchi had stowed all their supplies.

One thing remained for Flinx to try. Standing by the shadow of the azure overhang, he closed his eyes and thought furiously. From the skies, he imagined to himself, from the skies, a terrible danger! I need you, Pip, it's threatening me. Where are you, companion of childhood? Your friend is in danger! Can't you sense it? It's coming closer, and there's nothing I can do about it!

He kept up his performance for long minutes, until sweat began to bead on his forehead and his clenched fingers turned pale. Something touched him on the shoulder, and he jumped. Pocomchi's sympathetic eyes were staring into his.

"You're wearing yourself out for no reason, Flinx," his guide told him. "Calling won't help." A hand gestured toward the sweep of dense vegetation. "When something calls the minidrag, it goes. This is their world, you know. Or hadn't you noticed that Balthazaar is gone too?"

Flinx had been so thoroughly absorbed by Pip's disappearance that he hadn't. Sure enough, the old minidrag always curled about Pocomchi's neck and shoulder was nowhere to be seen.

"Since I found him at the age of five," he tried to explain to the little man, "Pip and I have never spent a single day completely apart from each other." His gaze roved over the concealing jungle. "I just can't believe he'd simply fly off and abandon me. I can't believe it, Pocomchi!"

The Indian shrugged and spoke softly. "No minidrag is ever completely tamed. You've never been on Pip's home world before, either. Don't look so brokenhearted. I've had Balthazaar fly off and leave me for several days at a time. He always comes back.

"In case you've forgotten, we have other things to do here. There's that trail to follow, and your ringwearer to find. We won't be skimming out of Mimmisompo for a while yet. When they want to, both Pip and Balthazaar will find our thoughts."

Flinx relaxed a little.

"They're wild things, Flinx," Pocomchi reminded him, "and this is a wild place. You can't expect the two not to be attracted by that. Now let's make up a couple of packs and start the hard part of this trip."

Moving mechanically, Flinx helped his guide prepare a set of light but well-stocked backpacks. When Pocomchi was helping him on with his own, showing him how the strappings worked, a sudden thought occurred to him.

"What," he asked worriedly, "if we find what we've come for, and then when it's time for us to leave for Alaspinport Pip hasn't come back?"

Pocomchi stared straight at him, his eyebrows arching slightly. "There's no use in speculating on that, Flinx. Balthazaar means as much or more to me as your Pip does to you. We've been through a lot together. But a minidrag's not a dog. It won't slaver and whimper at your feet. You ought to know that. Minidrags are independent and free-willed. They remain with you and me because they *want* to, not because they're in need of us. The decision to return is up to them." He smiled slightly. "All we can do if we come back and they're not here is wait a while for them. Then if they don't show . . ." He hesitated. "Well, it's their world." He turned and started off toward the trail.

Flinx took a last look at the sky above. No familiar winged shape came diving out of it toward his shoulder. Setting his jaw and mind, he hefted the backpack to a more comfortable position and strode off after Pocomchi. Soon the skimmer was lost to sight, consumed by stone and intervening vegetation.

Every so often he would turn to make certain that Ab was still trailing behind them. Then he would turn forward again. His view consisted of tightly intertwined bushes and vines and trees, parted regularly by the bobbing back of Pocomchi's head. The Indian's black hair swayed as he traced the path through the jungle-encrusted city. Sometimes the growth had recovered and grown back over the path, but under Pocomchi's skilled guidance they always reemerged onto a clear trail.

Although he knew better, he could think only of his missing pet. Emotions he thought he had long since outgrown swelled inside him. They were ready to overwhelm him when a cold hand touched the right side of his face with surpassing gentleness.

Angrily he glanced back, intending to take out his feelings on the owner of that chill palm. But how could anyone get mad at that face, with its mournful, innocent eyes and its proboscidean mouth where its hair ought to be, tottering after him with the stride of a quadrupedal duck?

"Worry, worry, sorry hurry," ventured Ab hopefully, "key to quark, key to curry. Black pepper ground find in me mind"—this delivered with such solemnity that Flinx half felt it might actually mean something. While he was pondering the cryptic verse, he tripped over a root and went sprawling. Pocomchi heard him fall and turned. The Indian shook his head, grinned, and resumed walking.

Flinx climbed to his feet and hitched the pack higher on his shoulders. "You're right, Ab, there's no point in tearing myself up over it. There's nothing I can do about it." His gaze turned heavenward, and he searched the powdery rims of scattered cumulus clouds. "If Pip comes back, he comes back. If not"— his voice dropped to a resigned murmur—"life goes on. A little lonelier, maybe, but it goes on. I'll still have things to do and people to go back to."

"Call the key, call the key," Ab agreed in singsong behind him. "To see it takes two to tango with an animated mango." He stared expectantly at Flinx.

"Farcical catharsis." The youth chuckled, smiling now at his ward's comical twaddle. What a pity, he mused, that the poetically inclined alien didn't have enough sense to make real use of his talent. But he had become used to tuning out Ab's ramblings, so he concentrated on the path ahead and ignored the alien's continued verbalizing.

"Key the key that's me," Ab sang lucidly, "I'll be whatever you want to see. Harkatrix, matrix, how do you run? Slew of currents and a spiced hadron."

They walked all that day and afternoon. When Pocomchi found a place suitable for night camp, the path still wound off into the jungle ahead. With the experience of an old trailwalker, and maybe a little magic, the Indian somehow managed to concoct a meal from concentrates which was both flavorful and filling.

The fullness in his belly should have put Flinx rapidly to sleep. Instead, he found himself lying awake, listening to Pocomchi's snores and staring at the sky. The trouble was that the weight in his stomach wasn't matched by a more familiar weight curled next to his shoulder. Eventually he had to take a dose of cere-broneural depressant in order to fall into an uncomfortable sleep.

Morning came with anxious hope that quickly faded. The minidrags had not returned. Silently they broke camp and marched on.

Pocomchi tried to cheer his companion by pointing out interesting aspects of the flora and fauna they passed. Ordinarily Flinx would have listened raptly. Now he simply nodded or grunted an occasional comment. Even Pocomchi's description of temple engineering failed to rouse him from his mental lethargy.

They paused for lunch in the center of a series of concentric stone circles. Shade was provided by a five-meter-high metal pillar in the center of the circles. It was supported by the familiar metal buttresses on four sides. The pillar itself, fluted and encrusted with petrified growths and slime, had corroded badly in places.

"It's a fountain," Pocomchi decided while eating lunch. He gestured at the silent tower, then at the gradually descending stone circles surrounding them. "I expect we're sitting in the middle of a series of sacred pools that were once used for religious and other ceremonies by the populace of this city. If subterranean Mimmisompo stays true to the Alaspinian pattern, then the water for this was piped underground to here, probably through metal pipes by gravity." One finger traced the spray of ghost water. "It shot out of the fountain top and then fell down these fluted sides before spreading out and overflowing from one pool to the next." Leaning forward, he took a bite out of a concentrate bar.

"Judging from the slight incline of the pools, I'd guess the drain is right about there." He pointed. "See the formal, carved bench? That's where a priest could sit and bless the *w*aters flowing out of the cistern. On the right of the bench there should be a—" Abruptly, he quieted and strained forward.

Flinx felt a mental crackle from his companion and stared in the same direction. "I don't see anything. What's the matter?"

Pocomchi rose and gestured. "There, what's that?" Still Flinx could see nothing.

The Indian walked cautiously toward the cistern outflow, hopping down from one level to the next. When he reached the region of the stone bench, he leaned over the last restraining wall and called back to Flinx. There was a peculiar tightness in his voice.

"Over here," he said disbelievingly, "is a dead man."

Chapter Eight

The remains of his concentrate bar dangled forgotten from Flinx's hand as he peered over the cistern wall. Sprawled next to one another on the right side of the sacred bench were three bodies. Their skullcaps were missing, and their black suits were torn and ragged in places. Two men and a woman, all very dead.

Each body was feathered with twenty-centimeter-long shafts of some highly polished yellow-brown wood. Five tiny fins tipped the back end of each shaft. Flinx guessed that each body sprouted at least sixty or seventy of the small arrows. Or they might have been large darts, depending on the size of their users.

"So, they followed us here," he muttered.

Pocomchi was searching the surrounding jungle with practiced eyes. "They did more than follow, Flinx—they preceded us. They must have watched us set down, then circled somehow to get ahead of us on the trail." His gaze dropped to the corpse immediately next to him. Like the other two, it was missing both eyes.

"They knew we'd come through here, so they set up

a nice, efficient little ambush." Water trickled from the lowest cistern into the outflow drain, an anemic remnant of the once-substantial volume which had tumbled through this place ages ago. Pocomchi kicked at it and watched it darken his boot.

"This isn't the first time this has happened," Flinx told him. His eyes weren't as experienced as Pocomchi's, but he could search the witnessing jungle with his mind. "The Qwarm were ready to ambush Ab and myself back on Moth. Something killed them there, too."

Pocomchi threw him a surprised look. "Really? I don't know who was responsible for saving you, then, unless there are Otoids on Moth I haven't heard about." Bending over, he wrapped a hand around one of the several hundred shafts, pulled it free, and held it out to Flinx.

The point was fashioned of crudely reworked metal, with five spikes sticking out of it. "This is an Otoid arrow," Pocomchi explained, turning it over in his hand. "They shoot them out of a *sikambi*, a sort of blowgun affair. Only they use an elastic made from native tree sap instead of their own weak breath to propel these. They're not too accurate, but"—he gestured meaningfully at the bodies—"what they lack in marksmanship they make up for with firepower."

"You're right," Flinx informed him, "there aren't any Otoids on Moth. What are they?"

"You'd think I'd have a simple answer for that one, wouldn't you?" Pocomchi replied, scanning the jungle wall once again. "Well, I don't. Nobody does, for sure. They're vaguely humanoid, run to about half your size. Furry all over except for their tails, which are bare. They're not very bright, but in the absence of the temple builders they've become the dominant native race. Manual dexterity helps them. Each of two hands has ten fingers, with three joints to each finger. They can climb pretty well, but the tail's not prehensile, so they do most of their traveling on the ground."

"An interaction, disreaction, can't you see it's time to be, to activate the ancient key," Ab murmured. "Peter Piper picked a peck of pickled pheromones."

The alien was waddling down the pool levels at high speed. Both men would have laughed at Ab's absurd locomotion if it weren't for the three dead humans lying in front of them.

"Ab," Flinx began, intending to bawl the alien out for disturbing them. Then he heard the rising hoots, the sort of war cry a human baby with an unusually deep voice might make.

Ab was pointing and curiously feeling several objects sticking out of his back. The points had barely penetrated the outer epidermal layer. Plucking one out, he handed it to Flinx and smiled broadly. "Poor boy toy toy," he commented. "Tickle fickle tickle."

"Come this way, Ab," Pocomchi ordered urgently. "No boy toy. You too, Flinx," he snapped, wrenching at the youth's pack. Flinx did not move. He was staring at Ab, who appeared to have suffered no ill effects from the dozen or so arrows sticking out of him.

All hint of casualness was missing from Pocomchi's demeanor now. "Let's move it. If they get between us and the skimmer, we're finished. Come on, or I'll leave you and your idiot to greet them on your own."

Flinx found himself running back down the trail they had laboriously traced this far. Ab kept pace easily. Cries sounded ahead of them, and Pocomchi came to a gasping halt.

"No good. They've got us cut off." He looked around wildly. "We've got to get around them somehow." Something made a thunking sound as it landed in the dirt barely a quarter meter from Flinx's feet. An Otoid arrow.

Flinx noted that Ab had acquired another dozen of the feathered shafts. If they bothered the alien, he gave no sign of it. Flinx decided that either the secondary skin was incredibly dense or else some internal mechanism was sealing off each wound as it occurred. Or perhaps both.

Time later to study the alien's remarkable physiology. Time if they managed to escape.

Pocomchi was on his knees, using his beamer on the nearby trees. He shouted angrily at Flinx, "What are you waiting for, Flinx, an engraved invitation? Or do you want your eyes to end up in an Otoid stewpot?"

Flinx joined Pocomchi in retreating back to a cluster of broken tree trunks and tumbled masonry. Dimly perceived shapes moved from time to time in the trees around them. Whenever he detected such movement, he fired.

Pip did not magically appear to save him.

Arrows glanced with metallic pings off the stone around him, made dull thumping sounds as they stuck in the thick logs. Every so often Flinx risked taking an arrow to reach out and pull Ab down next to him. While the murmuring alien did not seem to be suffering at all from the missiles, Flinx had no idea when his body might suddenly lose its immunity to them. Ab rolled over, pulling the shafts curiously from his skin and rhyming nonstop, utterly indifferent to the battle surrounding him.

"How many do you think there are?" Flinx asked, ducking as a brass-tipped bolt sparked off the rock near his head.

Pocomchi replied in between rising and firing, and ducking back under cover. "No idea. Nobody knows how numerous the Otoid are. Xenoanthropologists aren't even sure how they breed. And, as you might suspect, they aren't kindly toward visitors."

Abruptly he snapped off a lethal burst from his beamer. Flinx peered between rock and log, had a glimpse of a wildly gesticulating form falling through filtered sunlight and branches. He heard a distant crash as the native hit the ground.

While continuing to rain an impressive number of missiles on the three interlopers, the Otoids kept up a steady chatter among themselves. Flinx couldn't tell whether their conversation consisted of various forms of encouragement or of insults for their enemy.

Not that it mattered. It seemed that hundreds of green eyes, gleaming like peridots among the trees, confronted them. Like most men, he wasn't going to be able to chose his place and manner of dying.

He wondered what exactly the aborigines did first

with dead men's eyes. As he was wondering, there was a hissing sound in the air. A blue energy beam considerably thicker than the ones put out by their small hand beamers passed over Flinx's head. It struck with devastating force among the densest concentration of natives. A great yelping and screeching reached them as a monster tree, a cross between an evergreen and a coconut palm, came smashing down among the concealed Otoid. Flinx saw where the blue bolt had sliced cleanly through the trunk.

A second burst of cerulean destruction flashed above them, tearing through leaves, vegetation, and not a few furious natives. To give them credit, the awesome display of modern weaponry didn't frighten the Otoid away, although the hail of yellow-brown arrows slackened noticeably.

Flinx turned on his side and shouted in the direction from which the shots had originated, "Who is it, who's there?"

Both he and Pocomchi stared anxiously down the fragment of trail that remained in view. A figure stepped out of the bushes, cradling an energy rifle nearly as tall as Flinx. It was a heavy military model, Flinx noted, and was probably meant to be mounted on a tripod. Somehow its wielder managed not only to lift the weapon, but to operate it. Makeshift slings put most of the weight on the man's shoulders.

And the man was big as two men. He had a voice to match. "This way!" the figure bellowed at them, in a voice that sounded more amused than worried. Around came the muzzle of the massive rifle, and another thick bolt carbonized trees and natives alike. "Hurry it up, there, you two! They regroup fast."

Pocomchi was up and running then. Flinx was right behind, darting around rocks and bushes, jumping over fallen logs. Occasionally each man would turn to snap off a shot at the arrow-flingers in the trees. Ab kept pace easily, though Flinx had to make sure some flower or bug didn't distract the simple-minded creature.

While they ran, the bulky figure ahead of them stood

in place atop the slight rise, firing down into the clusters of howling, frustrated Otoid. They had almost reached him. Flinx found himself scrambling up a crumbling masonry wall the last couple of meters. Pocomchi was just ahead and to Flinx's right. The wall seemed a million miles high.

At its top stood their rescuer. Up close he was even more massive than he had looked from a distance. His white hair curled and fluttered in the warm breeze, and his face was half court jester, half mad prophet. Obsidian eyes, brows like antipersonnel wire, a sharply pointed chin—all were dwarfed by a nose any predatory bird would have been proud of. It rose like a spire from the sea of swirling features which eddied around it.

His trousers, bright mold-green, ran into boots that sealed themselves to the pants legs. Above the waist he wore only the rifle straps and a massive power pack for the weapon, which crossed a chest full of white hair like steel wool and resembled an ancient bandoleer. His arms were covered with a similar grizzled fur. Though those limbs were bigger around than Flinx's thighs, the man moved with startling agility, like a graceful gorilla.

There was a curse, and Flinx turned to his guide. A small, feathered shaft protruded from the back of Pocomchi's thigh. The Indian slid downward a little. His fingers dug at the rough rock; he trailed blood on the white stone as he fell.

Reaching out and across, Flinx caught the back of Pocomchi's shirt just in time to halt his fall.

"Hurry up, dammit!" the rifle-wielder shouted down at them. "They're gettin' over being scared. Now they're mad, and there's more of them coming every minute."

"My friend's hurt!" Flinx called up to him.

"I can make it," Pocomchi said through clenched teeth. He and Flinx exchanged glances; then both were again moving up the uneven stone facing.

Somehow cradling the huge rifle in one arm, the giant above them reached down one treelike forearm and got a hand on Pocomchi's shirt top. The material held as Pocomchi all but flew the last meter to the top of the wall. Flinx scrambled up alongside them.

Pocomchi took one step forward, his face tightening in pain, before he stopped to yank the shaft from his leg.

"We've got to get back to the temple," the big man rumbled, letting loose another recoilless blast from the rifle. He looked squarely at Flinx. "I can't cover us with this and carry him too."

For an answer, Flinx slipped his right arm between Pocomchi's legs and hooked it around the man's right thigh. Then he took the Indian's right arm in his left hand, bent, heaved, and swung the swarthy miner onto his shoulders.

"I can manage him," Flinx assured the bigger man. Both of them ignored Pocomchi's protests. "Just show me the way."

Teeth formed a line of enameled foam beneath that incredible nose. "It's a right good fight you two made of it till I got to you, young feller-me-lad. Maybe we'll all make it back unskewered."

With the man's powerful rifle keeping the pursuing Otoid at a respectful distance, they started down into seemingly impenetrable jungle. Flinx hardly felt the weight on his back.

Just when it appeared that they would run up against an impassible rampart of bushes and vines, the big man would gesture left or right and Flinx would find himself running down a gap only an experienced jungle hand would have noticed. Ab skipped along behind them, apparently enjoying all the excitement.

The sounds of Otoid crashing and racing through the trees alongside them grew louder, more perceptible. While the terrible fire from the heavy military gun cut down any aborigines who ventured too near, it still seemed to Flinx that they were tightening a ring around the fugitives.

Flinx's concern wasn't alleviated by the expression on the big man's face. Sweat was pouring down him now, and he was breathing in long, strained gasps, despite his strength. The tripod blaster was beginning to sap his reserves. It was not meant to be used like a handgun, much less to be carried and fired while on the run.

"I don't know, young feller-me-lad," he said blinking the sweat from his eyes and talking as they ran. "They may cut us off yet."

They ran on, until Flinx's heart felt like a hammer on his chest and his lungs shrieked in protest. The formerly light Pocomchi now seemed to be made of solid lead.

Then, just when he thought he couldn't move another step, he heard a shout from his huge companion. Wiping aside perspiration and a few soaked strands of hair, Flinx thought he could see a dark rectangle looming ahead of them. The ancient portal rose a good four meters high and two across. It formed an opening into a creeper-wrapped temple built of sparkling green stone. The temple appeared isolated from any other structures. Its color enabled it to blend inconspicuously into the surrounding forest.

The building was low, compared to many of the imposing edifices Flinx had passed in Mimmisompo proper—not more than two stories aboveground, flat and broken on top from the action of persistent, prying roots.

Apprehensively he studied their apparent destination. "In there? But it's small, and there's nowhere to retreat to. Can't the Otoid . . . ?"

"You can always try to make it back to your skimmer, lad," his rescuer suggested pleasantly.

Arrows continued to fall around them as they staggered, exhausted, toward the catacomblike entrance. One bolt whizzed past so close that it slit Flinx's shirt under his left arm. Glancing down and over, he saw that the point had nicked the skin and he was bleeding slightly.

Just ahead, several figures ducked down into tall grass. Emerald eyes glinted malevolently at them.

"It's no good," Flinx wheezed, defeated. "They're ahead of us now."

"How many?" the big man asked, crouching alongside Flinx and swinging the rifle around.

"I don't know, I don't know," Flinx panted, wondering if he would be able to stand again with Pocomchi's weight on his back. Next to him, Ab imitated his posture and offered a hopeful verse. Flinx was not comforted.

"Little devils know how to fight, how to hide themselves. If they ever get organized, they'll run the prospectors *and* the scientists off Alaspin." Flinx, in spite of his near-total exhaustion, found time to be curious. But the big man apparently felt he had said nothing remarkable.

"Got to chance it, lad," the man decided.

"Chance it, fance it, dance and prance it," agreed Ab excitedly.

"We can't stay here and we can't go back." He started to rise. "I'll go first. That'll give you a little time ... and some shieldin', if you can stay back of me. If we can just—"

Popping sounds came from ahead of them. Several fist-sized globes of red fire emerged from above the dark doorway in the temple.

Glancing higher, Flinx thought he could see a figure moving about in a long, narrow gap in the green stone. From that position it fired a weapon which produced the energy globes.

Where each ball struck there was a small explosion. Flames leaped briefly skyward, only to disappear and leave a man-sized pillar of light-brown smoke in their wake. Those Otoid blocking the approach to the temple broke and fled—those who were still able to. Red spheres pursued them.

"That'd be Isili," Flinx's blocky savior declared. "I thought for sure she'd be down in the diggin's. Lucky for us she heard the commotion." He rose to his full height. "She'll cover us. Come on." He started for the towering entrance, running with lumbering, pounding strides that reminded Flinx of the herd of toppers he had flown over only a couple of days ago.

Every muscle in his body strained, but he still found

himself falling farther and farther behind. Any second now, he expected the sharp, exquisite pain of a metal point to penetrate his legs or lower back. But every time an Otoid raised itself for a clear shot at the fugitives, or moved to pursue, a cottony-crimson globe of energy would touch it, and both would vanish in an impatient gout of flame.

Then, as he was tottering down carved stone steps, he realized that he was descending into the temple. The steps gave way to a level rock floor. Something thundered behind him. He experienced a moment of panic, but it was only a makeshift wooden door slamming shut across the temple entrance.

His eyes rapidly became accustomed to the slightly dimmer illumination in the modest chamber. Small, independently powered lamps were hung from the ceiling, mounted on rock outcroppings.

They reached the end of the entrance tunnel and emerged into a brightly lit cleared room. Here the surrounding walls were embellished with row upon row of magnificent carvings, mosaics of metal and stone alternating with deeply etched friezes depicting scenes from ancient Alaspinian social and religious life.

Flinx had little time to appreciate the sculpture as he sank, exhausted, to the floor, barely managing to set Pocomchi down gently. Ab strolled over to a pile of excavated stone and commenced examining some of the pieces.

Taking the stone steps three at a time, the man who had led him to at least temporary safety mounted to a gallery which ran around the top level of the chamber. The ornamental banister which bordered the gallery was also made of carved stone. It was a good three stories above the chamber floor.

Flinx saw him approach another figure, indistinct in the distance, and talk briefly. Then he turned and shouted down to Flinx. A slight echo shadowed his words.

"Relax, feller-me-lad! They've given up for now. They'll count their losses, remove the eyes from their dead, and ceremony for a while. Then they'll decide what to do."

"Surely," Flinx called up to him, "they won't attack a position as well defended as this temple?" The thick stone walls were making him confident. "Not with the kind of weapons you have," he finished, with a gesture toward the rifle the man had leaned against the nearby wall.

"Don't count on being safe tomorrow," the man advised him pleasantly as he descended the stairway. He indicated the gun as he reached the floor. "Any reasonable humanx wouldn't want to tangle with a Mark Twenty, but these aren't reasonable or human or thranx, lad. They're primitives, and primitive folk always have more courage than brains. Besides, each of 'em probably thinks that if he dies in battle the gods will favor him in the afterlife. At least," he amended himself with a modest wink, "that's my theory."

"Are you an anthropologist?" Flinx asked him uncertainly.

A great, roaring laugh filled the room, rattled around the engraved walls, and filled each niche and hollow with monumental delight. While the man enjoyed Flinx's question, the youth took the time to note the piles of supplies stacked neatly in various spots around the room. There was also an oversized mattress, a cell charger, and a compact autochef complete with moisture condenser. All signs indicated that here was an efficient, organized, long-term camp.

"Not me, young feller-me-lad," the man finally replied after regaining control of himself. "I'll claim science as a hobby, not a trade." Turning, he shouted up toward the high gallery and waved at the figure standing by the long window there. "Come on down, Isili! Sunset's on. You know they won't trouble us any more today!" Lowering his voice, he spoke conspiratorially to Flinx. "Isili's the scientist. Me, I'm just a menial . . ." He stopped, frowning.

"What's the matter?" Flinx watched as the man walked over to him and continued on past. He saw him bend over Pocomchi and realized that the guide had not said a word since they had reached safety.

"He's asleep?" he inquired hopefully.

The big man rolled the slight Indian over onto his stomach. The action revealed two broken shafts sticking out of the narrow back. With an angry grimace, the white-haired giant plucked both arrows free, then gently turned the Indian over onto his back. Flinx saw blood on the small miner's lips.

"Hey, grubber-man," the huge man inquired gently, "how do you feel?"

Pocomchi's eyelids twitched, his eyes opened. "How should I feel?" He turned his head and looked back up at the concerned face above him. "How did I get here?"

"The lad carried you."

Pocomchi raised his head slightly and smiled at Flinx. "Thanks, Flinx. Waste of time, I'm afraid."

On all fours, Flinx crawled over to sit next to the limp form of the man who had brought him this far. Pocomchi took in the expression on the young face. He shook his head slightly, and winced at the pain the effort caused him.

"Not . . . your fault," he assured Flinx. "My own . . . carelessness. Should have sensed them." He forced out a smile. The gesture was nearly beyond his rapidly fading capability.

"Anything I can get you?" the big man asked gruffly.

"How about . . . a shot of Tizone?" Flinx started. Tizone was so illegal that few people even knew it existed. The giant could only grin faintly.

"Sorry, grubber-man. Would I could."

"Thanks anyway." Pocomchi's voice was that of a ghost now, the syllables poorly formed. Within him life had shrunk to a soap bubble's consistency.

"I'm going to join Habib anyway," he rasped, staring across at Flinx. "I'm not religious, but the sanctimonious fool is there, I can feel him."

"Give him my best," Flinx choked out. "Though that's not much to give anyone, these days."

"Not ... your fault," Pocomchi repeated. His eyes closed. His lips moved, and Flinx had to lean close to hear. "If ... you ever see Balthazaar again ... give his neck a scratch for me."

"Two scratches," Flinx assured him, in a tone scarcely more audible than the Indian's.

The soap bubble popped, the spirit in the small body fled, and the third person who had been good enough to aid Flinx since his arrival on Alaspin was now just so much meat.

Slowly Flinx climbed to his feet, arranged his jumpsuit, and glared at the silently watching giant. "As soon as it gets dark, I'll make a run for the skimmer. Maybe they'll all be ceremonying, like you said, and I'll be able to slip through. You'd better not try to stop me. People seem to die in my vicinity."

Pursing his lips, the big human examined Flinx appraisingly. "Well, now, that's quite a speech, feller-me-lad. But, frankly, you don't look like much of a jinx. You're just a little bitty feller. And I'm about as unsuperstitious as they come. Besides, after they get through arguing and partying, they might just decide that they don't want any more of my Mark Twenty or Isili's popper."

Flinx paused. "You really believe that?"

"Nope," responded the man, turning to face the gallery above, "but it's a nice thought. Isili," he shouted again, "quit your gawking at the greenery and come meet our guest! Bet you the Ots don't even bother with us again."

A rippling, slightly brittle voice called back to them, "You're dreaming if you think that, Skua." But the figure put the weapon down and descended the stairs.

Trying to force Pocomchi's death and what he thought was his responsibility for it from his mind, Flinx studied the woman intently as she approached.

She was about a twentieth of a meter shorter than he was. Her skin was a rich olive hue, much like his own, but other features pointed to a different ethnic heritage. Terran-Turkish, he decided, taking in the doll-like face with its amber eyes, the too-wide mouth, and the natural waterfall of sparkling hair that looked like pulled filaments of pure black hematite.

She returned Flinx's stare for a moment, then ignored him. "They'll be back," she assured her associate, in that soft voice. Yet each word had an edge to it, suggesting that every consonant had been filed to a fine point before being uttered. What he could sense of her mind was as hard as duralloy.

Pretty she was, but not in a commercial sense. It was the kind of beauty which would appeal to the man with a taste for the exotic. Flinx thought of her as a rare dish. It might give you an upset stomach or you might remember it as uniquely satisfying for the remainder of your days.

He suspected that, beneath the jungle suit, her body was as wiry and tough as her thoughts. He nodded mentally. There were blatant differences in size, sex, appearance, and much else between her and the giant. But mentally there was a similarity of process and purpose, and that was undoubtedly what had joined them together.

Of the obvious differences, one was that she did not share the big man's desire to protect Flinx. "You've brought us a lot of trouble," she told him candidly. "We haven't had any trouble with the Otoid until now."

"You're also the first visitor we've had in weeks," her huge partner countered, "and welcome, lad."

First visitor . . . then they hadn't seen the bodies of the three Qwarm, Flinx mused. No point in mentioning them. He was already unpopular with the woman. The announcement that he and Ab were being chased by the brotherhood of assassins wouldn't exactly help change her attitude toward him.

She noticed Flinx's live companion for the first time, and her expression became one of distaste. "What's that grotesque thing?" At the moment, Ab was singing something about Usander, crystalware, and Peter the Great.

Once again Flinx had to explain his ward. He finished gratefully, "I can't say much except to thank you for my life, both of you." The woman didn't look at him as she muttered something inaudible. Flinx indicated the motionless form of Pocomchi. "I know my friend would have been too. If it hadn't been for you, Mr. Skua . . ."

"September," the white-maned giant corrected him, "Skua September."

"If not for you, I'd be dead and eyeless out there some place."

"Would have been better all around," the woman murmured, stalking over to the food supplies and viciously cracking the seal on a carton. She pulled a tube free, took a seat on a smooth stone, and sucked at the liquid inside the transparent plastic. Her gaze traveled from Flinx to September.

"Would have been better if you'd left them. Now we'll probably all die. Oh hell," she concluded, not looking at either man. "I guess I'd have done the same thing, Skua. I'm going up for another look."

September shook his head. "Isili, I told you, the Otoids will not attack during—"

"Since when did you become an expert on the Otoid?" she snapped back. "Nobody's an expert on the Otoid. I don't think they'll attack at night either, but it's not completely dark out yet." She climbed the stairway and reassumed her position at the long window above the gateway. Her gaze was turned outward, the pulsepopper cradled efficiently under one arm.

"Women!" September murmured softly, his expression unreadable. A hundred shades of meaning were encompassed by the single noun. He turned a bright smile on Flinx. "Would you like something to eat, feller-me-lad?"

By way of reply, Flinx indicated Pocomchi's body.

"What, not squeamish are you, lad?" wondered the giant disapprovingly.

"No, but don't you think we ought to bury him?"

"Sure," September agreed, walking over to the recently opened case of food. He removed several small, brightly colored cubes, dumped them into his mouth, and chewed. "You pick him up," he mumbled around the mouthful of organic slag, "and carry him outside. I'll toss you our smallest excavator through the doorway. Isili and I will do our best to cover you while you dig him a grave. I guess there's always a chance you'll make it back inside."

Flinx didn't reply immediately. Instead, he walked over to stand next to the food case. "Despite your untimely sarcasm, I'll have a couple of those concentrates."

"Sarcasm? Sarcasm!" the big man rumbled, spitting particles of food over the floor. "There's no such thing as sarcasm, boy. Just a few of us in this universe who accept the truth and deal with it accordingly. Sorry if I offended you, but outside the Alaspinport this world doesn't take much notice of tact."

Flinx mulled over his situation as he masticated a concentrate cube which tasted affectionately of beefsteak and mushrooms. He knew the concentrate bore no more relationship to a once-live steer than it did to a thranx *vovey.* But while it was artificial, it was a masterfully composed artificiality, and his dried-out taste buds conveyed the efficacious, nutritive lie to the rest of his body.

"What are you doing so far from the city?" September asked.

Flinx wasn't quite ready to answer that question. Not just yet. "I might ask you the same. You said she's the scientist?" He gestured up to where the watchful woman continued her sunset vigil.

"My employer, Flinx. It's stretching things a bit to say we're partners. Isili Hasboga. We're not too bad a team. She's as pessimistic as I am optimistic."

"Optimistic?" Flinx snorted. "On this world?"

"Ah, now who's being sarcastic, young feller-melad?" September inquired without rancor. "She's one of the most knowledgeable Alaspinian archeologists I've ever met. What's more, she's as avaricious as I, and that's greedy, lad. We have different reasons for wanting wealth, but the aim's the same. Isili wants financial independence so she can pursue the kind of research that interests her, instead of doing what some prissy institution wants her to. My desires, on the other hand, are more basic."

"Why'd she choose you?"

"I'm good at what I do," September replied easily. "I don't drink, narcotize, or simiedive on the job, and I'm honest. Why not? It's as easy to be honest as it is to be a crook."

"You're an optimist, all right," observed Flinx.

"She decided on this particular temple after two years of research," the big man went on. "She needed someone to do some of the heavy work and provide cross fire when required." Moving to the near wall, he patted the huge weapon resting there. "This Mark Twenty, for example. It's tough to see an Otoid in a tree. With this toy, you just blast the tree. Never met another man who could use one as a hand weapon."

"So she supplies the brains and you the muscle," Flinx commented. Refusing to be taunted, September simply grinned back at him.

Flinx wondered if the giant could be upset. Despite his outer boisterousness, there was much that hinted at an inner calmness and confidence which would put him above petty arguing. And yet, something in the man's mind—something buried deep, hidden well—suggested some terrible secrets.

"There's some crossover, lad," he finished. "I'm not the village idiot, and Isili's much more than a fragile flower, bless her curvilinear construction. What we find, we split evenly."

"If we find anything," a voice tersely called down to them. "You talk too much, Skua. Getting lonely?"

"Why, Grandma," September yelled back in mock surprise. "what big ears you've got."

She didn't smile back. "All the better for gathering reasons to have you discharged, and drawn up before a government court for violating the secrecy terms of employment," she countered. She glanced back out the portal at the near-blackness outside, then started down the stairs.

"Ah, the lad's no claim stealer, silly bog," September murmured coaxingly. She brushed past him. "What's the matter, no Otoid for you to fry?"

"One of these days," she snarled with a smile, "I hope one of those homicidal little abos puts a copper bolt right into your—"

"Now, silly," he chided her, "no dissension in front of our guest."

She might have had a retort ready, Flinx felt, but her attention was drawn from the wordplay to Ab. Walking past him, she inspected the alien closely, eyeing him up and down, walking a complete circle around him. For his part, Ab ignored her and continued his rhyming.

"Funny," she muttered to Flinx, "I think I recognize this fool, but from where I can't remember. What planet does it come from?"

"Not only don't I know Ab's world of origin," Flinx informed her, "but I wish he was back on it. Ab was a slave, performing in the marketplace in Drallar, back on Moth. I acquired him accidentally," he explained, leaving out a great many awkward details of Ab's acquisition. "He's harmless. He also," he added with a touch of awe, "seems to be immune to Otoid arrows and to massive electric shock."

"I'd like to have the first ability myself," she responded. Taking a stance directly in front of Ab, or at least where she decided his front was, she stared straight into his eye and said, hard and plain, "Where do you come from . . ." She glanced at Flinx. "What did you call him?"

"Abalamahalamatandra is what he calls himself, but he responds to 'Ab' " was Flinx's reply.

"Very well." She moved closer, almost standing on a green-striped blue foot. "Ab, where do you come from?"

A blue eye rolled at her. "Hetsels, hetsels, harmon nexus. Special nexus. Shoulder right and up a thousand nexus, spatial solar plexus."

Hasboga made a disgusted sound while September stifled a smirk, without much success. "That's one useful facility Ab has," Flinx commented, smiling himself. "He makes people laugh."

"He's more than a pet, then," the inquisitive scientist decided, studying Ab thoughtfully, "if he responds directly to questions."

"Not necessarily," argued September, leaning back against a broken stone. "He might be only a mimic. Little intelligence required for that."

"His comments are not repetitions of what's been said," argued Hasboga in return.

"I had a pet once," whispered Flinx, but no one heard him.

"Pet . . . scandal smith," decided Ab, promptly performing a quadruple handspring and landing on his hands. His trunk roved over the floor, sucking up pieces of dropped concentrate. So absurd was the figure of the inverted alien that both Flinx and September broke out in laughter, and even Isili had to smile.

"Funniest-looking creature I ever set eyes on," the giant declared. He brushed back the hair that had slid over his face. It fell straight down again, but not before Flinx saw what he had almost expected.

"The earring," he almost shouted.

"What?" September looked startled; then his thick brows furrowed with concern. "What are you staring at, feller-me-lad? You all right?"

"It's the earring," Flinx finally explained, pointing to the giant's head. "When you brushed at your hair, I saw it. You got a gold ring in your right ear."

Reflexively, September reached up and fondled the circlet, hidden behind his flowing white hair. "Well, yes, I do. Why so interested, lad?"

"I just—"

"Just a minute," Hasboga interrupted, stepping between the two men physically and verbally. "Before this goes any further, Skua"—she turned to confront Flinx—"we still don't know what *you're* doing here. Just because you're young doesn't make you trustworthy in my book. I'll buy your funny alien," and she jerked her head in Ab's direction. The alien was now standing on two legs and two arms, scouring the floor for crumbs.

"But what about you and your unfortunate friend?" she wanted to know. She jabbed a thumb at Pocomchi's body. "His kind I placed the moment I set eyes on him. Alaspin is infected with prospectors, like a pox. But you ..." She gave him the same thorough examination she had bestowed on Ab. "You don't look like a grubber, and you're too young to be much of a scientist. So what are you doing here in Mimmisompo?"

Chapter Nine

"You two are looking for your fortune," he finally replied, after a moment's hesitation. "I'm looking for myself."

If it came to a fight, for any reason, he knew he would have no chance against these two. He had to convince them he was telling the truth. They had been friendly so far, but they had the strength to be.

The problem lay with Isili, he felt. While not openly antagonistic, she was cautious to the point of paranoia. He tried to reach out mentally to her and received an impression of enormous emotion barely held in check. Surprisingly little of it was directed toward him or September. It was all wrapped tightly inside her. She was like the coil of an old-time generator: On the surface all was calm, but overload it slightly and wires would fly in all directions.

Taking a seat on a block of trimmed green stone, he explained about his search for his true parents. He censored those details which might upset or prejudice his hosts, avoided mention of Ulru-Ujurr and his flight from the Qwarm. His mere presence was unnerving enough to Hasboga. No need to make it worse.

He finished with his search for a big man, one with a gold earring and a small minidrag, who had tried to buy him over a dozen years ago.

"Twelve years, standard time," he said, staring hard at the watching September. "I was five years old. Do you remember it?"

Isili's eyes widened, and she stared accusingly at September. "A five-year-old child, Skua. Well, well." She gave Flinx a knowing look when the giant failed to respond. "He remembers something, for sure. This is the first time I've ever seen him speechless."

"Yes. Yes, I remember, lad," September finally admitted, looking and sounding like a man reliving a dream he had forgotten. "I did have a small minidrag with me."

"Did you leave Moth with it?" inquired a tense Flinx.

"No." Something trembled inside Flinx. He felt like a person with amnesia slowly regaining memory of lost events. "It finally left me in a bar. I was drunk. Minidrags can be temperamental. It probably decided I wasn't fit to associate with any more."

"I know how temperamental they can be," Flinx assured him. He forbade mentioning that Pip might have been the same minidrag September had lost. "I . . . used to have one myself."

"Then you do know. And you also probably know, lad, that on Moth it's a severe crime to import venomous creatures. So I couldn't very well march myself up to the nearest gendarmerie and ask for help. Not without being thrown in jail for letting a toxic alien loose on the planet. Sure, but I remember the slave auction." His memory of the incident appeared to grow stronger the longer he thought about it. "I bid on you. I was bidding on several in the same consignment."

"Several others with me?" Flinx frowned. This didn't fit. "What others?"

"I'm not sure it's a good idea to tell you that just yet, young feller-me-lad," the big man announced

softly. For some reason he appeared almost afraid of
Flinx, as if the youth were a bomb who might explode
at any second. Flinx could not understand. The dialogue was not following the scenario he had constructed in his imagination as to how this momentous talk
would proceed.

One way or the other, his last trail seemed to be
drawing inexorably to a dead end. Already, one possible link was broken. His meeting with Pip when he
was six years old appeared to have been accidental. A
coincidence only.

"For yourself?" he asked uncertainly.

September snorted. "I wouldn't know what to do
with a slave. No, lad, I was bidding for an organization."

The trail abruptly revealed a fresh length of itself.
Perhaps the giant wasn't the end after all.

"What organization?" he pressed the big man. "Does
it still exist? Could it be traced if it's disbanded, traced
to its responsible individuals?"

"Easy down, lad," September advised him, making
calming motions with both hands. "You've already told
us you found out about your natural mother last year."

"Yes. She's dead. She died before I was sold."
Silently he strained his erratic abilities, trying to see if
the information sparked any response in September's
mind. He was disappointed. The big man exhibited no
reaction he could detect, mental or otherwise.

"As to my natural father, I know nothing," he continued, "I do know that my father wasn't the man my
natural mother was married to. I'd hoped that by trac-
ing whoever was trying to buy me, I might discover
some new information leading to him."

"That makes sense, feller-me-lad," agreed an ap-
proving September.

"Nothing makes sense," growled Isili, who had listened to about as much of Flinx's problems as she
could stand. "What about us, Skua?" She was stalking
magnificently back and forth, her ebony mane flying,
her amber eyes glowing. "Nothing makes sense if all
the work we've put in here goes for nothing, and it will

if the Otoid persist after us." She stopped abruptly and whirled on him. "Months of planning, years of research, and we come up with nothing!" She wrung her hands in frustration. "I don't know why I tear myself up about it. I'm probably all wrong about this temple. We've been excavating for nearly two months and we haven't found anything beyond those." She indicated the exquisite carvings lining the chamber's interior. "And we didn't have to move a pebble to find them. Hieroglyphs, stories . . . what a waste."

"They seem unusually well preserved to me" was Flinx's comment. He found her attitude peculiarly unscientific.

She startled him by trying to read his mind. The force of her desire shocked him a little, although he knew she had no talents of any kind. She possessed a powerful mind, did Isili Hasboga, but it was not a mind of Talent.

"So you think the historical and scientific aspects of our grub should interest me more, do you?" she eventually inquired. "My *real* work is back home, on Comagrave. There's a site in the Mountains of the Mourners that's never been dug. No foundation or museum or university thinks it's worth excavating." Her eyes blazed. "I know better! They're wrong, all of them!"

Fanaticism in pursuit of knowledge, Flinx reflected, was still fanaticism.

"I know what's there," she rambled on, "under the garb mounds. And I'll find it, even though I have to mount and finance my own expedition. But for that I need credits. All of us need credits." She drew herself up haughtily. "That's why we're all on Alaspin. As you are neither a scientist nor a researcher," she concluded with a twinge of bitterness, "I don't suppose I can expect you to understand that."

"Maybe I understand more than you think" was his quiet reply. "I have a good friend, a young thranx who was once a student archeologist in the Church, who would have sympathized completely with your attitude at one time. She's since found other things to do." He wondered how Sylzenzuzex was managing without him in teaching the ursinoids back on Ulru-Ujurr.

"It's all for nothing anyway, now." She slumped. "Damn all unreasonable, xenophobic aborigines! Damn this world and its endless temples!" She sucked in a resigned breath. "Nothing now but to try to get out and try somewhere else, Skua. Maybe they'll leave us alone if we move to the other side of the city. But it's got to be somewhere in Mimmisompo. It's *got* to be!"

Flinx had no idea what "it" might be. It wouldn't have been discreet to inquire. Such a question would serve only to heighten Hasboga's suspicion of him.

But, having found the man with the earring, he could not let him go. Not till every question was satisfied. The internal portables brightened, compensating for the vanishing illumination outside.

"If you're finished with your grubbing," he told September, "I'll hire you."

"You, hire me?" The giant smiled condescendingly at him. "What'll you pay me with, lad? Stories, and entertainment provided by your poor ward?" He indicated the gallivanting Ab.

Flinx took no offense. He had come to expect such disbelief. "Whatever your cost, if it's in reason, I can pay it. How much?"

"That sounds like a sincere proposal," September confessed. Flinx thought the giant threw a mischievous glance at Hasboga. "I suppose if we *are* going to give up here . . ."

"Then both of you can go to hell!" Hasboga exploded, the barely suppressed anger finally erupting. She stormed over to glare down at Flinx.

"First you bring the Otoid down on us and now you want to steal Skua. Well, my skinny stripling, you're in no position to buy. Only to give. You owe me. We saved your miserable, barely begun life because on Alaspin help is rendered without question to those who need it. Don't you forget that." She turned away from him to confront an amused September. "And, mercenary that you are, Skua, don't forget that you and I have a contract. Of course, if you want to buy out from under me . . ."

"What, from under you?" Bushy brows lifted in mock astonishment. Flinx got the impression that maybe the relationship between these two was something other than wholly professional. He winced at the slap she gave the giant, but September only rubbed at the reddening place on his face and grinned more widely, almost approvingly.

Stalking away from them both, she threw herself down on the huge inflated mattress and buried her attention in a small, self-contained reader screen. For Flinx, there followed several moments of embarrassed silence.

"For a scientist she can behave awfully irrationally at times, feller-me-lad," September confided to him. He added, somewhat reassuringly: "These spells don't last much longer than they take. Watch." He winked.

Strolling over to the mattress, he sat down next to her. She ignored him. He pretended to peer over her shoulder at the screen.

"Now, Isili, it's not nice to act petulant before the lad."

"Get lost!" she snapped. "I'm busy."

"I can see that," admitted a seemingly startled September, his eyes bulging as he focused on the tiny screen. "I can tell what the man and the woman are doing, but the two tendril cats are—"

With an exasperated sigh, she looked up at him and spoke in a tone one would use with a child. "This is a perfectly plain theoretical tract, as you can easily see."

"Oh yes, I can see it, all right." Sitting back, he whistled solemnly at the ceiling. Flinx marveled at the man's élan, considering that they might all be dead the next night.

Rolling over, Hasboga sat up straight, put her hands on her hips, and glared at the giant. "Are you implying that I'm watching pornography?"

"Oh no," September started. "No, no, no, no. It's just that, in front of one so young . . ." He gestured toward Flinx. "And tendril cats, too." He clucked disapprovingly.

"Listen, you outrageous parody of a human being, if you think you can embarrass—" She stopped. September was grinning down at her. She fought to remember what she was about to say, but for the life of her couldn't get a grip on her half-disintegrated thought. Her mouth twisted and gradually broke into an almost shy smile.

The moment she realized what she was doing, her lips immediately clicked primly back to a firm set. "It's important work," she muttered lamely. She gestured weakly toward Flinx. "Go bother our visitor for a while and leave me alone."

Turning away, she went back to the viewer, but Flinx could sense that the dark cloud of fury which had been hovering over her had evaporated.

September obligingly walked back to flop down heavily in front of Flinx. "See? Silly's not such a bad sort. In fact, she's rather a good sort. Pity there aren't more like her." Commentary came from the vicinity of the viewer, but it was garbled and indistinct and not really angry any more.

"It's you that interests me right now, feller-me-lad. You've come a great way and a hard way to find me. You want to know about that day a dozen years ago, on Moth. I'll try to tell you what I can. That way, maybe I can learn a little too." He sighed. "I suppose you know who sold you, if you found out about your natural mother."

"I do."

"Do you know why?"

"I think so."

September shook his head. "I don't think you do. Not all of it. I can't tell you the rest, not yet. There are ethical questions involved."

Flinx's laugh was so harsh that he wondered at it himself. "You're talking to someone torn from his parents before he can remember, and sold like a piece of meat on a world not of his birthing."

"All right," September shifted agreeably, "call it a

business confidence, then. I probably will tell you, in time. But I need to think on it. Remember, I didn't have to tell you I knew anything."

"We'll let it pass for now," replied Flinx magnanimously, since he couldn't coerce the giant anyway. His next question he had to consider carefully. For a large part of his adult life he had framed it, rephrased it, turned it over and over in his mind, considered how he would present it to various people. He had developed and discarded a hundred different approaches. Now the moment to ask had come. This might be the last moment in a search that had taken him across half the Commonwealth and through stranger adventures than most people could imagine.

He forgot all preconceptions, leaned forward, and asked with unsophisticated innocence: "Are you my father?"

September took the question well. Maddeningly, he didn't venture an immediate reply. Indecision was the last thing Flinx had expected from the big man. September looked at the floor, using a landing-skid-sized foot to move rubble in meaningless patterns.

Flinx strained in the silence with all his desire, tried to bring his infrequent, awesome talent to focus on the man before him. The falseness or truth of September's eventual answer could be the most important thing in his young life. But, as so often happened, when he most wanted his abilities to function, they mocked him. Some days they could operate with the precision of a tridee beam, could pierce the nothingness between worlds. Now, even his own thoughts were unreadable.

When September looked up, he wore an expression of almost overwhelming earnestness. All thoughts of prevarication left Flinx. This man was not going to lie to him. He stared so long and hard that for a second Flinx wondered uncomfortably if the giant didn't possess unsuspected mental talents of his own. But while his gaze was intense, it was only from concentration.

"Young feller-me-lad, Flinx, believe me when I say I wish I knew."

Stunned, Flinx could only gape back at him. A yes he could have coped with. That was an answer he had been prepared to deal with a hundred thousand times in his imagination. A no would have been harder to handle, but he would have been ready for that, too. But "I wish I knew"?

So unexpected was the indeterminate answer that the youth who had organized the Ulru-Ujurrians, who had outwitted the Church and baffled Conda Challis, could only say lamely: "What do you mean, you don't know?"

"Don't you think I wish I did?" September half pleaded. "I am uncertain. I am indecisive, I can't say for sure because I don't know for sure. Positiveness of either possibility escapes me. I can't shade it yes or darken it no. There's no room for maybes, feller-me-lad. It's what I said plain, which means . . . I could be."

"Let's not play," Flinx said slowly, coldly. "Did you ever sleep with my mother, who was a Lynx of Allahabad, India Province, Terra?"

September shook his head, looking at Flinx as if for the first time. "What an unusual young man you are. You've got brains and guts, Flinx-lad. You're not by chance extremely wealthy, are you?"

"No, I'm not."

"Good," September commented with satisfaction, "because if you were, and I said I was your father, you'd have the natural suspicion of the wealthy and not believe me."

"How do you know I'd have any intention of sharing any wealth with you?" countered Flinx. "Maybe I'm looking for my father out of feelings of anger. Maybe I'd want just to blow your brains out."

"I wouldn't blame you," replied September. "But I never slept with your mother, of that I *am* certain. Nor have I ever been to India Province, let alone the city you mentioned. I've no idea who your mother was, and I doubt if I'd recognize her face or name if you confronted me with her this instant."

"No chance of that," Flinx assured him. "I told you, she's been dead since before I was sold."

"I'm sorry for that," September said, expressing genuine-sounding sorrow for someone he had just claimed never to have known.

Flinx's thoughts were full of speculation and garbage. "I don't understand this, I don't understand."

"Who does?" mused the giant philosophically.

"If you never even met my natural mother, let alone slept with her, then how could you possibly be my father?"

"Like most circles, it all ties together, feller-me-lad." September put both hands behind his shaggy head and leaned back. "Why do you think I was there on Moth that day, trying to buy you, and why do you think I didn't?"

"You didn't have the money to bid against Mother Mastiff," suggested Flinx. "The old woman who finally bought me." Then something else the slaver had mentioned came back to him. "You left the auction in a hurry, and there were a large number of police in the crowd."

"Very good, your sources have good memories," commented September. "I had the money to buy you, and the others. But I was a wanted man. Somehow the police knew I was on Moth. Since the reward for me was considerable, they came a-hunting. I had to leave fast. Purchasing you was one assignment I was never able to carry out. One of the few I've never been able to carry out. By the by, how much is it worth to you to find out if I really am your natural father?"

Flinx had never considered having to pay for the final word. "I don't know. I have to think on that one myself."

"Okay," agreed the giant, "so do I." He rolled over, pebbles scraping the floor beneath him. "We'll talk more tomorrow. Right now I'm feeling done in. Saving your life was an exhausting business."

Father or not, Flinx would cheerfully have strangled the big man over the delay. But there was nothing to do, and he did not want to risk antagonizing September.

He was not a man to be pushed. Besides, he told himself, he had waited this long, another evening would not make any difference. And he was completely worn out himself. Anyhow, he doubted that his hands would fit around September's enormous neck.

As it turned out, morning prevented any resumption of their conversation. Automatic scanners performed their function. So did the alarms they were connected to. The three sane occupants of the ancient temple chamber came awake to a clamorous howling.

"Otoids," said Hasboga curtly, grabbing up her pulsepopper and slipping off the safety. She ran for the gallery window as Flinx was still blinking sleep from his eyes. By the time he was fully awake, September had joined her atop the stone stairway. The two moved back and forth along the wide slit in the temple front, firing frequently at targets below. Dimly one could hear the incessant chatter of the Otoid.

Flinx joined them atop the stairs. Soon arrows began pinging through the narrow gap with disconcerting frequency. September cursed as fast as he fired. Standing alongside and watching the Mark Twenty cut down trees and leave craters in the earth, Flinx felt comparatively helpless as he snapped off an occasional burst with his own small handbeamer.

A bolt plunged onto the stone facing, falling almost vertically by September's right hand. He glanced upward. "They're atop the temple now," he muttered, "probably a mob of them. We can't hold this gallery much longer."

"The tunnel," Isili suggested, "fast!"

Flinx stayed between them as they ran down the stairway. They raced across the chamber floor. Around a slight bend in the inner chamber wall were five steps which Flinx hadn't seen before leading downward, Ab joined them and studied the entrance curiously.

"They'll open the door we built soon enough," September grunted. "This chamber has several back entrances, which we blocked up, but you can be sure they're just waiting for us to stick our heads out one of them." He indicated the low passageway at the bottom of the steps. Portable lights showed a dry stone floor.

September was gathering up food packets and shoving them into various pockets in the shirt he had donned on awakening. He pressed an armful on Flinx. "This tunnel is where we've done most of our digging. This is the only entrance—and exit, of course."

Several arrows pinged off the stone walls. September whirled, raising the muzzle of the Mark Twenty. Blue fire cleared the gallery window and left smoking stone and bodies behind.

"They might tire of this," he continued, speaking as if they hadn't been interrupted. "If they don't"—he ducked as a fresh bolt shot by overhead—"we'll have a choice of charging them or starving. But I don't think they can overpower us down in there."

Then Flinx was fighting his load of containers as he followed Hasboga down the steps and through the narrow, winding tunnel. September trailed, covering their retreat.

In the dim illumination he saw that the tunnel was roughly pyramidal in form, with a narrow strip of flat ceiling overhead. Delicate bas-reliefs ran in a single strip along each wall; a third decorated the small roof. Underfoot were smooth, alternating slabs of blue, green, and pure white stone, the white shining like glazed tile, while the blue and green remained convincingly stonelike. Ab loped along easily behind Flinx, singing querulously.

Finally they stopped. Panting, Flinx dumped his load of food containers. Hasboga settled her pulsepopper on a mound of recently excavated rubble while September found a resting place for his massive weapon slightly below and to her left.

Silence soon gave way to a deafening chatter as a horde of Otoid warriors came surging and hopping down the tunnel.

"Ready," September whispered expectantly.

Though the aborigine battle cries were thunderous, they were nothing compared to the roar of the two powerful guns as they fired away at the screaming, attacking natives. Flinx felt like a fly trapped in the landing bay of a cargo shuttle at the moment of touchdown.

The tunnel became a long, fiery gullet which digested stone and Otoid with equal indifference. With so much firepower concentrated in such a small space, Flinx's handbeamer would have been superfluous. He conserved it's modest charge and let Hasboga and September do the incinerating.

Eventually it dawned on the Otoid that they had reached a point beyond which nothing living could pass. With much howling and cursing, they retreated around the first bend and out of range. A deep swath of charred, smoking corpses constituted a disquieting reminder of their presence. Since the slight breeze blew always inward, the four inhabitants of the tunnel's end received the full brunt of that noxious barbecue.

"Now what?" Flinx wondered, glancing from Hasboga to the giant. Despite the apparent solidity of the stone walls, he was nervous. "Could they cave in the tunnel and trap us here? Or smoke us out?"

"As for the last," Hasboga told him, "that's no problem, though we might have to share tanks." She pointed to a pile of mining equipment in a corner. It included a pair of atmosphere masks for poor-air digging.

"The original Alaspinians built these temples well," she went on, indicating the walls around them. "With their primitive tools, I don't think the Otoid could break through the ancient cement sealing these stones. Even if they could, I doubt that they'd try it."

"Why not?"

"If they did that," September explained, "they'd never get our eyes."

"Eyes again," Flinx murmured. "What do they do with dead men's eyes?"

"Never mind, young feller-me-lad," was the grim reply. "It doesn't make pleasant conversation." Flinx decided not to insist on an explanation. If the subject troubled September, he wasn't sure he needed to know.

"Try to starve us out," the big man announced professionally, eyeing the far bend in the tunnel. "In any case, I don't think they'll try another mass rush like that last one for a while. They'll sit down and talk it over first." Leaving his rifle resting in place, he turned and slumped down against the wall of protective rubble.

Flinx took the opportunity to examine the section of tunnel they had retreated to. It wasn't so much a room or chamber here as it was a slight enlargement of the tunnel proper. Possibly the engravings set into the walls and ceiling were a touch more elaborate, a bit more plentiful. Three meters on, the tunnel assumed its normal dimensions, and a couple of meters beyond that the smooth walls ended in a dam of collapsed stone and rock. Despite Hasboga's assurances, it was clear that the Alaspinian temple was not invulnerable.

She noticed the direction of his gaze and said with a certain amount of enthusiasm, "We've been drilling and clearing this section, as you can see. We're trying to find out where this tunnel goes. I've studied thousands of temple schematics, and this tunnel has no counterpart in any of them that I've been able to discover. Also, those Alaspinian temples that do have passageways or tunnels have them laid out with sharp angles, regular and precise, all heading toward definite destinations. Usually they lead to other structures. This one makes no sense. It just sort of winds off uncertainly to no place. Compared to your usual Alaspinian road or passage, this one's constructed like somebody's small intestine."

"What do you expect to find at the end of it?" Flinx asked her.

She shrugged and smiled hopefully. "Storeroom, if we're lucky. Iridium temple masks, city treasury, anything else valuable the Mimmisompo priests wanted to hide and protect. Maybe even a religious scepter. They usually used crysorillium, and sapphire to decorate those scepters. Might even have some opalized diamonds."

"No doubt all of great scientific value," mused Flinx.

She threw him a warning look. "Don't criticize,

Flinx, until you've had to spend ten years on useless projects presided over by pompous asses with well-connected parents. Remember, I'd rather be doing some worthwhile research on my home planet. For me, this is a means to an end."

"Sorry," Flinx admitted. "I was—"

September broke in. "Apologies later, lad," he declared, rolling over to take up the trigger of the Mark Twenty. Angry hoots were drifting up the tunnel toward them. "Here they come again."

But the big man's concern was premature. The hooting came no nearer, though it continued not far from them.

September peered over the top of the shielding wall. "Probably having a final, violent disagreement over tactics," he theorized pleasantly. The hooting grew louder, and Flinx thought he heard sounds of fighting.

"Sounds like they're plenty angry at one another. Good! A couple of the warrior-primes are squabbling. They might end up fighting each other. Otoids have short tempers. It's been known to happen."

Hasboga nodded confirmation. "A few reports of natives attacking miners and outposts and ending up by massacring each other have been substantiated." She looked almost excited. "The only thing the Otoids hate worse than themselves are human or thranx interlopers. We might have a chance!"

"Lopers, mopers, lazy daze," came a high-pitched verse from behind them. "Moping, moping, eating maize . . . oh say can you see the canticle me."

September glanced briefly back at Ab. The alien was amusing himself at the far end of the excavation by juggling rocks with his four hands. Something struck the giant, and he eyed Flinx appraisingly.

"How about sending out your property as a decoy? It would tell us if they're too busy with each other to bother us." He hurried on before Flinx could reply. "There's a chance the Otoid will be so fascinated by him that they'll take him for a prize—he's got four eyes, to our two apiece—and they'll leave without risking any more dead."

"No," an angry Flinx replied. He said it firmly, so that there would be no mistake about it.

That did not keep September from arguing. "Why not, lad? You've admitted he's a burden on you. He's obviously madder than a bloodhyper and no good to anyone, and he might even slip through, depending on how many shafts he can take."

"Ab," Flinx responded very slowly, "is an intelligent creature."

September snorted. "It might save our lives."

"He's completely helpless," Flinx continued tightly, "totally dependent on our judgment. Furthermore, Ab trusts me. I wouldn't send him out there"—he gestured down the tunnel—"any more than I would a crippled cat."

"I was afraid of that." September sighed, looking over at Hasboga. "Our young lad is an idealist."

"Don't be too sure of yourself, September," Flinx warned him. "Idealism's an affliction I can put aside when I have to."

"Take it easy, lad," September cautioned him. "Isili, what say you, woman?"

Hasboga turned to stare at her associate, then looked across to Flinx. "The creature is the boy's responsibility and property," she declared, her gaze never wavering from Flinx's face. "We still don't know if the abos are fighting among themselves. Let's wait and see what they do. I'm not ready to vote for anything drastic until we start running out of food and water. Ab stays, if that's the way the youth wants it."

"Musical, musical, think time contusional," rhymed Ab, happily ignorant of the state of his fate and unaware that it had just been informally decided.

"We'll wait on then," September agreed, giving in gracefully. "I just don't like waiting, that's all." He returned his attention to the tunnel. At least the cool air would slow the process of putrefaction. If not, the stench of decomposing corpses could force them to use the masks as efficiently as smoke would.

Quite unexpectedly, the far end of the tunnel seemed to become darker. Flinx squinted, unsure that his eyes were relaying the truth. September leaned over the edge of their wall and tried to see around the first bend. The darkness jumped a little bit nearer.

"What are they up to?" Flinx inquired anxiously. "Filling up the corridor?"

"No," murmured the big man softly, "I don't think so."

It was Hasboga who first realized what the natives were doing. "They're taking out the lights," she informed them, even as another several meters of darkness appeared. "Rather than cover up the reflectors, they're just taking them down and moving them out of the tunnel."

"They won't take out the last three," September said grimly, hunkering down over the bulky stock of his rifle and shifting a little to his left. Howling and shrieking cut off further conversation as another mass of tightly packed natives came surging around the turn in the tunnel. September kept his weapon aimed near the precious light and shattered one alien after another as they tried to climb up to the unbreakable, self-powered sphere. Hasboga tried to hold back the rest of the screaming wave, and Flinx helped as best he could with his tiny pistol.

But they were so densely packed and there were so many of them that September was finally forced to bring his own weapon to bear in order to drive them from the corridor. One aborigine in the mob was able to reach the lamp. Triumphantly he wrenched it free from its mounting.

Shouting their victory, the mob retreated up the tunnel to safety, bearing the precious light with them. Now there were only two spheres left, one halfway down from the just-removed light to their position and the other a couple of meters in front of Hasboga. Beyond that, night had claimed the tunnel.

"They'll be regrouping again," September decided wanly, "for another charge. Buoyed up by their success. Some warrior-prime is in full control now." He used a hand to indicate the second light, partway to the tunnel bend. "If they get that one we're going to be in big trouble."

That led him to revive the discussion of a few minutes earlier. He gestured back toward the singsonging Ab. "What about it?"

Hasboga eyed the alien, turned a speculative stare on Flinx, then sighted back down her own weapon. "Not yet. They may not get the next light."

September growled softly but did not argue. As the prospect of death grew more real, Flinx noted, the big man's sense of humor was suffering.

Several hours passed before the peace and quiet was shattered by a terrible screaming and mewling. Flinx didn't jump this time, his ears were still numb from the last attack. But although they waited expectantly for the anticipated charge, it did not materialize.

"Why don't they come?" muttered Hasboga tightly, trying to see around the distant bend of a now-dark section of tunnel.

"Trying to rattle us," suggested September coolly, apparently unaffected by the spine-chilling cacophony. "Ignore it and stay ready. The noise can't hurt us."

"Not physically" was Hasboga's response. "Primitive or not, that's mind-tingling stuff."

The bloodcurdling concert continued, unendingly. It was beginning to make Flinx twitchy when it started to fade. Once begun, the cessation of the shrieking and moaning accelerated rapidly, until all was quiet again. Almost too quiet.

"By O'Morion," ventured September in amazement, "I think they've left."

"Maybe they did start fighting among themselves," guessed Hasboga, not daring to believe it.

"No, someone's coming," Flinx informed them, and then instantly cursed himself for saying it.

September's eye went back to the sight of his weapon. Several seconds passed before he thought to glance uncertainly over at Flinx.

"How do you know, young feller-me-lad? I can't see or hear a cursed thing."

"I have unusually good hearing," Flinx lied.

He was receiving impressions of some kind of mind up ahead. Beyond that he could sense nothing. His mind had been overloaded with input from emotionally wracked minds since the previous day, minds both advanced and aboriginal. Right now he couldn't evaluate the ones approaching them any more than he could separate granite from gneiss.

"I hear something, all right," Hasboga whispered, cuddling her pulsepopper tight as an infant. In the silence they heard the slight crunch of rock underfoot.

"Trying to slip a couple of good bowmen close to us, while we're worn out from the last charge" was September's decision. "One tactic that won't work." He adjusted the focus on his sight slightly and lowered the energy level—no sense wasting power on only a couple of the abos.

In the silence of the tunnel, only their own soft breathing could be heard. That made the gentle, pedantic voice that abruptly spoke sound louder than it actually was.

"Please don't shoot," it requested, in perfect terranglo but with a slight accent. "I do hope you are all uninjured."

"That's certainly a thranx voice," a wondering, confused September said firmly. He stood up and peered into the darkness. "Come on ahead, whoever you are!"

The crunching resumed. Soon a pair of figures emerged into the light. One was a dignified thranx of considerable age, evidently the one who had called out to them. His antennae dropped, and his chiton was turning deep purple. Both wing cases had been treated for the cracking of maturation, but the insect walked with sureness, and the shining compound eyes still held a brightness few young thranx possessed.

His companion was a tall, slim human of comparable age. His eyes were simple, and there were no ommatidia to throw back rainbows at the stupefied watchers, but they gleamed a little in their own way from beneath slightly slanted brows.

"As fast as we come, it's never been fast enough,"

the thranx announced tiredly. "None of you are damaged?"

"No, no," Isili Hasboga responded. She tried to see past the two figures into the darkness of the tunnel. "What happened to the Otoid?"

"I'd like to say," the tall human replied, in oddly stilted Terranglo, "that we landed among them, discussed the situation pleasantly, and convinced them to leave in peace. Unfortunately, they are belligerent far in excess of their intelligence." He appeared embarrassed. "Our skimmer is just outside the entrance to this temple. We have some heavy weapons in it."

"Frankly, it wouldn't disappoint us if you'd exterminate the little bastards completely," September declared, rising and brushing rock dust from his hands and clothes.

"I am sorry," responded the thranx, with frosty politeness, "we are not in the genocide business."

For a thranx to speak such perfect Terranglo was most unusual, Flinx knew as he moved for a better look at their rescuers. In fact, in his whole life he had only met one thranx who spoke the language of man like a native. That was . . .

"Truzenzuzex!" he shouted, stumbling forward past a dumbfounded September. "Bran Tse-Mallory!"

Chapter Ten

The two partners, prospector and archeologist, stared blankly as their young visitor exchanged noisy greetings with the two peculiar saviors.

Tse-Mallory was smiling his thin little smile, which masked more enthusiasm than it ever revealed. The Eint Truzenzuzex made clicking sounds in High Thranx indicative of greeting mixed with great pleasure, then added in Terranglo: "Again to see you is a delight, young Flinx."

September gazed open-mouthed at the evident reunion; then his brows furrowed in concentration and he simply watched and listened.

"I am warmed mentally and emotionally, though I cannot be physically," announced the thranx philosoph. "So I must . . . ask you to remove your arms from . . . around my b-thorax . . . so I can . . . breathe."

"Oh, sorry," Flinx apologized, removing his arms from around the old insect. Once again the eight breathing spicules pulsed freely. "But what are you doing here, old friends? Of all the places in the universe, this is the last that I'd expect—"

"Everything in its proper time plane, lad," Tse-Mallory broke in, making calming motions with both hands. "At present, I suggest we remove ourselves from this confined place. The aborigines who are left may elect to return. We would not be able to properly direct our skimmer's weapons from this deep in the earth."

"I'm for that," grunted September, willing to accept salvation without explanation. "The rent on this rat hole's been paid." He gathered up his Mark Twenty.

Led by Tse-Mallory, the little party of saviors and survivors started back down the tunnel.

Hasboga increased her stride to come up alongside Flinx. She was relieved, confused, and wary all at once. "You obviously know these two," she murmured accusingly.

"They're old friends, as I said," Flinx readily confessed.

"What are they doing here? Not that I'm sorry they appeared, you understand," she added hastily, lest she seem ungrateful, "but you told us you were here alone, except for the one dead in the temple."

"I told you the truth," Flinx insisted easily. "I was as surprised to see them as you and September were." At a sudden thought, he glanced back over his shoulder. Sure enough, Ab was still sitting back in the alcove, playing with rocks.

"Move it, Abalamahalamatandra!" he shouted impatiently.

Ab looked up from where he was squatting near the rear of the wide place in the tunnel. "Come some, fly high," he murmured, perhaps to himself, maybe to Flinx, possibly to nothing and no one in particular.

Twelve stones were arranged in a neat circle in front of Ab. With additional stones the addled alien was creating an abstract and seemingly meaningless design in the center of the circle. He had found the stones in a small hollow in the floor where his foot had fallen through during the fighting.

At his master's urging, he rapidly pushed the stones, diamonds, tanzanites, and a couple of fist-sized black emeralds back into the little hole. They fell the half meter to the bottom of the hollow. One of them bounced off an Alaspinian doubledevil mask, a meter high and wide, made of solid platiniridium and faced entirely with faceted jewels. It lay atop a small hillock of similar artwork.

"Go flow," ordered Ab as he scrambled to his feet and gamboled down the corridor after Flinx.

Emerging into the central temple chamber they had abandoned earlier, the tired survivors were greeted by the warmth and friendly daylight filtering in through the gallery window high above and through the once-dark doorway. Fragments of broken wood from the shattered makeshift door lay strewn all over the floor.

Hasboga took one look and moaned at the sight of the supplies they had been unable to take with them into the tunnel. Everything edible was gone, everything nonorganic broken, torn, battered into uselessness. The sleeping mattress was tiny flakes of plastic drifting in the gentle jungle breeze. Their autochef, the sole means of synthesizing a decent meal, was scrap metal, the smaller sections missing. Undoubtedly the cannibalized metal would find its way into hundreds of Otoid arrowheads.

"That's the end of it," she sighed, bending over and picking listlessly through pieces of a shredded dream. "I've no grant money to replace this." She probed through the rubble and held up a bent, half-unwound spool of study tape.

"How they hate us," she murmured. "Why?"

A hand the size of a good book covered her right shoulder. September looked down at her with a mixture of paternal and nonpaternal affection. "We'll scrape up the credit somewhere, Isili, if you really want to come back here one day. It's only money. I've been richer and broker than this a couple of dozen times in my life. The scale always balances."

"Not for me it doesn't," she replied viciously, throwing the tape into the rest of the vandalized pile.

She sniffed loudly. "I will not cry. It's unscientific and unbecoming and solves nothing."

"Damn right," agreed September, turning away from her so she could let the tears flow without embarrassment. "I said we'd raise the credit from somewhere, and we will!" He studied the Otoid bodies which lay strewn about the chamber. Several black-lipped holes showed in the temple walls. Both were testimony to the effectiveness of whatever weapons the two odd newcomers claimed to have in their skimmer. "They paid for it," the giant finished, examining the Otoid dead.

"Our sorrows to you," Truzenzuzex clicked, making a gesture which looked much like a sign of blessing, "but we should hurry. Those who would return would be angrier than the ones who lie quietly here." The aged philosoph watched as September moved to comfort Hasboga. "We don't know you and you do not know us," he pointed out. "We have access to certain funds. Your loss touches me." The valentine head swiveled slightly; he looked up at the tall human standing nearby. "Bran, may we not aid these two?"

Hasboga brightened and looked uncertainly from man to insect. "Noble sirs, we'd be forever in your debt!"

"We are not nobles," Tse-Mallory corrected briskly. "My name you now know. My companion"—he touched the insect's b-thorax lightly—"is a theoretical philosopher holding the rank of Eint among the thranx. We were both once of the United Church and served it."

"Who do you serve now, Tse-Mallory?" asked September.

The slightly wrinkled face smiled cryptically. "Our own curiosities. Your names, sir?"

"Isili Hasboga, my boss," September responded, ignoring the disgusted look she gave him, "and I'm Skua September. We'd appreciate any loan you could make us, humanx."

Tse-Mallory found himself looking eye to eye with a man twice his own mass. "September ... that name I know from something."

The giant grinned. "Can't imagine how or where from, Tse-Mallory, sir."

"I see you are not violently opposed," Truzenzuzex told his friend. "We can discuss matters of money and memory later, after we have left this dangerous place. If you will all hurry," he once more urged them, "our skimmer is hovering just outside."

Everyone moved . . . less one.

Flinx had not heard much of the preceding conversation. He stood off to one side, staring down at the eyeless body of Pocomchi. Now he turned sharply.

"Just a minute." While the others stopped to stare at him, he moved as if he had all the time in the world and started brushing dirt and dust and gravel off Ab. As always, the alien allowed himself to be cleaned without comment.

"Everyone's in too much of a hurry," he continued. "Me, I'm not going anywhere with anyone until I get some things straight in my own mind." Truzenzuzex stared at him disapprovingly, but Flinx was firm. "Not with you or with Bran, until we . . ." Something clicked and now he spoke rapidly. "You've both been following me. You must have been following me, or you wouldn't be here now. Unless you have some dealings with September or Isili, and judging from the little exchange I just overheard, you didn't know each other until just a few minutes ago."

September looked curious, Hasboga merely confused.

"I don't know why you've been following me," Flinx went on forcefully. "I want to know." After a brief pause, he added, almost indifferently, "It was you two who killed all those Qwarm back in the warehouse on Moth, when I was on my way to the shuttleport."

Hasboga's confusion gave way to the kind of worry and nervousness that mention of the assassin clan always engendered. "Qwarm? What's this about Qwarm?" She eyed Flinx as if he had suddenly turned into a dangerous disease.

"Quiet," instructed September. "Let them talk it out, Isili."

"Oh no," she objected, "not this lady. Credit loan or no credit loan, I don't want anything from anyone who's had dealings with the Qwarm." She smiled gratefully but cautiously at Tse-Mallory. "Thanks for your offer of aid, sir, but you can keep your money and your arguments with the Qwarm to yourselves. We'll raise the credit elsewhere."

Tse-Mallory finished listening, then turned back to Flinx as if Hasboga had never opened her mouth. "Yes, we killed them before they could kill you, Flinx."

That explained the fading mental screams and sounds Flinx had sensed while fleeing from the warehouse. Tse-Mallory and Truzenzuzex, those aged beings, had been concluding their grisly work. No doubt the Qwarm had been very much surprised.

"Then you *have* been following me," he declared, more curious than accusing.

"All the way from Moth," Tse-Mallory replied, "but you are only partially correct, Flinx."

Truzenzuzex raised a truhand and foothand, pointed to Flinx's left and behind him. "Primarily, Flinx, we've been trying to catch up with *it*."

For a second Flinx stood staring blankly at the philosoph. Then he turned and gazed silently behind him. So did September and Hasboga.

Ab noticed all the silent attention, giggled his alien giggle, and began to rhyme noisily at his new audience.

Flinx turned away from his charge, to eye the myriad corpses scarring the temple floor, the ruins of September and Hasboga's camp, and discovered that try as he might he couldn't find a thread of logic in anything that had happened.

September was apparently of the same mind. "You two have been chasing that crazy four-legged whaţsis," he announced in disbelief, "and killing Qwarm because of it?" He shook his massive head in amazement, that great proboscis cleaving the air like a fan. "You don't *look* like madmen."

"Neither are the Qwarm," Flinx added dazedly. "Why is Ab's death so important to them?"

"Abalamahalamatandra, you called to it back there in the tunnel," Tse-Mallory mused maddeningly, ignoring everyone's questions. "Ab for short. It has a name. Interesting."

"You're avoiding me, Bran," Flinx half snapped at the tall Oriental. "That's not the Tse-Mallory I know who pondered the inner workings of the Krang. Why do the Qwarm want Ab dead?"

"Not the Qwarm," corrected Truzenzuzex quietly. "Never the Qwarm. If they want anyone dead, it's you, Flinx, because of the trouble you've caused them. But to them Ab is only a statistic at the end of a voucher. They are hired by those who want others dead, in this case your accidental companion." The philosoph looked sad, angry. "The Qwarm clan is a lingering evil from unenlightened, pre-Amalgamation times. Why the Church and Commonwealth tolerate it I have never understood. As for Ab there are impressive forces that want him extinguished. Not simply dead, but obliterated, disintegrated."

"But why?" Flinx pleaded, uncomprehending. "Look at him." He gestured at the innocent, versifying creature. "Why would anyone want such a harmless creature killed, and why take such pains to do it?" Turning back to face Truzenzuzex, his next question revealed how much he had grown since they had last seen him. "Even more interesting, why would two individuals of your abilities want to go to the trouble of preventing it?"

"Why did you bother to rescue him that first time, before we could do so?" Tse-Mallory asked.

Flinx didn't look at him as he replied irritably, "I have a talent for getting my nose stuck in other people's business. I spend a lot of time trying to yank it out. Actually, I didn't intend to interfere. It was Pip who—" He broke off in mid-sentence.

"I do not see the minidrag," Truzenzuzex admitted. "Your pet is dead?"

"Not dead," Flinx corrected him. "But I don't really know. This is the planet of Pip's birth. The man who guided me here also had a tame minidrag, Balthazaar.

Both flew away together, in the middle of the night. Possibly forever, although," he added hopefully, "there's always a chance they'll return." His tone grew firm. "You're both trying to distract me. I'm not setting foot in any kind of skimmer with you two devious old men"—Truzenzuzex made a clacking noise—"until I find out why someone wants poor Ab killed and why you both want him alive." He shook his head in puzzlement. "It doesn't seem to me that either Ab or myself is worth all the attention that's been given to us."

Bran Tse-Mallory responded by glancing impatiently from Flinx to the rubble-and-body-littered temple entrance. "This isn't the place or time, Flinx."

Flinx folded his arms and took a seat on a nearby stone. "I disagree."

Isili Hasboga was picking sadly through the remnants of her scientific equipment. As she spoke, she brushed strands of hair from her face. "I have to agree with your friends, Flinx. The Otoid will come back, twice as many the next time. When they do return, I don't want to be here."

"Sorry, silly," said September. "I have to side with the boy." He flashed Flinx a look of support. "You've got some interesting friends for one your age, feller-me-lad. Stay obstinate. I'll stay, too."

"Very well then," whistled Truzenzuzex exasperatedly. "Bran?"

Tse-Mallory made a negative sound. He eyed September, who was rocking on his heels, humming to himself and supremely indifferent to the possibly imminent arrival of several thousand rampaging aborigines. "If you'll pick up that formidable-looking Mark Twenty, Mr. September, and come outside with me, we'll keep watch while these two chatter." September nodded his acquiescence and moved to shoulder the rifle. "Try to be brief, will you, Tru?" Tse-Mallory asked his companion.

"If there is one among us who is guilty of persistent loquacity," came the reply smoothly, "it is not I."

"Debatable" was Tse-Mallory's simple retort, as he

followed September up the steps leading out of the temple.

"Not without being guilty of the crime of debating!" shouted Truzenzuzex, but by that time Tse-Mallory and September were out of hearing range.

On the grass outside, both men took up positions on board the skimmer. "The lad indicated the thranx is an Eint and philosoph," September said conversationally. "What of you?"

"I mentioned we were at one time both in the service of the Church. I was a Chancellor Second."

September appeared impressed, though not awed. "Pretty high. Wouldn't have guessed it. Myself, I never had much use for the Church."

"Nor did Tru and I, after a while. That's why we left it." Jungle sounds drifted innocently out of the green wave, helped them relax a little. "And you, sir?"

"Oh, I've done a little bit of everything," September replied modestly, "and had a little bit of everything done to me." He did not elaborate, and Tse-Mallory did not pry.

Settling himself down on his four trulegs, Truzenzuzex folded truhands and gestured with foothands as he talked. Behind Flinx, Ab was arranging stones in a circle (ordinary stones, this time) and singsonging softly to himself.

"Flinx, what do you know of the double-world system Carmague-Collangatta and the planet Twosky Bright?"

Flinx thought a moment, then looked blank. "Little more than what you've just told me, their names. I've never been to either. I think they're all well-populated, highly developed worlds."

"Correct," said Truzenzuzex, nodding. "All three are important contributors to the Commonwealth economy; stable, advanced worlds. They're all going to die . . . or at least most of the people on them are— probably the worlds themselves, also."

"Their suns are going nova," Flinx guessed. He frowned. "That would be quite a coincidence."

"I would expect you to be an expert on coincidences, boy. Your assumption is incorrect. The situation is this. Many years ago, but not too many, a Commonwealth science probe mapping behind the dark nebula called the Velvet Dam discovered a sun disappearing into nothingness. Of course, it wasn't disappearing into nothingness, only into something that partook of the aspect of nothingness."

"I don't think I understand," Flinx admitted.

"You will. Your Lewis Carroll would have. He was a physicist himself, I think? No matter. The star in question was being smashed down into a rogue black hole. Such an object has been theorized, but this is the first one detected. Its course has been determined. We know enough to predict that only a small percentage of the populations of all three worlds could be rescued before their respective suns vanish into the rogue."

Flinx's own problems were forgotten as he tried to conceive of disaster on the scale Truzenzuzex was describing to him. He sat quietly, thinking, before it occurred to him to ask, "But why tell me this? What does it have to do with your being here?"

Truzenzuzex shifted his stance slightly, his claws making tiny scratching sounds on the tunnel. "Because your acquisition, your acquaintance, your ward, or whatever you wish to call him"—he pointed with a truhand at the rhyming Ab—"may be the one possible chance for those worlds' salvation."

Having nothing intelligent to respond to that incredible bit of information with, Flinx kept silent.

"A black hole is the ultimate state of collapsed matter, usually a star which has fallen in on itself," the philosoph explained. "In the case of the rogue, we believe that it may consist of not one but many collapsed stars. Dozens, perhaps hundreds. We do not have instrumentation capable of telling us by direct measurement, but we can approximate from the speed with which the star detected by the probe was absorbed. For a collapsar, the mass of the rogue is immense."

"How could anyone, especially Ab, least of all the creatures in the galaxy, help you? Nothing can turn or destroy a collapsar. At least," he added quickly, "nothing I ever heard of. I see no connection, Tru, sir." For a moment he displayed the attitude of a schoolboy ignorant of the answer to a teacher's question.

"I would not feel foolish at that failure," Truzenzuzex confided to him. "You have much company." Some bitterness crept into his voice. "Both the Commonwealth High Council and the Court of Last Resort of the United Church are of the opinion that nothing can be done to save the three worlds. They are attempting to rescue small groups of the three populations without causing panic, which will be inevitable. They refuse to consider the alternative."

"There's an alternative?" Flinx looked startled.

"We are hopeful" was all the philosoph would admit to. "But both Bran and myself feel that anything which might save billions of lives and uncounted trillions of credits, no matter how absurd it sounds, is worth serious and not jocular consideration. Our strongest assurance that we are on the track of something potentially helpful has been the frantic attempts of other parties to eliminate that hope. How your poetically inclined alien is involved in this I will tell you in a moment.

"While Bran and I are no longer connected to the Church, we still retain sympathetic connections in the bureaucracy. In the Commonwealth government, too. Through these we learned of the death sentence hanging over the three worlds in the path of the rogue. We felt as helpless and sorrow-filled as anyone. However, we elected to try to do something. Our specialty is the pre-Commonwealth, pre-Amalgamation history of this part of the galaxy. To make many weeks of tedious research brief, we learned of a possible connection between an ancient race and a similar destructive appearance of a rogue collapsar. Somehow, somewhere on this side of the galactic center, the menace was met and dealt with.

"That in turn led us to search for anything that might tell us what became of the device which dealt with the first rogue. Rumors of a being of unknown type were brought to us by our agents. The being was at that time reported to be in the city of Drallar, on Moth. This being sang nonsense rhymes and performed as a comic foil in a simple street entertainment. We were not on Drallar at the time, but we succeeded in obtaining copies of recordings from a tourist who witnessed the being's performance. This intellectual expressed astonishment that Bran and myself should be interested in such things.

"We were very excited when we saw the first images of your Ab," the philosoph went on. "He matches up with no known race. However, it was not his appearance, rather, one of his rhymes we heard while viewing the recording, which caused my breathing spicules to lock to the point of fainting and caused Bran to utter an oath I had not heard from him in eighteen years. You see, Flinx, one of the rhymes contained a mention of the race we believe successfully stopped the intrusion of a rogue collapsar approximately eight hundred thousand Terran years ago on the near side of the Shapely Center. That race was called the Hur'rikku."

There was a gasp, followed by a metallic clattering. Isili Hasboga had dropped the armload of tapes she had so laboriously salvaged. They sprawled across the floor. Several of them had cracked, and thin microscopic tape had unreeled from the twisted spools.

She made no move to recover the tapes. Her expression showed shock; her eyes were wide in disbelief.

Flinx saw something moving nearby: A truhand was plunging into a pouch in the philosoph's thorax vest. Perhaps it was the abrupt shock of Hasboga's reaction—perhaps his talent chose that perverse moment to function—in any case, he sensed what was racing through the elderly thranx's mind.

"No, Tru!" he shouted, rising and stepping between the insect and Hasboga. "She's not a spy, she's an archeologist. Wouldn't she know of the Hur'rikku?"

Truzenzuzex turned blazing compound eyes on Flinx and considered his words. The hand relaxed; the concealed weapon in the pouch never emerged.

All at once, Hasboga came out of her moment-long

trance. She turned her gaze to the floor, saw and remembered what had happened. Suddenly she was scrambling to retrieve her precious tapes. Occasionally she would glance back at the watchful Truzenzuzex, aware that something had upset him, but she never suspected that the old insect had been prepared to kill her simply on the basis of her reaction to what he had told Flinx.

"You are not a spy," he decided, the fire fading from his eyes. "I see that now."

"Me?" She looked back in confusion. "A spy? Spy for whom?"

"I will tell you in time," he murmured. "When you indicated a familiarity with the Hur'rikku I . . . Excuse me." He executed a thranx gesture of apology seasoned with contrition at his own stupidity. "Too many deaths are already involved in this matter. Bran and I can take no chances. The Commonwealth and the Church are already suspicious of our actions, and they dislike having others inquire into matters they consider wasteful. Then there are those who would like to see the rogue proceed unchallenged on its course of destruction."

"Who or what are the Hur'rikku?" Flinx was still a bit shaken from the severity of the kindly philosoph's murderous reaction to Hasboga's knowledge.

His antennae still aquiver, Truzenzuzex proceeded to explain. "The Hur'rikku are the half-legendary race who, scientists postulate, erupted from the region near the galactic center some nine hundred and fifty thousand years ago."

"They weren't half legendary," argued Hasboga. "They were completely legendary. Myths about them exist, but no physical proof has ever been found for which alternate explanations couldn't be provided."

"No physical proof, this is so," admitted Truzenzuzex. "But they frightened the ovipositors off the Tar-Aiym." His mandibles clicked in thranx laughter. "Of the Tar-Aiym we *do* have physical proof."

Flinx knew the truth of that statement from his experiences of over a year ago.

"We know that about the time the Hur'rikku are rumored to have begun their expansion outward from the galactic center, this entire section of space was dominated by the Tar-Aiym. Roughly half a million Terran years ago, the indomitable Tar-Aiym were thrown into a racial panic. It seems reasonable to assume that the Hur'rikku were the cause of this."

Hasboga made a derisive sound. Truzenzuzex ignored her and continued on. "The Tar-Aiym scientists constructed numerous new weapons to counter the Hur'rikku threat. One was the defensive weapon known as the Krang. Another was a simple plague. That destroyed not only the Hur'rikku but the Tar-Aiym themselves, and all life in the region we know today as the Blight, before finally destroying itself.

"At this point in time the Hur'rikku are mostly a legend. They exist because your friend Ab sings of them." A truhand gestured to where the alien was delightedly juggling a dozen rocks. "The Hur'rikku are like the rogue. Like it, we have no direct perception of existence. But we can see how it acts upon other objects. Similarly, we know the Hur'rikku existed because we know of their effect upon the Tar-Aiym. In fact, that is *all* we know so far of the Hur'rikku—that they existed. That and the fact that perhaps they may have found a way to counter the danger posed by a wandering collapsar—and a few other less-impressive myths."

"But you need physical proof!" Hasboga objected.

"Evidence need not be physical," was the insect's calm reply.

"You philosophical scientists are all the same," she said in exasperation. "You support hypotheses with dreams embedded in foundations of supposition."

Truzenzuzex was not upset by the disparaging of his chosen field. "So, Flinx, as little as we know of the Tar-Aiym, we know even less of the Hur'rikku. And yet . . . your alien talks of them."

Flinx turned disbelieving eyes on the humming Ab. "You think that Ab might be . . . ?"

"No." Truzenzuzex was quick to correct a blossoming misconception. "We do not think your Ab is a

Hur'rikku. The last Hur'rikku died five hundred thousand years ago. What Bran and I believe is that he is more likely to be a very old member of some race living on the periphery of the Blight, a race that retains memories of both the Tar-Aiym and the Hur'rikku and their exploits. The legends of the Hur'rikku and the collapsar are known. It is part of one legend that the Hur'rikku threatened to use on the Tar-Aiym worlds the device which had stopped their rogue. If true, that would go far to explain the unprecedented panic among the warrior Tar-Aiym."

Flinx turned to watch Ab's juggling act. Noting the smoothness of the blue skin, the supple arms and legs, the clearness in the four limpid blue eyes, he reflected that the alien didn't *look* old. He reminded himself that he was judging Ab's appearance by human standards. Among Ab's race, smooth skin and bright eyes might be signs of advancing senility.

"The legends seem to imply," Truzenzuzex went on, "that beside this Hur'rikku device, something like the Krang is a larva's toy."

Flinx was pacing the floor worriedly. "Couldn't we try to use the Krang against this new rogue?"

Thranx laughter spiced with sarcasm preceded the philosoph's response. "Just how would you move it, Flinx? You'd have to move the entire world of Booster, on which the Krang is located and from whose core it draws its power. Besides, if my initial supposition is correct and the Krang does generate a Schwarzschild Discontinuity it would not harm a collapsar. Quite the contrary."

He leaned forward and stared hard at Flinx. "Then there is the question of who could operate the Krang. I recall your saying that you had no idea how to operate it."

"Well, that's true also," Flinx almost panicked, trying to cover his mistake. Truzenzuzex had always been suspicious of Flinx's abilities. He hid his concern in wonder. "Something that would make the Krang seem to be a child's toy . . . incredible."

"An ultimate weapon." Truzenzuzex nodded slowly.

A sharp laugh sounded from nearby. "Ultimate weapons indeed! You and your tall friend are madder than this alien. No such thing as an ultimate weapon can exist. If it did, it would have destroyed everything in the galaxy by now, once it had been activated."

"Not if in activation it neutralized itself," Truzenzuzex argued charmingly.

"You can't convince me with semantics."

"I know, young lady. You require physical proof." More Thranx chuckling, a sound like seashells sliding against each other. "We think it worth trying to locate such proof, if it does exist. We have nothing to lose except three worlds."

Chapter Eleven

After a moment's silence, Flinx pointed back at Ab, "How do you know Ab knows anything more about the Hur'rikku than he's already said?"

"He appears to be a limitless fount of information, Flinx. Or haven't you noticed that he never repeats the same rhyme twice?"

"That may be so," Flinx conceded, "but he only talks nonsense."

"Much of it probably is nonsense that will always remain incomprehensible to us." Truzenzuzex was agreeable. "But some of it is not."

"How do you propose to get any more Hur'rikku information out of him?"

Truzenzuzex sighed deeply, an eerie whistling sound in the near-empty chamber. "We've chased him across two planets now so that I can do just that. But why don't you do it, Flinx?"

"Do what, sir?"

"Ask him. Ask him about the Hur'rikku."

"I . . ." Flinx noticed that the philosoph had switched on a tiny recorder attached to his thorax vest.

177

The insect was serious about this. Well, he could play along. Turning, he faced Ab and said sharply, "Ab! Abalamahalamatandra!" All twelve rocks fell to the stone floor, their juggler ignoring them save for a single blue orb. He gazed wanly at the stones until they stopped bouncing.

"What about the Hur'rikku, Ab?" Flinx asked, feeling like an idiot as he talked sensibly to his ward. "Tell us about the Hur'rikku. Tell us about how they stopped the collapsar rogue."

"Nine and five, five and nine, loverly to dine if fine. 'Ricku, 'Ricku, sing to hicku, haiku you, you key me."

"There, you see?" Flinx turned and spread his hands in a gesture of helplessness. "It's useless—he's crazy."

"Not completely," countered Truzenzuzex. "It's simply a matter of points of tangency. You have none. Bran and I have learned several. For example, *Neinenive* is a Geeprolian translation for Hur'rikku neuter. They had three sexes, it seems. Ab is trying to convey information, but it's garbled through maybe a dozen languages at a time, all of which he's trying to pronounce as Terranglo."

Flinx threw Ab a look of pure incredulity before returning his attention to the expectant philosoph. "You mean Ab's been making sense all along?"

"No. Some of his chattering seems to be pure nonsense. The trouble is separating out the sense. Or perhaps I am wrong and everything he is saying would make sense if only we had some way of breaking it down. His name, Abalamahalamatandra, for example. I wonder if that's just a collection of conveniently collected syllables, or if it actually means something." The philosoph rose from his squatting position. "Let us take your Ab along, probe and prod him, and see what other insightful nonsense he can spout."

Tse-Mallory and September clambered back down the steps and stood at the base. "Patience, ship-brother," Truzenzuzex called to his companion. "We are coming."

"Now," Tse-Mallory responded in Terranglo. "We've wasted too much time here. September and I killed two Otoid scouts a few minutes ago. They must be returning. There are also the Qwarm to consider."

Flinx started. He had almost forgotten about the professional assassins, with all the amazing talk of lost races, ultimate weapons, and a coherent Ab.

"You brought a fair-sized skimmer, sirs," said September. "I think we can all fit inside."

"We can if you take no more than that." Tse-Mallory indicated Hasboga, who was laden with tapes, real books, and a few modest Mimmisompo artifacts.

"Nothing here for me," September commented with a grunt. "I can always come back for whatever the abos leave."

"Why bother, Skua?" Hasboga wanted to know. "We found nothing here. We probably never would." Her gaze roamed the chamber floor a last time. "We tried the wrong building. I see no profit in returning. Next time we'll try somewhere else."

"Sure we will, silly," September said reassuringly. "We'll raise the credit somewhere, don't worry." He shifted the enormous Mark Twenty from his shoulder to a ready position. "Gentlesirs, if you'll lead the way I'll endeavor to keep an eye or two on the tree trunks, in case the need rises for me to incinerate one or two overcurious little green brothers."

"We will chance your expertise in the jungle." Tse-Mallory's mouth twisted in distaste. "Though I wish you'd phrase your intent in a less primitive fashion. All intelligent beings are brothers, you know. The Otoid as well."

A reflective grin split the giant's tanned face. "I had a brother once. Didn't like him either. I . . ." He cut the story short with an expansive gesture. "After you, gentlesirs and lady."

As they emerged from the sheltering stone walls of the temple, Flinx found himself nervously eying every branch and vine and creeper, convinced that a thousand Otoid were concealed nearby. At any second he expected to feel a rain of darts, loosed from the nearest trees.

Ahead of him, Truzenzuzex was murmuring deeply

in Low Thranx. Nonsense rhymes and songs emanated
from Ab with the usual unconcern of the mad. Only
now they seemed to be in response to the philosoph's
hypnotic mutters. Some were in Ab's mangled Terranglo, the rest in languages unknown to Flinx. But twice,
he thought he heard mention of the Hur'rikku, so perhaps the philosoph was learning something after all.
Privately, Flinx couldn't help but think his two wizened
friends were engaged in a fruitless chase founded on a
futile assumption.

All the jungle noises which assaulted his ears were
animalistic and indifferent. There was no sign of the
native Otoid. It was only a short walk to the hovering
skimmer.

Tse-Mallory employed a control panel on his belt to
deactivate the protective energy shield surrounding the
craft and then to have it sink to the ground for easy
boarding. It was a small cargo craft, much larger than
the tiny two-man ship Flinx and Pocomchi had traveled in.

That forced Pocomchi and Habib into his thoughts
again. Indirectly, at least, he was the cause of their
deaths.

Why, he mused in anguished fury, did so many
people have to perish around him, when what he
sought was neither wealth nor power but only
knowledge of his origins?

Tse-Mallory boarded the skimmer first, followed,
with the always unexpected agility, by Truzenzuzex,
then Hasboga and September. As soon as Flinx entered
the broad cockpit, with Ab bringing up the rear, Tse-
Mallory touched a switch and the canopy door slid
shut.

The engine whined expectantly. Soon they would be
back in Alaspinport, where he could press September
to finish his explanation, no matter how much the giant
tried to put off Flinx's questions this time. His gaze
rose curiously, why he didn't know, to the transparent
roof. Something moved against the clear sky. Squinting,
he stood on tiptoes and peered so hard the back of his

eyes hurt. Then Flinx was jumping up and down, shouting violently, "Stop the skimmer, stop, stop!"

Tse-Mallory hit a switch reflexively, and the craft, which had commenced a slow turn, came to an abrupt halt. September was struggling to reclaim his rifle from the cargo area, while Truzenzuzex was digiting the skimmer's heavy armament uncertainly.

"What troubles you, Flinx?" the philosoph inquired, glancing back over a shoulder turned Tyrolean purple.

For an answer Flinx continued to stare skyward, though he gestured with his right hand toward the control panel. "Put back the canopy," he requested. Tse-Mallory started to object. Flinx's voice rose almost hysterically! "The canopy—put it back!"

The human scientist exchanged looks with his thranx companion, who simply shrugged. Tse-Mallory activated a control, and the transparent polyplexalloy dome slid back into the body of the skimmer, leaving only transparent sides, doors, and front windshield in place.

Hasboga moved to stand alongside Flinx. She stared into the sky. "I don't see anything, Flinx," she said with surprising gentleness.

"There," he told her, pointing. "Coming toward us out of the sun . . . it has to be . . . I'm sure it is!"

Two shapes wove a descending spiral, dancing on the air. Two small dragon-forms stark against mountains of cloud. One was noticeably larger than the other.

A hundred meters above the skimmer, they finished their aerial choreography and separated. Balthazaar flew off in the direction of the sun. The other began a steady twisting dive toward the open skimmer.

"That's a dragon!" Hasboga gasped, reaching for her sidearm. Flinx put a restraining hand on hers.

"No, it's all right, Isili. It's mine. It's Pip." His voice was cracking, despite his best efforts at self-control.

A familiar diamond-patterned shape braked, pleated wings backbeating the air, tail and lower body hooked out and extended. Flinx raised his right arm out from his side. Pip dropped for it, tail curving around the

proffered perch. The pleated wings folded tight to the
body, and then the flying snake was ensconced in its
usual position of rest on Flinx's shoulder.

Reaching down, its master affectionately stroked the
back of the triangular head. While the minidrag, as always, showed no outward sign of emotion, Flinx could
sense a feeling of pleasure in his pet. Empathy cloaked
him like the warm glow of stones surrounding a wood
fire. Several moments passed in silence before Flinx
noticed that everyone in the skimmer was staring at
him.

"Your pet came back," Truzenzuzex finally said, explaining Pip to the still-uncertain Hasboga and September. "I am pleased for you, Flinx. I remember what
you two meant to each other." With that, he turned
and activated the skimmer controls.

Hasboga eyed the snake warily, but settled back in
her seat as the lithe craft picked up speed. Soon they
were speeding back toward Alaspinport, traveling just
above the waving grass of the savannas.

When the exuberance experienced on his pet's return
had faded some, Flinx thought to turn and look over
at September. The giant was enjoying the ride, since
someone else was doing the piloting for a change.
Thick fingers were running absently through his wild,
wavy white hair. His nose interrupted the view behind
him like a plow.

"Skua?"

September faced him and offered a pleasant, toothy
smile. "What is it, young feller-me-lad?"

Flinx glanced significantly down at his now-occupied
right shoulder. "My minidrag. His name is Pip." He
touched one leathery wing, and the snake shifted
sleepily. His attention returned to September. "Twelve
years ago, back on Moth, you lost a young minidrag,
remember?"

"I see what you're thinking, lad." September put
both hands around one knee, which resembled a knot
on a tree, and leaned back again, thinking. "All minidrags look the same to me, lad. As to whether your
Pip happens to be the one I lost, I'm guessing it's pos-

sible. I never named my snake, so there's no way of knowing, is there? Minidrags aren't common off Alaspin. I wouldn't know of any others that had been on Moth then. Might have been. If your Pip is the one, that would be an interesting coincidence, wouldn't it it?"

"Yes, it sure would." Flinx kept his voice carefully even.

"Signifying nothing." September finished with that, and turned his gaze to the scenery slipping past outside.

Flinx did likewise, watching the savanna roll past as Truzenzuzex and Tse-Mallory skillfully maneuvered the craft over low hills, around trees and upthrust, unweathered rock spires.

"Signifying nothing," he murmured softly to himself.

At Alaspinport, Flinx was forced to reveal that he had his own ship. That was fine with Tru and Bran. Flinx permitted them to commandeer it—on one condition. "I'm not through questioning September," he whispered to Tse-Mallory.

The scientist regarded him somberly. "You'll have him around for a while yet, Flinx. Hasboga has undoubtedly told him of our plans. For their own protection, we must take both with us until this matter is resolved. If not, they will be questioned by the Qwarm. I don't think they would be permitted to live."

Neither Hasboga nor September objected to a free trip off Alaspin, once it was explained to them what might happen if they remained. Both appeared to be under the impression that they would be delivered immediately to some larger, safe world like Terra or New Paris. Flinx didn't exactly lie about that, he simply neglected to tell either of them that they would be taking a long route around.

As they left the surface of Alaspin, Truzenzuzex's damnable curiosity prompted him to ask Flinx how he had acquired the impressive sum necessary to purchase and operate a private, system-jumping vessel like the *Teacher*. Flinx could not explain that the *Teacher* had been built by his precocious pupils, the Ulru-Ujurrians.

Yet it was extremely difficult to lie believably in front
of someone as perceptive as Truzenzuzex. So, in what
he hoped was a natural tone of voice, he explained that
he had purchased the ship out of the money given him
by Maxim Malaika as reward for his part in discovering
the Krang. When he ran out of money to operate the
vessel, he would have to sell it.

Truzenzuzex appeared to accept this facile explanation readily enough, though Flinx could detect a familiar twinge of suspicion in the philosoph's mind even as
he acknowledged the story.

Presently, they entered the *Teacher* with the insect
explaining that Flinx's fast ship was the reason they were
so long in tracking him down on Alaspin. Meanwhile,
Flinx went about the difficult task of assigning quarters
to everyone on a ship that had not been designed with
passengers in mind.

"We've always been just a step behind you, Flinx,"
Truzenzuzex said. "On Moth we had to stop and deal
with the Qwarm, while you made your way to the shuttleport. Then you outdistanced us because we were
forced to take a commercial ship to Alaspin, one which
stopped several times along the way, while you raced
here directly. We were lucky to find you as soon as we
did."

They entered the spacious lounge, spacious because
Flinx enjoyed space and the *Teacher* had that to spare.
The room accommodated them all comfortably.

The philosoph gazed around approvingly. "A fine
ship you have for yourself, Flinx."

"Adequate" was the youth's response.

"I do not understand where the name came from."

"A whim." Flinx managed only a half-lie this time.
"I've always had thoughts about being a teacher."

"An admirable profession. One to which too few
beings dedicate themselves. I find most, sadly, to be
teaching because they have good minds but no imagination. Teaching is charity for the intelligent."

Leaving the lounge to Hasboga and September,
Flinx led the two scientists to the pilot's compartment.

Three walls were embroidered with controls, the fourth showed naked space.

"Where do you want to go?" he asked, hands poised over the ship's instrumentation.

For the first time, Truzenzuzex and Tse-Mallory did not have a ready answer. Both glanced at Ab, who had trailed the three forward and was now rhyming at a rapid pace. Flinx couldn't tell whether the philosoph was making any sense of the alien's verses.

"Actually," Tse-Mallory had to admit, "we don't know yet. Somewhere in the Blight, but we need at least a clue from your Ab. For now, head in the direction of Hivehom. It's best if we leave Alaspin's vicinity."

Flinx conveyed the requisite orders to the navigation computer, which responded promptly, though it hesitated at the lack of a specific destination. A halo of deep purple formed at the nose of the ship, visible manifestation of the great KK drive's posigravity field. At minimal acceleration, so as not to interact with Alaspin's gravity well, the *Teacher* began to move out of orbit. Once they were the minimum safe number of planetary diameters out, the drive would be fully engaged and the ship would leap ahead at a multiple of the speed of light.

"There's a ship coming into orbit." Flinx gazed interestedly at a gauge on the console.

"Not much traffic to this world," murmured Tse-Mallory. To Flinx's surprise, both he and Truzenzuzex moved to activate several sensor controls and the large screen.

"Monitor configuration," Tse-Mallory instructed as he manipulated several controls.

"Monitoring." Truzenzuzex's delicate truhands made fine adjustments.

Flinx was prepared to leave the ship's controls on automatic. However, he turned curiously instead of walking from the chamber. "Wait a minute. What's all the excitement about?" While Pip shifted on his shoulder, he stared at the two scientists, who were watching instruments with intense concentration. Flinx's gaze narrowed. "The incoming ship . . . You still haven't told me who hired the Qwarm. I think I can guess, judging from what you told me about certain forces who want to see the rogue destroy Carmague-Collangatta and Twosky Bright. But I can't be sure."

"We intend to tell you, Flinx." Tse-Mallory spoke without taking his attention from the controls beneath his hands. "Does it matter so much to you? It's Ab they're after."

"I'd like very much to know why someone's trying to murder me because of Ab. That is," he added sarcastically, "if it wouldn't be too much to ask, since I've given you the use of my ship."

Both scientists were immune to sarcasm. Truzenzuzex's truhands continued to fine-tune controls, but he beckoned Flinx to his side with a foothand. "You wish to know, Flinx." The youth moved alongside him. "There they are." He indicated the shape neatly focused on the computer tridee tracker. "Do you recognize that configuration? You are a bright human. I am certain your guess is correct. Now, who would stand to benefit most by the damage to Commonwealth production and population the rogue collapsar would cause?"

Flinx considered his supposition in the new light of the image displayed on the viewscreen. It confirmed what he had suspected, all right. But seeing physical proof was a good deal more ominous than simply supposing.

September and Hasboga walked into the piloting chamber. "I thought," September bellowed, "that since we're on our way, it might be fun to . . ." Frowning, he stopped. He squinted hard at the picture on the screen. "Funny . . . that looks like an AAnn courier ship." Hasboga looked questioningly at him. He ignored her, crossing the floor in several huge strides to peer closely at the screen. "No . . . no, by Pallanthian's Ghosts, it's a destroyer!" He turned a no-nonsense gaze on Tse-

Mallory. "What's an AAnn warship doing inside Commonwealth boundaries?"

"Boundaries, Mr. September?" Tse-Mallory tried to look innocent. "You can't draw boundaries in space."

"No, but you sure can on navigation charts," September shot back. "No one makes mistakes light-years deep, not with automatic positioning equipment."

"No one said they had made a mistake," Tse-Mallory's voice was even, composed. He returned his attention to the controls in front of him. "You needn't sound so melodramatic, September. You rave like a tridee fisherfax. Everyone puts too much reliance on boundaries. Absurd, when the boundary of the AAnn Empire and that of the Commonwealth are hundreds of light-years high, wide, and deep. You can't build a fence, not even with the best deep-range monitoring systems. You can monitor worlds, but not parsecs." He quieted for a moment to watch as the AAnn warship slipped into orbit around Alaspin.

"There is nothing on Alaspin capable of resisting a regular warship. So the AAnn will not make trouble. On the contrary, they will probably claim to be experiencing trouble of their own and request assistance. Mutual aid for emergencies involving deep-space ships is thoroughly covered by the treaties."

"What happens," September wanted to know, "when a Commonwealth peaceforcer shows up and detects no sign of damage on board?"

Tse-Mallory smiled softly. "Mr. September, the AAnn will not linger about Alaspin. They will satisfy themselves that what they have come for, meaning Ab, is no longer on the planet. Then they will depart rapidly. No doubt they are tracking us at this very moment." Hasboga stifled a gasp. "But while they may know about this ship, through Qwarm informants, they cannot be sure Ab is aboard. They must check Alaspin first. By the time they know for certain, we will be a long way elsewhere."

"Protests will be lodged over the unauthorized orbit," Truzenzuzex declared. "Word will reach Terra and Hivehom. There will be accusations, denials, apologies, concluded with promises not to do it again. We have done the same thing within the Empire. So long as nonstrategic worlds like Alaspin are involved and nobody gets killed, there's not much the offended side can do short of starting an interstellar war. The AAnn know they're not strong enough for that, and the Commonwealth is too conciliatory for it. So . . . nothing will happen."

"It might as far as we're concerned." Flinx looked significantly at the philosoph, who nodded slowly in response.

"True, Flinx. The presence of this ship means that the reptiles have lost patience with the Qwarm." He permitted himself a small sighing sound of satisfaction. "That is not surprising, considering how ineffective the assassin's clan has been. They could hardly know who has been interfering with them."

Tse-Mallory chuckled at that remark.

Truzenzuzex turned a somber gaze on Flinx. "This does not mean, however, that the Qwarm are finished with you. So long as they continue to believe you are responsible for their difficulties, they will continue to try to kill you."

September ventured a summation, "So we're running from both the reptiles and the Qwarm."

"And the Commonwealth and Church as well," Tse-Mallory added.

Flinx looked uncertain. "Why them, too?"

"Remember, Flinx," the former Chancellor Second admonished him, "those organizations believe Ab is nothing more than a wild wish in the minds of two senile renegades."

Now it was Truzenzuzex's turn to laugh, a rapid clicking of all four mandibles.

"The Qwarm are trouble enough, but I would rather deal with them than with minor bureaucrats. If we are detained officially, I wouldn't be surprised to see some minor functionary turn Ab over to them to keep the Empire pacified."

"Slow down, just a minute." Comprehension was beginning to dawn on Hasboga's dark features. "If we're going to avoid Commonwealth officials, how are you going to set Skua and me down anywhere where we can raise financing?"

"We'll put you down on Burley, or on Terra, or wherever you wish," Tse-Mallory assured her, "as soon as we have completed our little experiment."

"If you think I'm going to run off into the Blight and heaven knows where else with you in pursuit of some crazy theory, while the Qwarm and the AAnn try to kill you, you're out of your minds!" Her fury was exceeded only by her incredulity.

There was a brief moment of disorientation. A slight shudder passed through the *Teacher* indicating that they had just exceeded light-speed. Pulled by the KK field, the ship continued to accelerate.

When no one said anything, Hasboga walked over to stand next to Tse-Mallory. Eyes flashing, she shouted up at him, "I *demand* you put us down on the nearest developed Federation world!"

The scientist sounded contrite. "Sorry, can't do that. We have no time to waste. The mere presence of the AAnn destroyer within the Commonwealth indicates that they are growing desperate. We can't risk delays or detours. I think they cannot follow us, but the AAnn are efficient. They may be able to pursue us based on the particulate matter produced by this ship's KK generator. We cannot afford to linger. Several billion lives are at stake."

Fuming, she turned away from him. "Oh, come on! You've as much as said yourself that the Hur'rikku device is half myth. You can't really expect to find anything."

Tse-Mallory's eyes could not mask what he felt toward her at that moment. "Those whose death seems certain will climb a rope made of one straw, if such a rope can be provided. We are searching for that straw. Isili Hasboga, no one's personal desires are going to obstruct this search until it is concluded."

Hasboga looked ready to argue further, but Flinx interceded. "Please, Isili," he pleaded with her, "bear with them. Truzenzuzex and Bran Tse-Mallory are good humanx. If they didn't have a good reason for what they're doing I would never have agreed to provide them with a ship."

"Easy to say," she snapped angrily, "when your own life is at stake anyway!"

So ferocious was her reaction that Pip started, and stared threateningly at the source of the angry emanations being directed at his master. Flinx calmed the minidrag. The flying snake settled back on his shoulder, but kept a watchful cold eye on the woman.

Flinx spoke softly but firmly. "If that's the case, why didn't I leave Ab behind to be killed by the AAnn? True, it might not take the Qwarm off my back, but the AAnn would no longer have an interest in me. So maybe I have a little more than just self-preservation at stake, wouldn't you say?"

"I'm sorry." She looked away. "It's just . . . I've just had several years' work ruined, first by Otoid arrows, now by finding myself involved in something I couldn't care less about."

Unable to argue further with Flinx, she turned her fury on September. "What about you, stupid? You worked nearly as hard on the excavating as I did. Now it's behind us and we're broke. *Broke!* Don't you understand?"

He gazed down at her gently. "A stranger to impecuniosity I am not, silly bog. Me, I'm just a little ole hydrogen atom drifting in the galactic wind. Actually, I find the direction of our present drift kind of intriguing. Probably not profitable, but sometimes it's nice to enrich something besides one's pocket." Turning, he took a chair near the rear of the chamber. "Besides, I've been on Collangatta. Not Carmague, though I could always see it, hanging green-and-white in the sky overhead, and not Twosky Bright, but I've been to Collangatta. I liked the Collas. They're a friendly open sort. They know how to enjoy life. They made me feel welcome, something that doesn't always happen to me on a newly visited world. They made me feel at home.

"So, silly, before I see their world freeze over and turn into a round grave frosted with frozen gases, I'll take a chance to save it." He gazed jovially at Tse-Mallory. "Best thing this undertaking has going for it, near as I can see, is that the Commonwealth doesn't think it's worth trying. That's a good-enough recommendation for me." She turned away from him huffily, and he rose and turned her. She struggled, but couldn't move those massive arms.

"Isili, all accumulated wealth does is make you worry about the tax collector, and it's getting harder and harder to fool the computers. Plenty of time yet to acquire the stigma of wealth. Or, in your case, of fame."

"Do you really think that's it, Skua?" She gave him a pitying look. "That I'm desperate to get back to my pet project so I can have my fax in all the tridee tapes?"

"Not entirely," he admitted. "You're a little too devoted to science for that. But then, you're not wholly immune to it, either. You're human, Isili. It's a curse we all have to bear."

"Speak for yourself." The smooth interjection came from near the console.

September let Hasboga leave his grasp and looked that way. "I stand corrected, Your Bugship."

"Nothing personal." Truzenzuzex's reply was couched as mild amusement coupled with gratification. "Look at it this way, Hasboga." She kept her gaze resolutely elsewhere. "You've been unlucky enough to fall in with a couple of old fools, and you know what the old human saying says about them. So you might as well try to help instead of hinder us. There's nothing you can do about it anyway. We can be as fanatical about saving lives as you can be about exhuming their remains."

She whirled. "You're all crazy, every one of you!" She stalked out of the cockpit, heading for the lounge.

September ought to have been upset. He wasn't, Flinx noted. The giant accepted everything with an equanimity which hinted at great mental as well as physical assurance.

Abruptly, Flinx decided he liked the enormous human, whether or not the man was his true father. No, he would not try to coerce further information on that subject from September. He was beginning to realize that such knowledge would flow from September in his own time, and that patience would gain far more information than arguing.

Rising from the chair, September moved to follow his employer. He winked at Flinx. "Alcohol has a way of dissolving anger the way acid does plastic, feller-me-lad. Isili won't be really happy until she's digging up ancient junk again. But I think I can keep her fury at a level where she won't drive us all insane before this voyage is over."

Chapter Twelve

Long days passed as the *Teacher* chased its own field through emptiness. Tse-Mallory and Truzenzuzex employed a substantial part of the ship's computer in probing Ab, trying to make sense of rhymes which sometimes employed terms and words from six different languages at once, some of them no longer spoken anywhere, some using words that were fourthhand translations from the original. It was exhausting, frustrating work, made no easier by Ab's good-natured desire to make everything sound like Terranglo.

"We have formed a hypothesis," Truzenzuzex was saying to Flinx one day as they sat in the lounge listening to Ab burble endlessly nearby. "Bran and I have decided that not only is Ab not speaking nonsense, but that *everything* he says makes sense. We simply haven't the time or equipment to track down everything he is saying, to translate it properly. Half of our translations are largely intuitive, and the rest at least partially so."

Flinx's gaze went upward, to where Pip was darting lazily among the three-dimensional false clouds in the

simulated late-afternoon sky projected by instrumentation in the walls. "Everything seems to make sense to
Ab, but then, everything a madman says makes sense
to himself." He glanced at Ab. "I don't know how
you'll ever find the world you want from him."

Ab abruptly turned two blue eyes on Flinx. "Cannachanna, banarana, lemon pie and apple vana. What
ticks inside the helical mix?"

"There, you see?" Flinx said. "It's the same as . . ."
He stopped and stared at the philosoph. Tru was sitting on the thranx loungeseat, gazing blankly into the
distance. "Tru?"

Truzenzuzex stared a moment longer, then turned to
Flinx. "That's it."

Flinx felt groggy. *"What's* it?"

"The world . . . maybe." The philosoph was muttering to himself as he raced on four legs and foothands
for the lounge computer terminal. Still dazed, Flinx followed.

"It is an old Visarian name for a main sequence star
inside the Blight. The star is RNGC 1632 on Commonwealth charts." He was shouting commands to the
computer while trying to talk into the intercom at
the same time.

Tse-Mallory appeared in the room in response to the
more coherent instructions. The tall scientist was only
partially dressed, still wet from an unfinished shower,
and quite indifferent to his near nudity. "What's happened, ship-brother? Something at last?"

"Cannachanna, Bran."

While Truzenzuzex worked with incredible speed at
the terminal, Tse-Mallory walked over to sit next to
Ab. Water glistened on his body under the bright artificial light as he regarded the alien, who was playing
with his fingers.

"Cannachanna, remember. Remember Abalamahalamatandra." He was gazing unblinkingly into one blue
eye, doing things with his eyes and voice and hands.
"What about Cannachanna?"

Ab winked all four eyes in sequence and sang
pleasantly, "Go, go, go, fast, fast, fast. Needle-pie

death from underwear past. Kalcanthea tree for I am
. . ." and on and on, as usual.

But that was enough; it was a confirmation. Tse-
Mallory and Truzenzuzex came as close to kicking up
their heels as Flinx had ever seen them.

"The computer," Truzenzuzex said, when he got his
breath back and finally responded to Flinx's questions,
"has accepted the reference, given a transposition, and
plotted a course. We are on our way, at last. Praise to
the Hive!"

The most astonishing transformation the information
produced occurred not in the two scientists, but in Isili
Hasboga.

"You mean the Hur'rikku actually existed?" she
asked Tse-Mallory, her eyes shining in disbelief and
wonder.

"So it would seem. We're heading for a Hur'rikku
world right now. It's located in the proper position for
such a world, on the far center-side of the Blight.
That's where the Hur'rikku expansion would have
reached to when they encountered the Tar-Aiym. It's
also the logical place to establish a threat, to mount a
major weapons system."

"I can't believe it," she said, "I can't believe it. Such
things don't happen in real life."

"The incredible always happens in real life," Tse-
Mallory chided her. "It's the expected which makes up
most fiction."

"A Hur'rikku world," she was murmuring. "A
Hur'rikku world." She looked up with such naked
desire that Flinx was embarrassed. "We'll be the first
humanx to see it. Do you . . . do you think I might
have a chance to do some fieldwork?"

Tse-Mallory smiled; his voice was full of assurance:
"Hasboga, we're *all* going to be doing a great deal of
fieldwork. Or do you think we're simply going to orbit
the world the Hur'rikku inhabited, find a continent-
sized sign in symbospeech saying 'Ultimate Weapon—
Follow the Arrow,' and walk right up to it?"

She was so excited at the prospect of being the first
archeologist to set foot on a legendary world of a

mythical race that she hardly heard Tse-Mallory's stern sarcasm.

Flinx had been through the Blight once before. It looked no different from any other section of normal space, save for having a slightly higher population of stars than the Arm in which the Commonwealth lay. It still gave him the shivers. Once these myriad worlds had been home to dozens of intelligent races. Now only lower forms lived there, all higher varieties having been exterminated in the ravening plague unwittingly unleashed by the panicked Tar-Aiym half a million years ago.

Even those two usually aloof beings, Tse-Mallory and Truzenzuzex, were affected. They kept themselves busy with Ab and stayed out of the control cabin, stayed away from its wide port and its panorama of stars. Instead, they discussed abstruse philosophies in arcane languages, or played games of such complexity with the ship's computer than an onlooker could not even figure out who eventually won, much less how the game was played.

Three weeks passed when they announced that Ab possessed an approximate vocabulary of twenty-eight trillion words, in three million, four hundred sixty thousand languages, of which at least two million were no longer used and two hundred four thousand were purely mathematical.

These figures did not indicate the mind of an idiot.

Isili Hasboga, now expectant and happy, reveled in the comparative luxury of the *Teacher*. It was her first time on a private craft, since position and finances had always relegated her to economy-class transports whenever travel between worlds had been necessary.

What Hasboga found impressive merely amused September. His interest was in the practical workings of the ship. There were times when the giant worried Flinx, such as when he found September staring intently at some aspect of the *Teacher*'s construction. Eventually he relaxed, telling himself that if the giant discovered anything unusual about the ship, he would probably ascribe it to some vagary or peculiarity of the firm which had constructed it. Which would be true. Just so long as no one guessed at how peculiar the *Teacher*'s manufacturers were.

Flinx found he was left pretty much to himself. The ship ran without help. Checking and rechecking its smooth operation took little time. He had to find other excuses not to stare out the ports. What made him and the two scientists truly uncomfortable was not the emptiness of the inhabitable planets around them, but the inescapable deep-down fear that somewhere on one of those worlds a viable remnant of the Tar-Aiym's unstoppable plague still lurked, waiting to infect some unsuspecting explorer with an age-old malignancy.

The system of Cannachanna looked no different from many others Flinx had seen schematized on the ship's screen. There were only three planets circling the hot K-type sun. And unless the Hur'rikku were suited to extraordinary extremes of temperature and pressure, they could not have lived either on the massive, frozen gas giant circling farthest out or on the sun-blistered globe that skimmed scorchingly close to the primary. That left only the middle planet of the three. Though farther from its sun than Earth was from Sol it would still be a hot world. But at least it possessed an atmosphere humanx could breathe. It could support life. It was the only possibility.

"Of course," Tse-Mallory reminded everyone as they started surfaceward in the shuttle, "we have no evidence to show that the Hur'rikku were anything like ourselves, or even that they were a carbon-based form."

But then, they had little evidence of any kind concerning the Hur'rikku.

That this world had been inhabited by some race was amply confirmed by the *Teacher*'s scanners. All four major continents were dotted with ruins. They were extensive enough to indicate that at one time in the distant past the world circling Cannachanna had supported a sizable population.

With nothing else to go on, Truzenzuzex and Tse-

Mallory opted for touchdown near the largest city they could find. It was located near the west coast of the northern hemisphere's largest continent. The shuttle landed softly under Tse-Mallory's skilled direction, as Flinx stared out at a sky the color of molten iron. The star Cannachanna shone through the pulsing redness like an engorged blood vessel.

Pure white sand *shushed* under the shuttlecraft's skis as they touched down. Only a slight crosswind made the landing other than ordinary. Instrumentation indicated that the vast, mountainless plain they had set down on was hot. It was after midday, and the outside temperature registered nearly 45°C in the fresh shade of the shuttle.

The little group stepped down the ramp onto the white sand. Flinx and Hasboga were sufficiently dark-skinned not to require protection from the sun beating down relentlessly through crimson-hued clouds. Truzenzuzex was practically comfortable, except for the dryness of the air. He was the one who recommended and produced proper creams and sprays from the ship's dispensary to protect the more delicate skins of Tse-Mallory and September.

While the others stood in the shade of the shuttle wing, Truzenzuzex led Ab out onto the surface. Ab immediately kneeled and rhymed as he traced incomprehensible designs in the sand.

They listened intently as the philosoph addressed them: "Ab cannot be hypnotized, though the Tunnels know Bran and I have tried. But through various techniques I think I can gain his attention more closely than one could using normal speech. Doing so somehow depends on the pitch of one's voice.

"These last few days prior to our arrival Bran and I have been querying Ab constantly about the weapon. Since he has not provided us with any directions, we feel we might just as well start here and move from city to city, in the hope that something will trigger Ab to provide the proper response."

"Do we have to stay here?" Hasboga was staring yearningly at the distant city. Towers of well-preserved metal and unknown materials loomed tantalizingly over gypsum dunes.

"Hasboga, we are not here for simple exploration. My own curiosity presses me toward the city; common sense and a more desperate need hold me back from it." Truzenzuzex looked sad. "It must be this way, at least until we find what we have come for."

Hasboga was not appeased. "First you drag Skua and me all this way and then you tell me I can't so much as have a close look at one of the greatest discoveries in the history of humanx science. Here we are on the world of a race no one really believed even existed." She kicked angrily at the sand, sending a powdery white spray downwind.

They were standing on a world of hot ice, Flinx thought.

Tse-Mallory eyed her reprovingly. "This world will always be here, Isili Hasboga. Whereas Carmague-Collangatta and Twosky Bright will not be, unless we can find the weapon and make it work."

"Even if the thing is here, it probably isn't functional. You realize that, of course." September's gaze shifted from Truzenzuzex to Tse-Mallory.

The tall scientist smiled back at him and shrugged slightly. "We're nothing if not optimists, September. It's in the nature of humanxkind to defy the odds."

"That's the difference between us," September said, turning his attention also to the distant, archaic metropolis. "It's in the nature of Septemberkind to ride with the odds. That's how I've lived as long as—" He saw Flinx gesturing for attention. "Something happening, young feller-me-lad?"

Flinx was pointing at Ab. "He's going to do something."

Tse-Mallory's reply to September was forgotten. Even Hasboga's interest was distracted from the city.

Ab turned in place as if searching intently for something no one else could see. Finding a direction, he waddled off toward the southwest. When he got roughly ten meters from the shuttle, he stopped and hunted around his feet. After concluding a careful survey of the sand he was standing on, he sat down with a thump, reached out with three arms, and commenced etching a fresh slew of abstract patterns while singing to himself. He was as happy as any three-year-old in a sandbox.

"Wonderful." Hasboga threw her hair back and ran both hands over it. "The end of the noble quest. What do we do now?"

Though obviously disappointed, Truzenzuzex didn't show it in his reply. "We could not reasonably expect that the alien would immediately lead us to the weapon. Now we must begin our search in earnest." Hasboga's expression brightened, and the philosoph hastened to add, "From the air."

"Why the air?" she wanted to know, downcast.

"Before we commence the laborious task of examining these cities on foot, there is a chance Ab may recognize or be stimulated by some larger pattern."

Gathering up Ab, who as always came along without a fuss, they returned to the shuttle. The ramp was sucked in behind the last boarder, the engines engaged, and the little vessel turned to rise into the wind.

Behind, a few human and thranx footprints remained in the sand. Gentle wind began patiently to erase them.

Beginning with the largest on each continent, they went at high speed from city to city. Soon they were traveling over far smaller urban centers than the one they had set down next to. At each new city Truzenzuzex and Tse-Mallory would glance hopefully over at Ab. Each time Ab would stare delightedly at the new landscape beneath the shuttle, would rhyme ceaselessly, and then Truzenzuzex would read the computer interpretation of what Ab had said and the shuttle would change course once again.

Several days of such searching convinced Tse-Mallory that they might be on the planet a long, long time. Hearing this, Hasboga grew nearly as hot as the air they were flying through. She insisted on being set down in some city, *any* city, to pursue her work.

Unable to refute her arguments, Tse-Mallory and

Truzenzuzex finally agreed. She might discover something useful to them, and it would be quieter on board the shuttle without her.

September opted to join her, as much because the aerial search was beginning to bore him as for any other reason. They disembarked on the outskirts of the first city they had visited, taking along ample supplies and sufficient weaponry to defend themselves, although there had been no sign of hostile life.

Indeed, this world boasted little in the way of animal life and not much in the way of vegetation. Most of Cannachanna II's surface ran to desert, some low, some high. The largest living thing they had found so far was a sort of nervous-looking pink cactuslike plant which soared fifteen meters or more into the angry sky and was several meters around at the base. Its root system, Tse-Mallory observed, must be astonishing.

Water flowed below, rather than on top of the land. There was little in the way of large bodies of fresh water. The land showed the sameness as the cities. And each city was like the next, differing only in size. They were full of crumbling, disintegrating stonework and pitted metal structures, inhabited now only by insinuating winds and fading memories. The *Teacher*'s shuttle flew over each with the same hopes, departed with identical disappointment.

"The Tar-Aiym built better cities but fewer, judging from what we saw of Booster." Truzenzuzex was staring out at the desert sliding past beneath them. "That fits with what we know of the Hur'rikku's rumored prolificacy and helps to explain the Tar-Aiym's fright."

"You're sure that Ab's not one of them?" Flinx indicated the alien, who was strapped into a chair facing a wide viewport.

Tse-Mallory shook his head. "The shape of the doors we have seen on low passes is enough to demonstrate that, whatever else Ab is, he is not a Hur'rikku. They were much smaller than Ab, smaller than ourselves. Closer to the Otoid of Alaspin, if you need a race for comparison. Whereas the Tar-Aiym, as near as we can tell from similar evidence on their world of

Booster, were massive creatures, far larger even than your friend September. And yet," he mused, staring out over the wastelands of metal and rock and sand, "the tiny Hur'rikku succeeded in terrifying the greater Tar-Aiym to the point where they lost control of their military science and created something which ultimately destroyed them all."

Truzenzuzex looked unhappy as he preened his antennae with a truhand. "We are wasting time, I fear. We cannot spend forever on this world. Another week, and I recommend returning to hire additional, nongovernment help." At Flinx's look of surprise he added: "It is in my nature to be impatient, friend Flinx."

As the shuttle banked sharply to leave the city they had just inspected, the philosoph slumped in his lounge-seat. "Ab still shows no indication of responding to anything on this world. I fear that he might not react to the weapon even if we passed directly over it. And since we have no idea what to look for, if it does not resemble a humanx weapon we could pass the thing by in equal ignorance. How many cities have we inspected, ship-brother?"

"Fifty-five, counting the last."

Truzenzuzex made a sound indicative of mild disgust mixed with personal recrimination. "We could check out a thousand fifty-five, I'm afraid, without any hope of success."

His companion smiled back at him stolidly. "Possible, but we must examine those thousand and however many more. Three worlds await our—"

Truzenzuzex waved resignedly. "Yes, I know, I know. But it seems so hopeless. If we could only pry some clue, some hint as to where the weapon was kept, out of Ab, we might find it. On Booster the location of the Krang was evident from its size, its position of isolation and importance, and the uniqueness of its construction. We have detected nothing similar on this world, nothing out of the ordinary in any city."

It was then that Flinx, keyed by Truzenzuzex's words, had one of those rare moments of intuition which he could never predict. Yet that flash of intuition probably was not the result of his special talents at all. There was nothing extraordinary about the thought that occurred to him. It might simply have been that he, unlike the scientists, could think only of simple possibilities. He had already voiced half a hundred opinions on the possible location of the weapon prior to this one. None had been worthwhile. But this one definitely was.

"If I," he said casually, rubbing the back of Pip's head, "had built a really powerful weapon, I'd want to make awful sure that if it went off accidentally no one would get hurt."

"In the ocean, perhaps?" mused Tse-Mallory uncertainly. "But there are signs that the oceans were heavily used, perhaps as a food source. We have seen no place of sufficient isolation to construct or locate such a weapon."

Truzenzuzex left his antennae alone. "Not on this planet, no. I would not put a device capable of destroying a collapsar on any inhabited world."

Tse-Mallory merely nodded slowly, comprehending. The philosoph went to the shuttle controls and reset its course for the camp set up in the northern hemisphere by September and Hasboga several weeks ago.

"We have studied this world in hopes of finding something huge and different. The weapon could be small and ordinary-looking as well. But before we try combing every building, I think it behooves us to try your theory, Flinx."

Flinx shook his head. "But if it's in this system and not on this planet, how do we find it?"

"Your same thought holds, Flinx." Truzenzuzex leaned away from the controls. "Any race cautious enough to place such a dangerous device off its world would take care not to lose track of it. They would want to know where it was at all times. As yet we have not monitored persistent surface sources of radiation for any energy traveling out into space. Such energy should be produced by the most sophisticated, reliable machinery the Hur'rikku could construct. They would be designed to be long-lasting and self-repairing, in case of peripheral damage."

September was sick of the desert and rejoined them willingly and gladly. Hasboga reacted to the word that they might be leaving the planet permanently somewhat less enthusiastically. She was on the verge, she assured them, of uncovering secrets of the Hur'rikku which would keep Commonwealth researchers busy for decades. September half convinced, half coerced her onto the shuttle.

"We may have to return tomorrow, if this idea reveals nothing," Tse-Mallory said in an effort to placate her. "We may not discover any energy being beamed offplanet. A few circumpolar and equatorial orbits should be enough to tell."

Hasboga fumed and argued and cried and having no choice, gave in.

Sensors on board the *Teacher* had previously recorded over a hundred sources of radiation from still-functioning Hur'rikku machinery. Many seemed to be homing beacons. These were located on the outskirts of vast urban areas, near spacious plains that might once have been shuttleports or some other kind of staging area.

Three such beams were still broadcasting with enough power to reach deeply into space, well beyond where an incoming craft would need to pick them up. One beam emerged from the ground near the largest city on the south polar continent and dissipated itself in the general direction of Sagittarius. Flinx was more tempted than he could say to try to follow that immensely powerful radiant arrow to its ultimate destination.

But they desperately needed to locate something somewhat closer to home. So Flinx had the computer plot the beam's course for future reference. Someday, perhaps . . .

A second beam led the *Teacher* and its anxious occupants to the fourth moon of the peripheral gas giant. They traced it to some small ruins, better preserved than any they had seen on the inhabited world itself.

There was some erosion, however, since the moon possessed an atmosphere of its own. They had difficulty convincing Hasboga they couldn't afford to linger near the wonderfully intact Hur'rikku structures.

The third beam directed them to a fourth planet, one the ship's instruments had not detected during their initial rapid approach to the Cannachanna system. That was not surprising, however: The fourth planet was less a world than a drifting moon, about a third the size of Earth's. It orbited Cannachanna twice as far out as the gas giant did. It was a bleak, meteor-scoured globe, relentlessly uninviting, coated with a thin crust of frozen methane and ammonia. It had no free atmosphere. One side always faced sunward; the other perpetually gazed at the abyss of interstellar space.

They found a tiny receiver on Cannachanna IV. The beam from the Hur'rikku world ended there. A quick search of the receiving installation revealed only receiving equipment. There was nothing remotely like a free-standing device or weapon. Everything was tied in to the receiving station.

The team commenced a slow, low-orbit probe of the moon-world's surface. Detectors showed nothing below them but reflective frozen gas and dead rock.

Truzenzuzex was watching the monitor's monotonous reports flow dutifully to readouts in the piloting chamber. "This is the end, I suppose," he said dolefully. "We might as well attempt to follow the first transmission to Sagittarius." He shook his shining, jewel-eyed head. "I fear I am almost too old to make such a journey."

Tse-Mallory's expression was equally disconsolate, even as he tried to sound optimistic. "There is still a chance. We have not finished the survey yet. And we can always return to the second planet and begin again. The supposition we're pursuing may have been in error."

"True," agreed the philosoph.

"Gentlesirs." Flinx glanced back from his position by the monitors. "There's an artifact ahead of us."

That announcement precipitated a rush by the two

scientists toward the smaller screens located in the main console. Sure enough, according to the instruments they were approaching a comparatively small solid object of indeterminate composition. It remained stable above the small planet and lay in a straight line with the transmission ending on the rocky globe's opposite side.

With all instruments operating and alert for any sign of a reaction from the device, the *Teacher* nudged cautiously closer.

A fourth voice added itself to the general discussion: "See flivver run and diver, hopscotch moplatch, puddin'n thatch a house and teach a mouse." Ab lectured them in that vein for half an hour, then turned away and resumed his solitary singing.

Truzenzuzex ran the entire recorded dialogue through the vocabulary they had laboriously constructed for Ab. It produced one recognizable Terranglo word: *"Bang."*

The philosoph could hardly contain his excitement. "Gentlesirs, I think we've found our weapon."

But the actual sight of the artifact, when they had drawn near enough to inspect it visually, was disappointing. Certainly it displayed none of the visual awesomeness of the quiescent Tar-Aiym weapon, The Krang—or, for that matter, the impressiveness of many humanx weapons Flinx had seen or heard of.

September was urged forward, to venture his opinion. It was not complimentary. "A single SCCAM shell would make basic particles of that thing. That's the most pitiful excuse for an ultimate weapon anyone ever dreamed up."

"A germ," Tse-Mallory pointed out, "does not look particularly impressive either, but a certain variety once wiped out every creature in the Blight, including both the Tar-Aiym and the Hur'rikku."

Flinx edged the ship in until they were floating only fifty meters from the artifact. It was about a hundred meters in length, a roughly cylindrical shape with four curving sides which met at two pointed ends. Things that looked like long antennae protruded another few meters from each of the two ends. It resembled a four-sided banana, only it was straight instead of curved.

The artifact was a rusty-brown color, but it didn't look quite like metal. Starlight and the observation lights of the *Teacher* gleamed off its sides. It had a candy-slick luster reminiscent of plastic. But it wasn't a plastic, either, Flinx mused as he studied the readouts.

Where two curved sides met, the material assumed a translucence completely out of keeping with its otherwise solid appearance. Turning a work beam on the surface through one port, they discovered that the entire substance was translucent, although no matter how powerful the light shined on it, one could only see about a meter into the thirty-meter depth of the artifact.

The light also revealed that all four sides were engraved with a tiny, surprisingly florid script. Small protrusions and indentations broke the smoothness of the sides with a decidedly random regularity.

They could find nothing that looked like an entrance port, muzzle, trigger, exhaust, generator—in short, nothing that would lead an onlooker to believe he was examining a weapon. It was a hundred-meter length of metal-glass-plastic something that was determinedly innocuous in appearance and inert in state.

At the scientist's urgings, Flinx guided the ship in a slow circle under, around, and back over the top of the long alien form. Then the *Teacher* slipped between the small planet and the device. If this maneuver interrupted any vital transmission or broadcast, it didn't show in the continued inactivity of the device.

Tse-Mallory looked anxious. "That's the weapon, all right. Ab confirmed it. It's *got* to be the weapon." Flinx had never seen him so nervous.

Alongside him, compound eyes regarded the motionless artifact unblinkingly. Then the philosoph moved to activate specific sensors on the control console.

Hasboga appeared, looking sleepy. Her lethargy vanished when she saw the artifact. September quieted her, tried to explain what they had found and what they were doing. She listened, but her real attention was reserved for the inscriptions cut into the device's flanks.

"A diffusion scan won't penetrate the material." Truzenzuzex's gaze moved from one readout to the next. "Still no evidence of any movement relative to the planet below or to our ship. Nor is the artifact emitting any radiation—at least, not any variety this vessel is equipped to detect. And there is no connection of any sort to the surface below." He turned from the controls and regarded them thoughtfully. One truhand rubbed idly at his lower mandibles.

"This exceptionally unexceptional ghost from the Hur'rikku past *must* be the weapon. We have Ab's one significant, if colloquial, reference to it. We have the fact that it *is* here, in the safest place to store a powerful weapon in this system. Yet it persists in maintaining a pose of innocence. What we have observed on the Hur'rikku world does not prepare me to accept this as a deception. I confess I do not know how to proceed to prove it is otherwise."

"How is it supposed to work?" Hasboga edged closer to the curving main viewport, beyond which the device drifted. "Not that I care how big an explosion it makes, you understand."

Tse-Mallory did not smile. "We don't know that it explodes."

"Well, does whatever it's supposed to do. But I'd like to have a closer look at those inscriptions on it."

"You may have your chance," said Truzenzuzex. "We may have to decipher them in order to learn how the device operates. Certainly the mechanism has not manifested itself to us."

"The inscriptions might not be instructions," Flinx pointed out prosaically. "They might simply say 'This ultimate weapon manufactured by H'pel's Ultimate Weapons, Inc.', or something like that."

A valentine-shaped head swiveled to face him. "We'd best hope otherwise, Flinx."

Tse-Mallory indicated agreement. "I feel like a Neanderthal cornered by a Smilodon. Someone has just handed me Mr. September's Mark Twenty and I have ten seconds to figure out how to use it. Probably I'd

end up employing it as a club." He gestured at the
floating enigma. Lights from the *Teacher*'s ports shone
eerily on the dull-colored surface. "If we aren't careful,
we're liable to end up like that Neanderthal, looking
dumbly down the barrel of a Hur'rikku weapon while
we pound on its trigger. We'd better be careful which
of those protrusions and indentations on its surface we
stick our manipulative digits into. I'd much rather learn
how to activate the device from a distance. However,"
he added, without evident concern for his personal
safety, "if someone has to jump up and down on it to
make it go off, that is what we'll do.

"But we won't do it here, where it will do no good.
First we must convey the device to the present location
of the rogue." He turned his gaze on Flinx. "There's a
planetless binary system in the path of the rogue. We
should reach that spatial vicinity at the same time as or
slightly after the rogue if we depart from here now and
drive at maximum velocity for rendezvous. We will
have the rare opportunity to observe the influence of a
massive collapsar on another stellar object. We will
also see," he said, directing his words subtly to Isili
Hasboga, "what will happen to the suns of Carmague-
Collangatta and Twosky Bright if our research turns
out to have been incorrect."

"Suppose that's the case." Hasboga looked subdued.
"What will you do then?"

Tse-Mallory smiled very slightly. "Then Tru and I
will go hunting down the next best legend." He glanced
back to Flinx. "I think there is ample room. The cargo
hold is standard?"

Flinx nodded. "The *Teacher* was modeled on a
small freighter. I haven't had any occasion to handle
freight"—another small lie—"but there's no reason why
the hold shouldn't be functional." He indicated the
Hur'rikku artifact filling the port. "The ship's hold
should be able to contain several objects that size."

The *Teacher*'s attitude was altered so that the great
cargo doors in its tail were facing the object. Flinx operated the hatches and watched telltales indicate that
the huge metal panels were performing properly.

The hold was little more than a vast open sphere within which all kinds of cargo could be stored at null g. At present the cavernous space was empty. There would be plenty of room for the Hur'rikku device.

Gradually Flinx activated the posigravity tractor beams, used for manipulating large cargo. Every muscle in his body was a touch tenser than usual. No one knew if the powerful tractors would have an adverse effect on the artifact. Only instruments indicated when the tractors locked on, however. The artifact remained as quiescent as before.

"Slide it into the ship, Flinx," said Tse-Mallory, watching different sensors. "Slowly."

Through the use of rear-facing tridees they were able to see the artifact. Tse-Mallory looked up, smiled, and nodded with a touch of impatience. Several minutes had passed.

"It's all right, Flinx. You can bring it in now."

Flinx glanced up from the controls, confusion and uncertainty mixing in his expression. "Bran, that's what I've been trying to do. The tractors are set on maximum pull—but the thing's not budging."

Chapter Thirteen

Truzenzuzex and Tse-Mallory checked instrumentation, confirmed that the ship's cargo handlers were operating properly. Everything read normal, performed efficiently—yet the artifact refused to enter the *Teacher*. Flinx had an idea, which Tse-Mallory quashed.

"Why don't we just back the ship around the object?"

"No good, Flinx," Tse-Mallory explained. "If the tractors can't move the object, then I'm not sure it will move along with the ship. Try again."

Flinx did so, then tried a third time, each time at a different setting, using the four tractors in differing configurations.

Hasboga looked awed. "It hasn't moved a centimeter." She stared at the screens.

"Young feller-me-lad?" September looked from the screens over to the control console. "What's your manipulation capacity?"

"Two hundred and fifty thousand tons, dead-weight

mass, per tractor. I've tried employing them along the same axis, one million tons of pulling power. No good—it doesn't move."

September looked thoughtful as he stroked his chin. "Even if that artifact is unusually dense stuff, I don't imagine it weighing anywhere near that much."

" 'Unusually dense' leaves a great deal of room for variation, Mr. September," said Truzenzuzex. "The duralloy this vessel is made of is composed of exceptionally dense metals." A truhand fluttered in the direction of the screens showing the device. "That object may be composed of super-dense material."

"Maybe it's as dense as the collapsar," ventured Hasboga.

Truzenzuzex stifled a laugh; the woman was not a physicist. "If that were so, then our device would weigh as much as several galaxies. I think that unlikely. We will have to find something more powerful to pull with."

"Or push with," Flinx murmured.

Truzenzuzex made a sound indicative of agreement mixed with hesitancy. "There are other ways to employ a KK field."

"I see what you're thinking, you two." Tse-Mallory looked doubtful and not a little worried. "I don't know. It's risky, very risky."

"But worth trying." Flinx was sure it would work. "Instead of trying to pull the device, we'll position the *Teacher* behind it, line up on course, and push with the field."

"Why not just pull it with the field?" Hasboga asked.

"No," Tse-Mallory replied, "we have to try to push. A Kurita-Kinoshita field is spherical when formed, but when you pass light-speed it becomes teardrop-shaped. The tip of the drop extends only to include that solid matter which is firmly connected to the field projector, meaning the ship. It's possible, but if the field contracted sufficiently, and it should at the speed we'll be traveling, then we could lose the artifact."

"We are much more certain of retaining control of it

if it is riding in the front bulge of the field." Truzenzuzex was gesturing with all four truhands and foothands now. "Assuming that the field exerts sufficient pressure to move it, which is by no means certain."

"We could lose the artifact that way also, Tru."

"That is so, ship-brother," the philosoph conceded. "But can you think of anything else to try?"

"No. No." Tse-Mallory had to admit there was nothing else to do but try it.

"I'm not sure I understand your worry, Bran," Flinx confessed.

Truzenzuzex tried to explain, although spatial physics was not his area of expertise either. "Even in the leading bulge of the sun mass, the Kurita-Kinoshita field is narrow, Flinx. The higher the speed, the flatter and more angular the bulge. If we should misjudge slightly coming out of Kurita-Kinoshita space, space-plus—or improperly form the field—then all or part of the Hur'rikku artifact could emerge into normal space while we are still in space-plus. The result would be either partial disintegration of the object or, if it drops whole into normal space, its loss. We would continue to travel at plus-light-speed velocity, while the artifact would be kicked out at an angle from our present course into normal space, at a speed of several . . . well, before we could so much as twitch an antenna, let alone slow speed or reverse direction or both, the artifact would have long vanished. Our chances of relocating it in free space would border on the infinitesimal."

Flinx looked crushed. "Maybe we'd better try something else, then."

But it was the querulous Tse-Mallory who objected to that idea. "No, Flinx. Tru is right. We have to try pushing with the KK field." His eyes wandered to the waiting artifact. "Even if it is resting in a stasis field, no stasis field can resist the pressure of a KK drive."

"You left out one thing," September interrupted. "Known. No known stasis field can resist a KK."

Flinx edged the *Teacher* around until the great curving disk of the field projector was properly positioned with regard to the floating artifact. Truzenzuzex had the computer check all positional calculations four times to make certain the field would engulf the Hur'rikku device from precisely the required distance.

"All clear here," said Tse-Mallory, looking up briefly from the readouts he was monitoring. "Engage the drive, Flinx."

Within the immensely complex instrumentation of the ship, Flinx's subsequent instructions were computer-conveyed to the appropriate sections. A diffuse sphere of radiant purple energy began to form in front of the *Teacher*'s projector. No one in the ship's piloting chamber could see the field begin to take shape. It was hidden in front of the projecting disk. So was the Hur'rikku artifact. But the field appeared in the form of changing readouts and shifting dials on the chamber's instruments.

Very slowly, the *Teacher* began to accelerate out of the Cannachanna system. It passed through the space where the alien device had been floating. Since it was no longer there, it was proper to assume that the artifact was now perilously ensconced slightly forward of the KK field's gravitational nexus.

Muted congratulations mixed with expressions of relief on board the ship. "It's got to be there," Flinx confirmed after an instrument check. "We're using twice the power to accelerate half as fast as normal. The ship is handling the load all right, though."

Tse-Mallory lapsed into thought, pleased but puzzled. "I thought that once the artifact was moved, the stasis field would either collapse or be left behind. Yet if Flinx is correct, Tru, the stasis field is traveling with the device."

"There may be no stasis field involved. Our first guess, involving super-dense construction, may be the correct one. There is also a type of stasis field that is not really a stasis field in the way we know it. A theoretical state of matter that is called FCI, fixed cosmic inertia." His mandibles moved idly, nibbling at one another. "I wonder, I wonder. Such a state of matter has been postulated but not proven mathematically. Not yet. An FCI object would *appear* to be motionless, Bran. Yet what one would see would not be the object itself, but only its most recent manifestation. The real object would consist of undetectable but very real energy built up within the object itself. The object moves, or seems to, with us. But the energy it has built up trails behind it."

"Tru," a bewildered Flinx, interrupted, "you're leaving me behind, too."

"Briefly, Flinx," the philosoph explained, "what we may have ahead of us is an object that appears to move but in reality is motionless—the universe shifts around it. If we could *move* it, it would release its true inertial energy." He shook his head. "I still do not understand how that could be sufficient to affect a collapsar." He moved to a computer terminal. "I have work to do, gentlesirs."

Straining to move something which Truzenzuzex insisted wasn't really moving, the *Teacher* raced out of the long-dead system, carrying them at maximum speed back through the Blight. Flinx tried with every instrument on board to detect the trail of energy which Tru hypothesized the Hur'rikku device was leaving behind it. He found nothing.

However, if what Tru suspected was correct, then the artifact had been building up FCI force for over a half million years. Trying to imagine what such power could do (if indeed it existed) if released in one small place simultaneously left Flinx a little dizzy.

So instead he found a small ball, and he and Pip played a lot of catch.

What no one had yet detected, since it had taken great care not to be detected, was another ship, which had arrived in the system of Cannachanna shortly behind them. Instead of following them to the world of the Hur'rikku, it had been content to remain just behind the horizon of the gas giant, concealed by that protosun's energy fields and extensive tenebrous atmosphere.

It had remained there, monitoring their activity without rest. While its occupants had to take care not to be observed, a caution which somewhat inhibited the efficiency of their surveillance, they were still able to track the *Teacher*'s hasty departure and plot its course.

As soon as the *Teacher* passed into space-plus, this small but very fast craft sped at engine-warping velocity to a thinly populated world on the fringes of the Commonwealth. There it made contact with a mining colony which was as efficient in its true function as it was at its geological deception.

By now the *Teacher* was many parsecs distant. That did not matter to the crew of the small vessel. In conveying their information to the inhabitants of the station, they had accomplished their assigned task.

The beings who had piloted that ship and who ran the purported mining station below were neither human nor thranx. They had longish mouths filled with sharp, pointed teeth, and expressions which conveyed their utter contempt for anything not like themselves. Their skins were hard, shiny, and scaly, the minds beneath crested skulls active and devious.

Carefully scattered throughout the Commonwealth were others of their kind, some disguised surgically to resemble men. (None were disguised to look like thranx, for these were a bipedal, two-armed folk, in no way insectoid. Their blood, unlike that of Earthly reptiles, was warm. And though they preferred a warm, dry climate, they now moved vigorously about the cold world they occupied.

There were several functional mine shafts around the station. The AAnn occupied this borderline world by treaty with the Commonwealth, so appearances were important. The mine shaft beneath the station itself contained, not valuable mineral deposits, but a subatomic-particle acceleration communicator, known more commonly as a deep-space beam.

Metamorphosed into a stream of charmed positively charged quarks, a message could be flashed from accelerator to accelerator, world to world, at dizzying speed, far faster than a restricted tridee beam. A tridee beam employed high-speed leptons to carry its messages. Tridee leptons and Kurita-Kinoshita sun fields traveled through space-plus. But the less-than-perceptible quarks moved through something so esoteric it could not be properly described, and so had been labeled null-space, or space-minus.

At each successive receiving station the positively charged charmed quarks were carefully redirected and reaccelerated to their next destination. Eventually they would reach an ultimate destination. Instead of being reaccelerated there, the unstoppable beam would be read by a subelementary-particle counter and its message deciphered. Only another counter lying directly in the path of the message could intercept it, and the chances of that ever happening were as remote as the region where such beams eventually ended up. Only an enormous vessel, not smaller than a dreadnought, was large enough to contain a deep-space-beam station.

So the *Teacher* raced on, oblivious to the fact that its probable destination had been guessed. Its inhabitants were of mixed emotions. But no matter what each individual wished for in the way of an eventual destination, all hoped that their journey would soon meet with success.

Months later, they finally arrived in the vicinity of the Velvet Dam. A swirling blackness, the dark nebula hid everything behind it from view of any humanx-occupied world.

"That is what the rogue will be coming through in less than nineteen years, on collision course with the sun of Twosky Bright." Tse-Mallory studied the shuddery emptiness coolly. "Unless we do something to stop it. It will announce itself to general and amateur astronomers then because of the hole it will leave behind as it sucks in gas and particles from the nebula."

Flinx stared at the vast black brush stroke through which only a few large suns shone faintly and tried to imagine it with a hole cut out of its middle. The scale of the danger they were soon to confront was beginning to be appreciated. It was one thing to talk about a collapsar, another thing entirely to confront it.

Under Tse-Mallory's instructions, the *Teacher* altered its course slightly for the last time, to rendezvous with the predicted position of the binary system and the onrushing collapsar. The Hur'rikku artifact remained in position ahead of the field center.

September compared their feat thus far to a seal swimming the Atlantic Ocean with a ball balanced on its nose. Flinx knew what the Atlantic Ocean was—it was one of Terra's three major bodies of water. But a seal?

"It looks kind of like a Largessian, young feller-me-lad," the giant informed him. "Only smaller, without hands, and with a smaller head."

That description enabled Flinx to conjure a picture, though it was difficult to imagine one of the lazy natives of Largess swimming an ocean while balancing anything on its nose.

Days passed, and the ship gradually decellerated under the two scientist's careful supervision. They could still drop the device in a trillion cubic kilometers of empty space. Having successfully brought it this far, neither man nor thranx was prepared to risk losing it. Finally they slowed to a point where everyone experienced a brief instant of somewhere-elseness and nausea. The *Teacher* had returned to normal space.

Ahead of them should be the twin-sun system newly catalogued as RNGC 11,432 and 11,433. Everyone hurried to the fore observation port, in the observation-piloting blister, as the ship was positioned to provide them with a view.

No one spoke about the sight which greeted them until Tse-Mallory said quietly: "Gentlesirs and lady, we are a few days late. The rogue has already arrived."

What lay slightly to one side of them as the *Teacher* slowed to a stop was a sight that almost precluded description. The rogue, the multiple collapsar, could of course not be directly observed, but its effects could. And they could be heard, as was amply proven when Flinx opened all sensor equipment to monitor the precise position of the rogue. A violent, teeth-grating scream filled the room before Flinx, in a cold sweat, could lower the volume.

Hasboga winced, her hands covering her ears to shut out that inorganic wailing. Her eyes were squinched tightly closed. Next to her, September reached out with a comforting arm. No humorous twinkle was in his eyes—not now.

Flinx turned the sound level down to where the howl was bearable, but he could not bring himself to cut it out entirely. There was something mesmerizing about that shriek, an effect caused as much by the knowledge of what was behind it as by the sound itself. He became aware of his own rapid breathing, and forced himself to calm down.

"What *is* it?" Hasboga glanced up at September and leaned against his massive shoulder. "I've never heard anything like it in my life."

"I doubt anyone has, Isili." September wore a peculiar expression as he regarded the phenomenon visible through the port. "A man being killed slowly has a tendency to scream. Interesting to learn that a star reacts the same way."

"You are romanticizing," Truzenzuzex commented. "That so-called scream is only the result of torn-apart matter releasing energy as it is sucked into the collapsar."

Flinx reflected that although the philosoph's explanation was more accurate, September's provided a more effective description.

Leaving the controls on automatic, he moved in for a better look. RNGC 11,432 was an orange, K-9 supergiant. Its companion star, which rotated counterclockwise as opposed to its giant brother, was far smaller but much hotter, a yellow-green furnace.

From each sun, according to the direction of its rotation, a long tendril of glowing matter extended to Flinx's right. One curled in a tightening clockwise spiral to vanish into nothingness; the other twisted inward from the opposite direction. Around both tendrils clustered a vast, diffuse cloud of energy particles and gases which had also been pulled from both stars. A black circle rested in the center of that cloud, a circle that looked like a black cutout on fluorescent paper. At its center was a minuscule point with the mass of suns.

How many stars lay crushed and collapsed to that point? Dozens, hundreds—maybe thousands. How much of the universe had the wanderer already gobbled up? Flinx envisioned whole galaxies with thin black lines running through them, forming the trail of the wandering rogue where suns, worlds, populations had disappeared.

Was there a pit in Andromeda? Perhaps a hole in the midst of the Magellanic Clouds? Yet that was the force they were going to try to counter with the metalglass-plastic something riding in front of the *Teacher*. Something which September had estimated could be reduced to less than dust by a single SCCAM projectile.

Even the old philosoph's description of what FCI could mean seemed insignificant by comparision with an object which presently was draining the mass of two stars as easily as a sponge could soak up two drops of water.

Too bad for Carmague and Collangatta, Flinx mused silently. Too bad for the bright star of humid Twosky Bright. Too bad, too sad for the untold vanished worlds already destroyed in unknown galaxies unimaginable ages ago.

They could throw a billion SCCAM shells, a hundred suns at the rogue. Nothing could destroy it. The billion SCCAM projectiles would add infinitesimally to the collapsar's mass. The hundred suns would add a bit more. Both would only make the rogue that much more powerful, that much more destructive.

Flinx was on the verge of suggesting they turn and go home when Tse-Mallory looked over at him and said matter-of-factly, "I suppose we might as well get started."

September commented without smiling, "You don't mean that now that you've seen the thing you're going to try to do something with that little-bitty hunk of iron or whatever it is?"

Truzenzuzex regarded the towering human seriously. "The legend says it can do something. We are here. We will remain or track the rogue until we learn whether it can or not. We have nothing to lose."

"Listen," September argued softly, "the biggest bomb imaginable would only add to the rogue's mass, right?"

Truzenzuzex and Tse-Mallory did not reply.

"Stubborn, I see. Well, it's in a good cause. I wonder how much a miracle masses?" He guided Hasboga toward the door.

"Where are we going, Skua?"

"To the cabin. I'm wasting my time trying to argue with brain-cases. They may set that device off. It won't stop the collapsar, but I wouldn't be surprised if it destroys *us*. If I can't talk them out of it, I want to die the best way I know how."

"How's that?" she inquired mischievously. As they left the room he was leaning over and whispering in her ear.

The philosoph watched them depart. "Fatalist." He looked peeved.

There was something other than a touch of reproval in Tse-Mallory's voice. "True, Tru, but a fatalist with style." More serious, he faced his friend. "He's right, you know. We may accomplish nothing here other than our own destruction."

"Does that mean you believe we have a choice, ship-brother?"

Tse-Mallory reacted almost angrily. "Of course not! Flinx, activate the engines and back us away."

Using minimal power, the *Teacher* left the mysterious Hur'rikku device once again floating freely in space. Or, Flinx reflected, if you believed Truzenzuzex's theory, space shifted around the stationary device.

Under the scientist's instructions, he positioned the ship broadside to the device. It sat there in view of the starboard observation port, as innocuous-looking, enigmatic, and inert as it had been in the system of Cannachanna.

Flinx had given himself over to the advice of two far wiser heads than his own. A request for new instructions produced a disconcerting reply from Tse-Mallory.

"I don't know what to do next, Flinx. I suspect the next logical step is for some of us to go outside and see what we can make of those protrusions and depressions on the artifact's surface."

Truzenzuzex agreed. Both were preparing to don suits when an insistent, deceivingly gentle beeping from the main pilot's console distracted Flinx's attention. Leaving the two scientists to their discussion, he walked over and studied the active readout. It was one he hadn't had occasion to use often before, but there was no mistaking that urgent call. He wanted to make certain before causing any alarm, so he switched to printout for confirmation.

SHIP OR SHIPS APPROACHING

"Bran, Tru," he called out, louder when they didn't respond immediately. While he waited for a response, Flinx began activating other sensory instruments and demanding information. Both scientists came over, saw the brief readout, and moved rapidly to monitor other consoles.

Lighting up the main screen provided them with a picture of eleven dots arranged on a grid. Other sensitive machines added distance, direction, and velocity. They were not seeing the ships, of course, only the energy manifestations of their respective drive fields.

Compared to the other ten dots, the one traveling approximately in the center of the configuration was enormous. "That's a dreadnought," Tse-Mallory observed with frozen indifference. He glanced glumly at his companions. "Analysis of drive fields indicates they're not humanx vessels. It's a war sphere, all right."

"A battle formation, this deep in the Commonwealth?" Flinx couldn't believe the AAnn would go to such extremes. But then, it would require a fleet a hundred times the size of the force nearing them to attack and possibly destroy three fortified worlds. Probably the AAnn were taking what appeared to be a reasonable gamble to insure that the rogue was not diverted from its predicted path.

"This is a very sparsely explored, uninhabited region of Commonwealth-claimed territory, Flinx," Truzenzuzex pointed out. "Anyone could slip in and out of here undetected with comparative ease and safety."

"How much time?" Tse-Mallory eyed his shipbrother hopefully.

Truzenzuzex studied the instruments below faceted orbs. "A dreadnought, several cruisers, the rest destroyers or research vessels." He glanced over at Bran Tse-Mallory. "They will drop into normal space in ten minutes." Thranx did not perspire, but Flinx had the impression that the philosoph was trying to.

"If we're going to get away . . ." Flinx said, starting toward the pilot's console. A strong hand caught his left arm in a gentle but unbreakable grip of restraint. Pip stirred nervously on Flinx's other shoulder, and his master also sensed the seriousness in the tall scientist's mind.

"We cannot simply leave, Flinx. We must make an attempt to use the device. It may be that it is activated by what it eventually destroys. In this case, that would be the collapsar itself."

"How," Flinx asked very slowly, "would we do that?"

Tse-Mallory smiled like a Churchman. "In order to prevent the approaching ships from interfering, the artifact would have to be accelerated rapidly toward the rogue. We know of only one way to move it."

Flinx turned to a port, to where two distant stars were vanishing from existence, and he tried to imagine suffering the same fate. It was not pleasant to contemplate.

Chapter Fourteen

"We have no other option, Flinx." Truzenzuzex sounded sad, but quite as unshakable as his human associate. "If we take it with us, the AAnn will surely pursue. We certainly cannot risk letting the weapon fall into their hands. This way, by destroying it—and, only incidentally, ourselves—we can at least insure that does not happen."

Flinx tried to calm Pip, who was hunting with slitted eyes and pointed tongue for whatever was causing so much turmoil within his master. But he did not fly at Truzenzuzex or Tse-Mallory, for their present thoughts where Flinx were concerned were ones of genuine sorrow and fondness.

"We have a minute or two to search the artifact's surface," Tse-Mallory commented. "I'll see if I can discover anything. If not, just leave me out there. At least, if driving the device into the rogue works, I'll have a nanosecond to enjoy it." He started for the nearby observation lock where the suits were kept, then paused. "There's a light on here." He turned a quizzical gaze toward Flinx. "A malfunction?"

225

Flinx instantly began searching the ship with voice and instruments. Both registered two additional bodies: September and Hasboga.

There was no sign of Ab.

A sharp whistle sounded from both the console and the door leading toward the lock. Flinx knew that signal from every emergency drill he had ever been run through on a commercial ship.

"He's cycling the outer lock!" Truzenzuzex moved to press his mandibles to the curved edge of the starboard port, trying to see around it.

Flinx fumbled with the controls on the nearest intercom: "No Ab! Don't do it—wait!"

"Let him, Flinx. Perhaps Ab knows what he's doing." Tse-Mallory sounded hopeful.

"It's not that, it's not that," Flinx explained wildly, gesturing at six tiny lights on the lock door. They formed a pretty pattern. "There isn't a suit on board, for human or thranx, that will properly fit him!"

Tse-Mallory scratched the back of his neck while he walked to stand by his ship-brother. "Maybe our friend Ab doesn't need a suit. Maybe . . ." and then he was working hurriedly at a part of the computer that had not been employed for months.

A sharp pop and whistle sounded over the intercom. Slowly Flinx turned it off. He spoke almost inaudibly. "It doesn't matter now. He's outside. There's no air in the lock." The innocent, stupid, but harmless alien had become his responsibility. There was no rhyming, no singing in the observation blister now, nor would there ever be again.

It was Ab who had led them to the Hur'rikku device. Despite that, Flinx had forgotten him completely in the excitement and tension of the past weeks. Not that that was a decent excuse.

"Flinx, come here." Truzenzuzex was beckoning with a truhand and foothand together. "I think you might be interested in what's happening outside."

Flinx ran to stand beside the staring philosoph.

Ab's body was drifting slowly toward the long red-brown artifact. It appeared that all four eyes were open. All four arms were extended at right angles from the pear-shaped body and angled downward to meet the four extended legs. If the attitude the alien's limbs had assumed was unintentional, it constituted the most regularized rigor mortis Flinx had ever imagined.

A human would be twisted, contorted, and dead from the cold vacuum by now. Ab might be also, but something about the precise arrangement of those eight limbs led Flinx to think otherwise.

"He's definitely moving toward it," Tse-Mallory observed, his voice tight.

"What could be more natural?" Truzenzuzex was awed past astonishment. "He is curious and wishes a closer look. But I still do not understand. Why should he be curious? Bran, everything we have studied, everything we have surmised about the Hur'rikku, tells us that this Ab thing cannot possibly be a member of that race. Bran?"

Tse-Mallory did not glance up from the readouts he was poring over, from the instrumentation he was manipulating. "Quiet, brother. I'm working."

Truzenzuzex knew Bran as well as he knew himself. He did not even trouble his brother with a reply.

Flinx's shock at what occurred next was so overpowering that a startled Pip flew off his shoulder and fluttered nervously around the domed ceiling of the room.

Three meters from the artifact, the body of Abalamahalamatandra split into four equal parts. Each section held an eye, an arm, and a leg. Moving independently by some strange method of propulsion, each Ab-quarter positioned itself independently facing one of the artifact's four sides approximately opposite its equator.

Together, in a unison too precise to be accidental, they moved toward the rust-brown surface. About that time Flinx noticed the similarity between the configuration of each interior part of the Ab-quarters and several depressions and protrusions on the artifact. Only idly did he note that there was no blood or dangling organs visible where Ab's insides should have been. Those interior surfaces were irregular but unbroken.

They touched the artifact simultáneously. Four arms slid into four matching holes. Four legs did likewise, twisting and curving to fit. Four eyes contacted flat, stubby projections. Flinx could have sworn that, just before touching, the eye nearest the port winked at him.

All four quarters of what formerly had been the creature called Ab had merged smoothly with the Hur'rikku artifact. You could hear breathing and little else in the observation blister of the *Teacher*.

Tse-Mallory looked up, rubbed his eyes, and spoke. "He named himself well, or was well named." Truzenzuzex and Flinx looked over at him. "I put our Ab vocabulary to work on something we ought to have worked on first—his name. Abalamahalamatandra. A composite from four different languages, two being derivatives from other languages, one derived from yet a third. Together they form a couplet in a language three hundred and fifty thousand years dead, which the computer then compressed according to the rhyme scheme Ab used when announcing his name. I got one word I'm pretty positive of out of the whole business." He paused, then said anticlimactically: "Key."

"An informational key as well as a mechanical one," Truzenzuzex mused as he turned his gemlike gaze back to the port. "Certainly it was willing enough to impart information. We simply didn't know enough to understand the answers."

"Ab's a machine." Flinx too was staring back out the port. "The AAnn must at least have suspected what he is. No wonder they wanted him destroyed."

"Slow down, Flinx." Tse-Mallory tried to caution him. "We know only that Ab's a machine, some kind of key. We still don't know if he's the right kind."

"All that nonsense," Flinx was muttering to himself. "All the years he must have wandered about aimlessly, taken in hand by different races and different masters. I wonder how many secrets, how much knowledge, he babbled to people who didn't understand."

Behind them a readout buzzed for attention. It recorded information from several external sensors. Tse-Mallory, the closest, moved to read the information.

"Something is, according to this, happening to the artifact. Also, we have three minutes to get away before the AAnn war sphere arrives."

A soft yellow glow appeared and enveloped the entire Hur'rikku device. "There!" Flinx pointed. Where the four parts of Ab had touched the device, four black circles suddenly appeared. Inside those dark holes nothing could be seen. Part of the interior of the artifact was apparently gone, yet they could not exactly see through it. When the black circles appeared, the yellow aura vanished.

Within the artifact, something that was not normal space had been created. Flinx was so intrigued that he forgot to panic. Yet nothing more happened. There was no titanic explosion, no steady hum as from an activated machine, nothing. The artifact continued to sit in free space, unchanged save for four holes in its sides which met to form . . . nothing.

"We can't wait any longer if we're going to get away," Tse-Mallory announced, examining a readout. "But is it activated? Nothing's happened, no change in energy flow according to our instruments. What else has to be *done*, dammit!"

"Bran," Truzenzuzex said slowly. "I just don't know. But the Ab-thing has certainly done *something*. I think we'd best leave the device alone. It's a chance, but humanx society has prospered because of the chances individuals within it have taken. Also because our survival drive is so strong. At the moment, my own is working overtime. Up the universe, ship-brother. Let us depart, and trust in the rhymes of the fool who was not."

Without another word, Tse-Mallory activated the KK drive. "I want to see whether we're going to be remembered as prophets or fools. We'll stay in normal space and see what happens, unless the AAnn come after us. I'm betting they'll be more interested in the device."

As they moved out of the immediate vicinity of the Hur'rikku artifact, Pip returned to Flinx's shoulder.

Immediately thereafter the AAnn war sphere assumed a cluster position around the ancient remnant of that mysterious dead civilization. On board the *Teacher*, three anxious faces studied long-range detectors.

"They've encapsulated it." Tse-Mallory idly checked another screen. "No sign of pursuit."

"We are of no concern to them now," Truzenzuzex pointed out. He was worried, terribly so. "We may not know for years, decades, or in our lifetimes if we have made a proper decision. The device may take that long to function, or the AAnn that long to learn how to operate it." The philosoph noticed Flinx's drawn expression, and chittered his concern.

"It's just that I'm only now starting to realize what Ab might be capable of doing," Flinx explained, "and thinking about all the time I spent in his company. Or its company. I don't know of many machines with personality. Ab had that."

Looking like a cluster of enormous metallic soap bubbles, the AAnn flagship had slowed to a stop alongside the artifact. From the honor chair aboard the dreadnought, Baron Lisso PN studied the dwarfed silver of metal-glass-plastic with great satisfaction.

Messages of congratulations at that very moment were undergoing composition and would soon be broadcast via the deep-space beam which ran the entire length of the enormous vessel to secret bases within the Commonwealth. From there they would be relayed to the Empire.

There would be joy in many burrows, the Baron reflected. After many long years of service to the Emperor and the Pack of Lords, he might hope to find himself raised to that status, or even to be made an adviser with a chance of succeeding the Emperor himself.

The desperate humanx ploy, ineffectual as it would

likely have been, had been stopped. Not only that, but the object of all their enterprise had been captured. It floated outside the warship. Now there remained only tests to be run before it could be brought safely aboard. Baron Lisso PN didn't believe anything—much less the relatively tiny object outside—could interrupt the course of the collapsar. That was a myth. But myths often had some foundation, so it would be best to be cautious until the ancient artifact's harmlessness had been assured.

"Bring the object into the storage hold. Use the method described to us by our informants within the Commonwealth. Back us around it. Our tractors are far more powerful than anything the tiny humanx vessel could have mounted, but we will push it when we leave, if that is required.

"But it is best to study under convenient conditions."

While the other ships of the war sphere watched alertly for the approach of any humanx or Commonwealth force, the massive dreadnought laboriously adjusted its attitude so that the rear of the main globe backed up to the Hur'rikku device. Doors slid aside, revealing a vast, airless, illuminated compartment within. Carefully it backed over the artifact, encapsulating it. The massive four-sided panels slid shut behind.

Several leading archeologists and other scientists shunted over to the dreadnought from two fully equipped laboratory vessels, accompanied by members of the dreadnought's military-sciences staff.

They were greeted by the Baron and his executive officer in the zero-gravity vacuum of the cargo hold. The small group of suited AAnn drifted, studying the artifact visually while a huge battery of instruments examined it with senses no living creature possessed.

"Honored One," the executive officer said, "a message relayed from the periphery ship *Analosaam*. They report that the humanx vessel continues to flee in normal space and request orders to pursue and destroy."

"Request denied." The Baron was unimpressed by their prize. It would not be much of a trophy to haul

back to Sectorcav. "Having failed in their futile attempt with this relic, they may be trying to tempt one
or more of our ships into following within detection
range of a Commonwealth or Church outpost. That
would precipitate a useless incident. Let our presence
here remain undetected.

"As for any story they may choose to relate concerning us, without proof no one would believe a tale telling of an Imperial war force penetrating this deeply
into the Commonwealth simply to capture a device the
Commonwealth government does not believe in anyway. Before anyone could arrive here to check their
story, we shall be gone homeward."

"Home." The word was breathed softly by the
physicist on the Baron's right. Personally, he was even
less impressed than the noble by the Hur'rikku artifact.
Instrument readings relayed to him via his suitcom
indicated that the object floating before them was
emitting not a *doam* of energy, was not composed of
explosive materials, and was to all appearances as inert
and harmless as the caps on his two front incisors. He
was anxious to render his opinion. Then he could return to the hot, shifting sands of his own home.

One by one the scientists present gave their opinions.
All agreed that if the device before them had once
been a weapon, the rot of ages had destroyed its viabil-
ity. But by all means bring it back to Sectorcav. Its inscriptions and interior would interest the archeologists,
at least.

"Does that mean we can inspect it more closely?"
the Baron inquired impatiently. He too was ready to go
home.

The chemist in charge felt confident enough to reply.
"As long as one avoids the still-uninspected protrusions
and depressions, I should think it would be quite safe,
Honored One. We are monitoring for any change in
the object's status, but I personally anticipate none."

"Sure," a physicist-metallurgist added, "if it was capable of functioning, the humanx would already have
activated it."

"Logic and truth," agreed another, with a positive twitch of his head.

Propelled by gentle kicks off the curving wall and the encircling walkway, and trailing control cables, the group moved toward the device. A few tugs on the cables brought them to a drifting stop alongside it.

"What are those black circles that appear to be solid on the surface of each plane?" the Baron, no neophyte scientist himself, asked the others.

"They may not be solid, according to some readings, Honored One." The scientist sounded puzzled. "They show properties of solid surfaces and of vacuum simultaneously. It is an interesting but not necessarily dangerous phenomenon . . ."

Tse-Mallory's face was an unreadable mask as he looked up from the screen. "Still no signs of their giving chase. I think they'll be content with having stopped us. Resolution at this distance is difficult, but I believe they've taken the artifact on board the dreadnought."

Truzenzuzex's usual placid demeanor broke for an instant, as a foothand slammed with surprising force against the metal beneath the bank of instruments. "Something should have happened by now, if the device was going to do anything. The machine Ab—"

"Ab was no machine." Flinx sounded bitter. Their foolish but charming ward had apparently quartered himself on a whim. "Ab was somebody."

"It is something humanxkind has long suspected." Seeing how emotionally Flinx was reacting, the philosoph tried to comfort him by changing the subject a little. "For example, you humans used to anthropomorphize certain advanced machines long before it was learned that instincts were more accurate about such mechanicals than minds."

"I'm afraid it's finished, ship-brother. We must try another legend. Otherwise it will all be over for the people of the three worlds."

Flinx turned his gaze away from the screen. Out the rear port of the observation blister he could still see

clearly the twin suns RNGC 11,432–3. The AAnn war-
ships were far too small to be detected by the naked
eye.

The position of the two spiraling trails of matter
being drawn off the two suns had altered as the rogue
traveled deeper through the system. While it was probably only his imagination, he thought that the circum-
ference of both stars had shrunk noticeably. With a
stomach-wrenching thought for the doomed people of
Carmague-Collangatta and Twosky Bright, he turned
back to his companions and discovered September eyeing him questioningly. The giant and Hasboga, having
discovered that annihilation wasn't imminent, had returned to the observation chamber.

Truzenzuzex and Tse-Mallory's hunt had reached an
unsatisfactory conclusion. Now it was time to resolve
his own.

Eyes full of blue wisdom watched him, almost
seemed to sense his question. "This ship is emergency-
coded to respond in a dangerous situation only to my
voice, September. I can let you and Hasboga off or
keep you aboard until I get satisfaction. I want answers
and I want them now."

Oddly, September seemed to approve of Flinx's announced intentions rather than reacting angrily to
them.

"You never told me what you were doing on Moth
trying to buy me. And you mentioned others, too. I
want to know why you were at that auction."

"I like your ship. Keep me on it as long as you
want." Was the giant laughing?

Flinx walked over, put hands on hips, and stared up
at that graven visage. September towered over him. He
weighed more than twice as much as the youth and
could have broken his bones with one hand. Provided,
however, that the small, alert shape coiled about
Flinx's right shoulder did not interfere. Many men had
found that "however" to be a fatal one.

Not that September intended to react belligerently.
" 'Pon my soul, young feller-me-lad, if I don't think
you're threatening old Skua." He smiled petulantly.

Flinx turned away, angry at himself now. "I'm sorry. I don't like a universe where threats replace reason the way rock replaces bone in a fossil. I especially don't like to threaten friends."

Eyebrows of white lichen lifted in surprise. "So you regard me as a friend?"

Flinx spoke without looking at the giant. "I'd like to think of you as one."

There was an odd catch in September's voice. "I'd like that, feller-me-lad. So ... I'll tell you what you want to know."

Flinx whirled and immediately tried to stifle his excitement. He took a seat while September sat, lotuslike, opposite him. Hasboga turned her attention to the stars, a little miffed at being ignored.

Tse-Mallory and Truzenzuzex remained glued to their respective instruments. Flinx knew neither would concede failure until it was irrevocably displayed for them. Creatures of theory, they were the most pragmatic and empirical of men.

"A little less than twenty standard years ago," September began, "I found myself devoid of credit and prospects. I've been poor several times in my life, lad. It's not nice. I was depressed, my brain wasn't functioning right ... the reasons need not concern you. I took a job I probably shouldn't have.

"There was a firm, small, but associated with some very important persons, I later found out. Their motives were good. They believed they could, through the use of their combined abilities, improve humanity. Physically, not morally. For their theories to prove themselves, normal conditions were essential for the raising of their 'improved' children. They found an ideal launching device in couples desiring to have children in which the father was sterile. There are many organizations which supply viable sperm to such couples. It provided the firm with an ideal, inconspicuous cover.

"Needless to say, the couples purchasing sperm were not told that it had been improved." The giant looked away. "I didn't find out what was going on, you must understand, until after."

Flinx forbore asking until after what.

"The couples thought they were buying standard spermatozoa full of high-class genes. They had no way of knowing that those genes had been toyed with. I applied and was accepted as a sperm donor." He allowed himself a slight grin. "I'm sure it was because of my size and strength, not my overwhelming brilliance. Remember, I had no idea what was going to be done to what I'd sold. There were numerous other donors besides myself, of course.

"How many or how often they donated I don't know. I donated several times. Donated, hell—sold. And now you can see why I can't say if I'm your father or not, Flinx. It could have been my sperm that was implanted in your mother, or it could have been any one of many others. Even a chromosome match now couldn't tell us, because of the alterations made in certain genes by the firm's technicians."

"How did you eventually find all this out?" Flinx found himself bizarrely fascinated by the tale. Alteration of genes ... improvement of humanity—he was not so sure he was an improvement, but the explanation went a long way toward explaining the source of his erratic, peculiar talents.

"Most of the first group of altered offspring were born on Terra or on worlds close to it. Most of them were born normal, but there were some, perhaps a fifth, who were born malformed or genetically damaged. Sometimes the damage was pretty gruesome.

"The firm's organizers, remember, were essentially decent beings, men and women, human and thranx. They were properly horrified, broke up the firm and disbanded. The government got involved. There was a lot of talk of criminal proceedings, but the government couldn't find anyone to prosecute, because they had, and still have, no idea that the children were damaged as the result of prenatal manipulation.

"To protect themselves as much as possible, the firm's organizers set about a program of what you might call building up a case for the future defense. They employed a network to recover as many of the healthy children they'd produced, or to learn their whereabouts and identities, as they could. Unfortunate malfunctions they had destroyed." September's voice was flat.

"In order to preserve secrecy, this network used as many former employees as possible. They explained that just by donating, I could be considered an accomplice by a vengeful government. So I took the job."

Flinx didn't inquire if September had tracked down any unsuccessful children.

"I was about to buy you at the auction on Moth, to bring you back to Terra. They're raising several other healthy but abandoned or orphaned altered kids in a special school back there. Meanwhile, the government was beginning to learn things. They knew nothing of the children, but several members involved with the firm had been arrested. They would recognize me. So when a lot of local police showed up at the auction, I had to leave in a hurry. I intended to come back later and repurchase you from whoever finally bought you."

"Why didn't you, Skua?"

"Because shortly afterward the network collapsed, some employees talked in exchange for immunity, and most of the founders of the original firm were arrested. Judging from the hysterical stories in the tridee faxcasts, I thought it would be a good idea to quietly drop my association with the network and with the firm. I managed to lose myself for a while."

"What happened to the founders?" Flinx's excitement was beginning to return. Father or not, September might not be the end of his trail. "What about their records?"

"Sorry, feller-me-lad, I don't know for a fact—but I do have big ears." He wiggled them for emphasis. "From what I heard, the firm's records were destroyed in a fire."

"Well, the experimenters then." Flinx tried to remain hopeful.

"Public revulsion forced some unusually stiff penalties. Most of those involved were sentenced to selective neurosurgery." Flinx slumped. He knew what that meant. "That part of their memories dealing with the firm and its activities was erased. Their personalities and most of their knowledge remain, but nothing about the firm or its activities."

"I thought that was against Church doctrine."

September nodded. "It is, but public outcry was pretty violent, feller-me-lad. The Anti-Science League had a field day, as you can imagine. Sometimes Church opinion prevails. In this case the Inner Chancellors and the Last Resort probably thought it prudent not to insist. A rift in Church-government relations wouldn't have benefited anyone."

"But . . . you *could* be my father."

"I don't deny it, lad. Can't." He stretched his legs out, winced. One had gone to sleep. "From what I know of you, I'd be proud to be, but," he was forced to add, "it could have been one of several dozen other donors."

"What if I'd been one of the malformed ones?"

"Young feller," September said seriously, "most of those poor predamned souls never knew it when they were killed. Some of them were born without senses, some with new ones. Without arms, or legs, or both. With extra limbs or two heads or no head. And there was lots worse. Remember, most of the altered children turned out healthy—if anything, they *were* a bit stronger, a touch smarter than the average. I'm not defending the firm now, understand. Just telling you fact, and the fact is that that one initial batch didn't turn out too bad."

First batch, Flinx thought. An icy fury built within him. Pip moved nervously. He was an ingredient in a scientific stew. He was . . .

Something September said came back to him. "Some were born without senses," he'd said, "and some with new ones." If his awkward abilities were the results of that misguided genetic manipulation, then there might be others possessed of similar confusion and talents, uncertain, terrified, unsure of their own unpredictable abilities.

And what of September? What went on beneath that granite forehead, behind luminous azure eyes? Maybe-son stared up at possible-father. Neither said a word.

"What could their function be?" Baron Lisso PN questioned his science staff as he used a guideline to maneuver himself over to the nearest black circle on the Hur'rikku artifact. One physicist pulled herself over next to him. She held a boxy affair in both hands. It looked like a small dumbbell, with a bright red plastic square pierced by the handle. A cluster of buttons and switches and other controls adapted for manipulation by a clawed hand studded the box's surface. Several small disks fronted it and were directed at the mysterious black circle.

"Instrument readings remain inconclusive, Honored One," she declared. "We cannot penetrate the black areas. Until we are more certain of their nature, I hesitate to subject the artifact to any form of particulate inspection. Contact with energy or matter might set the weapon off."

"Bah," said the Baron. "We have already determined that if it was once a weapon, it is presently dysfunctional."

Under the withering stares of the other homesick scientists, the single remaining protester found herself backing down.

"Honored One," she managed to finish worriedly, "no precipitate action to take."

"It puts out no energy, takes in no energy. It is dead, millions of time units dead. Yet you do not wish us to proceed with examination. The inscriptions, for example," and he gestured at the engraved script covering the artifact's flanks, "will provide much information once they are deciphered. Perhaps some will aid in our mission to obliterate those warm-skinned humans and stiff-jointed thranx who infest so much of our present portion of this galaxy."

Reaching out, he traced one long character with a gloved hand. The moment he contacted the artifact, the single querulous scientist unwillingly sucked in her breath. Nothing happened. Turning, the Baron eyed her condescendingly. Her suit tag indicated she was called Di-Vuoyyi LMMVCT. The suit hid most of her shape, but not all of it. Her hips were wide. Perhaps later, after her unnecessary caution had been lost, he would endeavor to show his ability to be forgiving and compassionate to mistake-makers. In his quarters, on the blue dune.

With the hand he tapped the peculiar, as-yet-unidentified substance. "Dead, inert, harmless, as anyone can see." He drew back his hand, compensated for the movement in zero g, and smacked the surface hard. "Why do you not trust your own knowledge, *lya-nye*? Why do you doubt your own evident wisdom?" He moved until he was directly opposite the edge of one of the dark gaps in the artifact's surface.

"We cannot see into this space, yet there must be a space there. In the presence of instrumental indecision, we AAnn have always reacted efficiently." So saying, he reached out a hand, fingers spread, and shoved against the darkness. His hand passed through the black surface and vanished; and for a length of time just this side of instantaneous, he became the first and only one of his kind to touch Elsewhere.

Matter in Elsewhere triggered the device. Of course, the device was not actually there, within the AAnn warship. It was somewhere half a million years back in space, where the system of Cannachanna had once been. It was connected to its present manifestation by an unimaginably vast buildup of FCI energy. When Baron Lisso PN triggered it, that energy and the actual device slipped, avalanched through a different state of space.

It all came together inside the AAnn warship. There was no explosion as a result, however. The accumulated energy simply gave the slingshotted artifact a little shove. The Hur'rikku device was a needle. What it did was punch a tiny hole in the fabric of the universe.

Into the other universe.

Elsewhere waterfalled into Here. The Baron vanished. The scientists around him vanished. Everything in the immediate spatial vicinity, which consisted of eleven armed vessels of various sizes and their crews, vanished. They disappeared in tiny flashes of supernal brilliance, going out of existence like moths in a firestorm.

Only an electronic angel on board the *Teacher* saved Flinx and his companions. The computer detected the danger and threw the ship into space-plus just in time to save it from annihilation. Since that annihilation was racing toward them only at near light-speed, the *Teacher* didn't have to accelerate enormously. Only rapidly.

When they started picking themselves off the deck, it was the resilient, armored Truzenzuzex who was first on his feet and back at the consoles. Long-range scanners were activated, and the scene forming behind them came into view. There was no need to increase their velocity. They needed only to travel a little above light-speed to outspace the pursuing destruction.

Flinx and the others crowded around the screen. So stunned was the youth that he didn't notice a terrified Pip had vanished out the passageway.

"Gone." Tse-Mallory studied the detectors in disbelief. "They're gone, Tru. All eleven ships. Not a trace of them."

"Somehow they activated the device," murmured Truzenzuzex. Awed, he studied the picture on the screen. "Humanx, pay attention. What we are witnessing is unique."

Out of the region where the AAnn war sphere had drifted seconds before, something had emerged. An intense sphere of pure white brilliance, it was bordered by a black fire that could not be seen through. A tentacle of that blackness which was more than black seemed to shine as it stretched outward. That was impossible, of course. Nothing could glow black.

It was a distortion of every known physical law, yet it existed, even if a normal spectrum would have been appalled by it. From several hundred million kilometers away, a similar tendril of intensely glowing white fire was extending out from the event horizon of the collapsar.

"It's drawing matter out of the black hole, out of the rogue," said Tse-Mallory in a stunned whisper.

"That's crazy." September knew enough to sound confident about that. "Things fall into black holes. They don't come out of them again. Ever."

"Nevertheless, that is what is taking place, or else we and the instruments on board this vessel have all gone mad." Truzenzuzex's flashing compound eyes moved constantly from screen to other instruments. "I would not wager on that possibility. But then, I would never previously have wagered I would ever actually see an expandar. A *white* hole."

As it left the event horizon of the collapsar, the stream of incredibly dense matter pulsed with increasing intensity, until it was so bright that the *Teacher*'s compensators were hard pressed to stop down the light to where it wouldn't burn out the detectors: It approached the expandar slightly above the angle of approach of dark material from the latter's event horizon.

Mutual attraction altered angular momentum. Both streams twisted, turned, spiraled in toward each other. At the center of the two entwining spirals, they met.

On board the *Teacher*, a gauge which measured levels of radiant energy exploded. Another simply snapped. They had been pushed beyond the range their designers had imagined existed.

Where the two tendrils, brilliant and black, came together, a sphere of multicolored, incredible energy formed. It grew and steadied as they watched.

"Imagine that at one time all the matter in the universe was concentrated in one collapsar," Tse-Mallory mused. "It finally meets a weak point in space. The point gives and the two universes or more meet. What you get is a very Big Bang. What you get, maybe, is the new energy which later coalesces to form our present galaxies."

"You also get something which totally annihilates matter," Truzenzuzex pointed out. "An efficient irresistible weapon." The philosoph looked pale. "How do you stop an immense concentration of matter? Why, with an equal amount of antimatter." Light in the observation blister bounced off his eyes as if from a crystal chandelier. "Thank the Hive we never explored the trap after Ab set it. Any amount of matter, a single touch, probably would have been enough to set it off. But that's not what shakes me." He paused a moment to collect himself.

"We were going to drive the Hur'rikku device and ourselves into the collapsar. Had we done that, there would have been no gradual matter-antimatter annihilation, as we are seeing now. The white hole would have been created within the collapsar. All, *all* of the collapsar matter would have been destroyed at the same time.

"If that collapsar contains the remains of a hundred million suns, all would have turned to energy simultaneously." He rubbed at his mandibles. "I've always wanted to know what a quasar looked like, gentlesirs and lady—but not from close up!"

He turned back to the screen. "The flow of matter into antimatter appears relatively constant. That matches what the instruments tell us. We have a new star, gentlefolk. A rainbow star."

Tse-Mallory looked up from the console. "Tru, the motion of the collapsar has changed. No," he added quickly at the expression of alarm on the philosoph's face, "it's not moving toward the white hole. No quasar in *our* back yard. It looks like they're both going to orbit around the new star, if you can call it a star. Distance between the two remains, I'm happy to say, constant."

"How long will it burn?" wondered Hasboga, her arm around September's left. "It's beautiful."

"You'll be able to see it for a few million years at least, I'd guess," said Tse-Mallory. "But that's not where the real beauty will come from." She eyed him quizzically.

"The Velvet Dam," explained Truzenzuzex. "The extensive dark nebula that lies between here and the Commonwealth worlds. When the energy from this steady annihilation reaches it, it will turn a dark nebula into the most magnificent sight in our galaxy. I would not be surprised if the colors become visible on Terra and Hivehom in the daytime. We will not live to see it, I am sorry to say. But we have made a wonderment for our grandchildren and the generations to follow."

They continued to watch until the clashing colored energies of the rainbow star had faded to a small spot of brilliance on the screen. Then Flinx put the *Teacher* on course for Twosky Bright, the nearest major Commonwealth world. Primarily thranx-settled, it would be a good place for Truzenzuzex to communicate the knowledge of their accomplishment to officialdom. He could also help raise research funds for Isili Hasboga, who brightened at the announcement of the philosoph's intention to help.

Flinx paused, a hand going reflexively to his shoulder. The familiar form was not there. He did not remember when Pip had left him, but it had been some time ago, he was certain. For a second he panicked, thinking back to that awful time on Alaspin when he feared his pet had abandoned him forever.

That was no worry here, however, and he relaxed. The minidrag had to be somewhere aboard the *Teacher*. In fact, he mused, the minidrag had been absenting itself for longer and longer periods ever since they'd left Alaspin. No doubt, he thought reluctantly, the experience of brief freedom had made his beloved pet permanently more independent. He would have to cope with it.

It was no problem to excuse himself to go hunting for Pip. Everyone else's attention was focused elsewhere. Truzenzuzex and Tse-Mallory were deep in a discussion of the new phenomena now receding behind them. September and Isili Hasboga were equally engrossed in each other.

So Flinx went prowling through corridors and cabins, shouting out Pip's name. The minidrag had to be somewhere in the living quarters or the few other pressurized sections of the ship. Working his way methodically back and down from the observation blister, he eventually reached his own cabin.

"Pip! Come on out, Pip. It's all right. My mind is calm now."

An answering hiss sounded from behind his bed. He frowned. It was an unusually soft hiss. Was Pip sick? Maybe, he thought worriedly, that was the reason for the extended absences. He took an anxious step toward the bed.

"Pip, are you all . . . ?"

Something that resembled a tiny missile shot past his ear, droning like a herculean bumble bee. He froze. A second shape whizzed by him, then another, followed by three more. He stood in befuddled amazement in the middle of the room as four, five, six tiny winged shapes dove and hummed around his head.

There was a much throatier hiss from behind the bed. Immediately all six shapes dashed over the covers in ragged formation.

Flinx found Pip coiled neatly on a rumpled blanket on the other side, sequestered comfortably between the bed-bulk and the metal wall. As he watched, the winged sextet settled itself neatly around the much larger diamond-patterned Pip, looking for all the world like a squadron of stingships hovering around a mothering cruiser.

Looking up, slitted eyes stared directly into his own. Flinx felt a warm mental thrum pass between the minidrag and his own sensitive mind. It was the second time he had become a father today—first to a new kind of star, and now to six undeniably cute cable-shapes of winged poison.

"All these years we've been together," Flinx murmured comfortingly, "and you turn out to be a she."

No wonder he—she, he corrected himself—had vanished with the impressively muscled minidrag Balthazaar. No wonder their return and parting had resembled the conclusion of some unseen aerial ballet. Neither minidrag had abandoned his master. They had merely taken a brief sojourn in response to a higher directive that itself was part of the jungles of Alaspin.

"You ought to have told me, Pip," Flinx said reprovingly, but he was unable to restrain a broad smile. As if in response, six tiny empathic shapes soared up at him. They buzzed him, picking curiously at his ears, pulling his hair, fluttering in front of his eyes with the ravenous curiosity of all newborns. Pip watched to make sure everything was all right, then nuzzled her triangular head deeper into the folds of the blanket.

Undoubtedly, Flinx mused, she was seeking maximum warmth—but all the same, it *could* have been something akin to embarrassment.

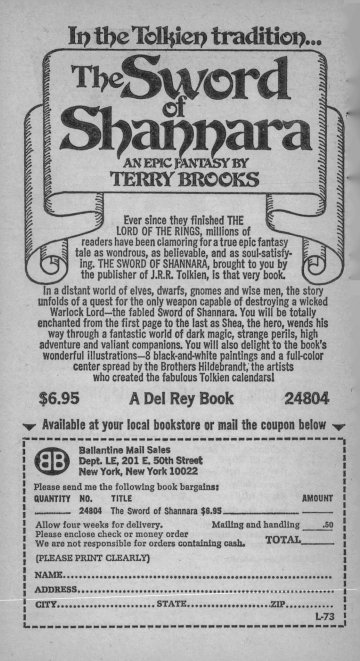